Text Classics

NADIA WHEATLEY was born in 1949 in Sydney. Her award-winning publications for children, young adults and adults include picture books, novels, short stories, biography and history.

Nadia began writing full time in 1976, after completing a postgraduate degree in Australian history. Her first book, *Five Times Dizzy*, was published in 1982. *The House that Was Eureka*, published three years later, grew out of her research into the Sydney Anti-Eviction Campaign of 1931 and a subsequent visit to the house in which the bloody Newtown eviction battle had occurred. Shortlisted for the 1984 *Australian*/Vogel award, the novel went on to win the New South Wales Premier's Children's Book Award in 1985 and to be commended in the CBCA Awards in 1986.

Nadia Wheatley's classic picture book *My Place* (illustrated by Donna Rawlins) was the Children's Book Council of Australia's Book of the Year for Younger Readers in 1988 and has recently been adapted as a television mini-series. Her biography of Charmian Clift won the New South Wales Premier's Australian History Award in 2002. In the same year the collaboratively produced *Papunya School Book of Country and History*, for which Nadia provided the written text, won the Young People's History Award.

Nadia Wheatley has been nominated by IBBY Australia for the prestigious 2014 Hans Christian Andersen Award for Writing—the highest international recognition given to a living author whose complete works have made a lasting contribution to children's literature.

Her latest book is *Australians All: A History of Growing Up from the Ice Age to the Apology*. Nadia lives in Sydney.

TONI JORDAN was born in Brisbane in 1966. She has written three acclaimed novels. Her debut, *Addition*, has been published in seventeen countries and her most recent, *Nine Days*, won the 2013 Indie Award for Best Fiction. Toni lives in Melbourne.

ALSO BY NADIA WHEATLEY

The House that Was Eureka
Nadia Wheatley

Text Publishing Melbourne Australia

textclassics.com.au
textpublishing.com.au

The Text Publishing Company
Swann House
22 William Street
Melbourne Victoria 3000
Australia

First published by Viking Kestral, 1985
This edition published by The Text Publishing Company 2013

Cover design by WH Chong
Page design by Text
Typeset by Midland Typesetters

Printed in Australia by Griffin Press, an Accredited ISO AS/NZS 14001:2004
Environmental Management System printer

Primary print ISBN: 9781922147189
Ebook ISBN: 9781922148254
Author: Wheatley, Nadia, 1949– author.
Title: The house that was Eureka / by Nadia Wheatley ;
introduced by Toni Jordan.
Series: Text classics.
Subjects: Homelessness—Juvenile fiction. Unemployment—Juvenile fiction.
Eviction—Australia—Juvenile fiction. Depressions—1929—Australia—
Juvenile fiction. Australia—Social conditions—Juvenile fiction.
Dewey Number: A823.3

CONTENTS

The Ghosts around Us
by Toni Jordan

IN 1985, the year Nadia Wheatley's extraordinary *The House that Was Eureka* was first published, I was eighteen, unemployed and desperate, and sleeping on the floor of my boyfriend's brother's flat. I would wake early on a Saturday morning and circle job ads: those few that said 'no experience required'. For a while, the only work I could get was selling aluminium siding door-to-door. My 'job' was to convince people who lived in broken-down houses in the western suburbs and were home during the day (so probably not working either), and who answered the door to clueless teenagers, that they needed to buy cladding. On credit.

The work was commission only. My two-week

stint of walking miles every day earned me, oh, roughly: nothing. After that, I was interviewed and missed out on a job as a receptionist in an office-furniture showroom. I've never sobbed so hard, before or since, than when I received the 'regret to inform you' letter. I thought I was good for nothing. I thought my life was over before it had begun.

I was sometimes hungry in those early years, yes. And frustrated. I was surrounded by people who cared about me, though, and was never in any real danger of homelessness or starvation. My sense of desolation was not based on practical considerations. I'd been brought up to believe I should have two simple goals: to get a job and then, if you work hard and live a stable life, a mortgage. A mortgage, that shimmering Holy Grail, was the only thing that could save you from being at the mercy of a landlady.

This is the world Wheatley shows us. *The House that Was Eureka* is about two families in two different times: in 1931, in the middle of the Great Depression, and in 1981, during the economic downturn of the early 80s. These families live fifty years apart, but there is a great deal that's similar: jobs are the source of freedom, of economic strength, of the ability to care for your family.

But there were also significant differences. In

1931, as opposed to the 80s, the dole was given as food or coupons. That's why evictions were commonplace, and why communities sometimes banded together to prevent them. There was simply no cash for rent. Families would find themselves on the street, their belongings dumped beside them. Some families, especially those with young children, took desperate measures to prevent losing their homes.

In *The House that Was Eureka*, Lizzie's father and brothers and supporters were determined not to let unemployment lead to homelessness. They make the fateful decision to defend their home against the police coming to evict them. They barricade themselves in, as if Sydney is a war zone. They are preparing for a riot.

> Lizzie peered through the spy crack and saw Pa's face on the other side. Heard him grunting.
>
> 'Heave-ho!' she heard, and Pa's face and the spy crack disappeared. They must be building the sandbags higher. Five foot high they were already at the door, and six feet thick. No way the cops could get in the front. For the window to the loungeroom was boarded up too, with sandbags six feet thick behind it...Not that the cops would even get to the front door, for the front fence and gate and the little front yard were criss-crossed

back and forth with roll upon roll of barbed wire, going up about six foot high.

The House that Was Eureka is gritty and realistic in its accounts of everyday life in a depression and a recession. Part of the thrill of the novel is the confident way that Wheatley balances the personal and the political, like the message that Lizzie writes in whitewash on the footpath in front of the landlady's house:

DOWN WITH SCABS AND CLASS-TRAITORS.
NO EVICTIONS FOR THE UNEMPLOYED.

In Wheatley's hands, it's not just a cheap slogan. We can feel Lizzie's fear and anger. We understand what's brought her to that point.

The House that Was Eureka was commended in the Children's Book Council of Australia awards in 1986, and it won the New South Wales Premier's Literary award for young people's literature—yet despite writing for a young audience, Wheatley never backs away from the politics of real life. By meticulously weaving actual events and people and newspaper clippings with her imagined ones, she creates a novel that speaks for people rarely shown in fiction. She changes the way her readers see the world.

Intellect and theme and politics are well and good. In the end, though, what matters is what's at the heart of a novel. At the heart of *The House that Was Eureka* are four young people: Lizzie and Nobby, in 1931, and Evie and Noel, in 1981. The thing that connects them is the house itself, where both families live: it's a rambling Newtown terrace with a balcony and a scullery. It has changed little in fifty years. Wheatley possess great technical skill in showing us the similarities and differences in their times and lives and in gently weaving her characters' stories together, but, when reading this book for the first time, I didn't notice any of it. My notepad was on the table beside me but I didn't make a jot. I was too involved in the story and the people; I was turning pages, busting to see what happened next. The later stages of the novel have a dream-like quality, as the shifting realities of Evie and Lizzie and Noel and Nobby intersect and collide. My heart was pounding for the final fifty pages.

History is never really past. We all live with our memories, every day, and stories and traditions are passed down to us. In 1931, when Lizzie was dealing with her father's unemployment and the family's eviction, my grandmother was fourteen and beginning her working life in domestic service. My childhood was filled with memories that are actually hers: her love of fresh bread and dripping, her fear of being caught in the outside loo when the dunny men came, her gratitude to the nuns for teaching her to read, her enduring distrust of green vegetables. The past lives on. It is always a part of our lives. To me, this is the central idea of the novel. There are ghosts everywhere around us, if only we could see them.

The ending of *The House that Was Eureka* especially pleased me. Wheatley treats all her characters with compassion, even the landlady, 'the despot'. Many of the characters pay a dreadful price for the riot and hers is among the heaviest to bear, though Wheatley's subtle lessons left me wondering what it was about the despot's own past that led her to those fateful decisions.

My period of teenage unemployment was brief. Just a few weeks after the shocking loss of my potential career in office-furniture administration, I was finally hired: my job was in a mailroom in the Department of Physiology, at the University of Queensland. From there, I was even luckier. After a while, my supportive bosses allowed me to work back at night to make up time spent at lectures during the day.

My experience of unemployment did not define me. When I finished the final page of *The House that Was Eureka*, I hoped for the same for Evie. I hoped her years of teenage despondency left her with nothing more than an appreciation for work, and an empathy for people down on their luck. Right now, as the world struggles through the global economic collapse, kindness is more important than ever.

The House that Was Eureka

For Issy Wyner,
who showed me the meaning of labour history

The tradition of all the dead generations
weighs like a nightmare on the brain of
the living.

KARL MARX, *THE EIGHTEENTH
BRUMAIRE OF LOUIS BONAPARTE*

PROLOGUE

...It was the gun dream he was dreaming. He had it more and more as time went on.

Crouching in darkness, underneath a bed. Looking up, he saw the criss-cross of the bed-wire, beneath the mattress. Not far away there were suddenly bullet-bangs. Out that way, in front. Though of course in the dream he didn't know where the bed was, so didn't know where that way was. He lifted up the counterpane a bit, and peered out.

There were legs outside the cubby-house of his bed. Legs from the knee down, running back and forth, some in old brown or black-dyed trousers, others in long white underpants, mostly barefoot; and outside the bed too there were yelling sounds, louder than bullets. Some close and loud; a dozen or so men's voices; though in the dream he could never hear what they yelled. And voices too out that way (wherever that way was); not as close, but loud; a mighty roar of voices, like when you hold a seashell to your ear; then bullet sounds too from the other way.

Under the bed, he had a gun that now he loaded, carefully slipping in a bullet; then hid the gun inside his coat. The gun changed from time to time: sometimes a rifle, or a revolver; sometimes a machine-gun, or even a red water pistol.

He held it close to his body and began to climb out from under the bed. Then he'd wake up.

BOOK ONE
Winding Up

This is the house that Jack built;
He laid each brick and fastened each board
For wages laid down by State award.
Now Jack lives in the slums
　　　Worried by bums
　　　Who gather the rent
　　　For the noble gent
　　　Who lives in the house that Jack built.

ANON, *THE TOCSIN*, 1930s

1

Evie was sixteen, but Mum always reckoned she was a very young sixteen. By the time mum was sixteen she'd been working for a year; by the time she was nineteen, she was having Evie. In the album there was a photo of Mum at sixteen and she looked as mature and polished as she did in her wedding photos, when she was twenty-four.

Evie took the framed wedding photo out of one of the boxes. They were moving in tonight, and with all the packing cases around full of plates and saucepans and useful stuff it was more interesting and homelier to decorate the place than to unpack properly. Evie put the wedding photo of Mum and Ted up on the mantelpiece in the downstairs front room. Then the baby photos of Maria and Jodie, and the three baby photos of Sammy. Then the family photo they'd had done by a proper photographer last Christmas in the loungeroom at their old house: Ted and Mum standing at the back, Mum very attractive still, well groomed and made up, tall and suntanned in her green slack suit; and Ted blond, smiling too much for Evie's taste, with a shirt out over his slacks to hide his beer gut, but still not too bad (Evie gave him that) for forty-three. Then Maria, nine, Jodie, eight, and Sammy, four, sitting at the front on the lounge, all with blond hair like Ted's, that white-blond colour gone a bit green from chlorine swimming pools. And then Evie kneeling beside them at the end of the lounge, neither sitting down like the kids nor standing up like the adults, neither blond like Ted nor dark-haired like Mum, but a one-out and middle-ey sort of Evie.

'Evie-Evie-Evie-Peevie!' Sammy ran in in her pyjamas, singing one of Maria's Evie-songs. She jumped from the armchair onto Evie's back.

'Bed!' Evie said. 'Back to bed!' She'd put Sammy down an hour ago but the kids were being loopy tonight. Everything was everywhere. The beds hadn't arrived yet and Evie couldn't find the sheets so they'd all be sleeping just with blankets on mattresses on the floor.

'I want *Mr Funny*.'

'I told you, I don't know where it is.' Mum had been working all week and so Evie had done most of the packing, and everything was topsy-turvey. 'I'll read you something else.' But Sammy started to howl. 'You and your *Mr Men* books.'

'What's *she* doing down here! I thought I asked you to take her up an hour ago.' Mum came in and fossicked around through the piles on the lounge till she found the car keys.

'Listen, love, Ted and I are going back with the trailer for another load, so get those other two to bed will you, there's a good girl.'

'You're going *now*?' Evie said. It was already dark.

'Yeah love, I want the sheets and things, God only knows where you packed them. We'll be back by eleven, twelve at the latest, you'll be all right.' Mum often left Evie to babysit when she went to the club, and she knew Evie never got scared.

'Listen, you make up your bed in here on the divan tonight – you can fix up that back room tomorrow. Night-night, sweetie...' Her lipstick left a kiss on Sammy. 'Be a good girl for Evie. And put the skids under those other two, won't you, love.'

Evie heard the car start as she hauled Sammy over her shoulder for an upside-downer. She struggled out the dark obstacle course in the diningroom, then up the pitch-dark narrow stairs. Ted had told Evie to buy light bulbs and she had, but then she'd gone and packed them somewhere she couldn't remember.

'Can't that girl do anything right?' Ted had complained to Mum. 'No wonder no one'll give her a job.'

By the time Ted had gone to put the light bulbs in and Evie realized they were lost, it was too late to buy any more. Mum had gone in next door to 201 and borrowed two bulbs from Mrs Cavendish, so they had lights now in the loungeroom and kitchen, but the upstairs was like a tomb.

'Oopsadaisy. Oh don't carry *on*.' As Evie turned on the tiny landing where the stairs divided, Sammy bumped her head. Sammy bawled and Evie plodded on past the bathroom to the back room that was to be Sammy's, felt around with her foot for a mattress, and plunked Sammy down. 'What a weight!'

11

'She's ten-ton-Sam, the fatso-man,' Evie sang as she held Sammy to stop the tears. Then found a blanket and tucked it around her. 'Go to byes now. Evie will stay with you.'

Evie felt guilty, because it was her fault about the darkness, and about the *Mr Men* books being lost. So she'd stay till Sammy went to sleep, and then go and fight those other two. She could hear them jumping and squealing up in the front room.

'Oooooo, I'm a ghost...' *Crash.* 'Watch it, Jodie!'

'How can I watch anything in the dark?' Jodie said reasonably.

Evie knelt beside Sammy on the mattress, knelt and looked out the open back window. There was a bit of moonlight, you could just make out a few shapes. About a metre and a half below the window was the corrugated-iron roof over the old breezeway and scullery. It was joined on to the roof over next door's scullery, for on this side 203 and 201 shared a wall right the way along.

'Make up a story,' Sammy murmured.

'Once upon a time,' Evie said, 'there was an old, old house, and a new family moved into it.'

'What were their names?'

'Oh, Evie, and Sammy, and Maria and Jodie.' Evie was bad at inventing things.

'*Then* what happened?'

Sammy's voice was drowsy; she was about to drop off. Evie watched the cloud shadows moving over the corrugated-iron roof. There was a narrow passage running down beside the kitchen and scullery on the right side, next to 205's fence. In this light it was a long dark pit, disappearing into the blackness of the tiny backyard. The shadows made Evie shiver.

Silver now, a foot-shape of silver formed itself on the roof below her as the clouds shifted. Then a black lump moved fast up the wall beneath her, to the window-sill. Down along that passage was blackness. Evie shivered.

For down there, in the scullery, Evie would be all alone. The family upstairs would be tight in their beds, and anything could creep along down the dunny-can lane, in the back gate, down the passage, up the breezeway, and into Evie's room. Evie was to sleep in the old scullery.

Maybe she should do what Mum suggested, and keep her things up here in Sammy's room and make up the divan in the loungeroom each night. Or follow Ted's idea, and sleep up here with Sammy. (Or do what she wanted to do, and move out.)

But it'd be good, down there alone. If she was upstairs, she'd spend half the night getting drinks of water for Sammy and taking her to the toilet, and if she slept in the lounge she'd have to wait till Ted finished watching television. In the scullery, she could lock the door so the kids couldn't muck up her things.

'But what happened?' Sammy drifted awake again, her voice cutting into Evie's thoughts.

'Nothing.' Evie was bad at inventing things.

'But what happened to the lady?'

'What lady?'

'The one you were telling me about. In the story.'

'There wasn't any lady.'

'Yes there was. The one that was talking to you.' Then Sammy stuck her thumb in her mouth and went to sleep.

A couple of hours later, Evie sat in the upstairs front room that was to be Mum and Ted's. She was sampling the whole house, like playing musical rooms. From this one she could just hear Jodie snoring in the room behind. Then that was drowned by the cold whine of a mouth-organ, coming from next door. And now a voice took over, a kind of nasal chant, as if whoever was singing had a blocked nose. Evie could just make out that it was that Bob Dylan song about the answer blowing in the wind. As the mouth-organ started up again she realised that whoever was playing was going over and over the same bit, then changing songs midstream. This time he was singing about how it was all over now.

(What was?)

Evie went out onto the balcony, stepping gingerly for the boards were gappy and she was scared they mightn't hold her weight. It seemed okay. From out here you could now catch a boy's voice floating out the balcony door of 201. He wouldn't want to sing up here at night when Ted wanted to sleep, or Ted would blow him in the wind all right. Though come to think of it, Ted couldn't do much, because 201 were the owners and Ted said he'd been lucky to get rent so cheap around here.

The music stopped. Evie studied the street. There was still a bit of noise, people getting in and out of cars, though it must be half past ten or so by now.

It was sure going to be different, living in here in Newtown.

Out at Campbelltown, where they'd lived before, houses were all separate, on blocks of land, and the streets were wide and quiet. Here in Liberty Street you were only allowed to park on one side, and even then it was hard for two cars to pass. And out at Campbelltown all the houses were new, at most only as old as Evie.

'I don't know, darl,' Evie's mum had complained when Ted had decided on the move. 'If your boss wants you for that big contract in the city, then we've obviously got to move. And if this is the only house we can afford, well, we'll make the most of it. Somehow, but, I just don't go much on the idea of living on top of a hundred years of other people's dirt.'

And Evie's friend Roseanne had been even more extreme. 'Just think, in a place that old, people must have *died* there! I'm never going to live in a second-hand house.'

...A second-hand house full of dirt and dead people, Evie thought now; and Evie all alone, with only the sleeping kids.

What if someone did break in? Or if a gang came? You read about gangs hanging around suburbs like this.

Evie imagined them breaking in the back door to the kitchen, or climbing over the scullery roof and getting in Sammy's window, or even getting in from the next-door balcony – the partition between the balconies of this place and 201 was only wood, and there were cracks and little holes. Evie felt eyes through the partition.

Don't be so stupid, Evie.

Evie stopped thinking about eyes through the partition. Evie was renowned for being dull. English teachers at

15

school had always complained of her lack of imagination.

Down in the street a car backfired like a bullet, and Evie jumped. Mum and Ted would be home any minute, and there were gangs at Campbelltown anyway, so it wasn't any different from being alone at their old place...

Still, if a gang *did* want to break in, Evie thought, that was how they'd do it: in the kitchen door or (if they couldn't do that) over the scullery roof, or through this partition (though that'd mean they'd have had to have got into 201 first; unless the owner of 201 was a friend of the gang).

Evie screamed. Not loudly, but loudly enough, loudly as would anyone who saw eyes move behind two neat round holes. Then much more loudly when the gun barrel slid fast out at her through a crack.

The boy stuck his head and the gun around the partition, and laughed. 'Bang!' he said. Evie recognized the gun as a toy rifle of Maria's.

The boy was funny-looking, or at least his head was; that was really all Evie could see. There was something old-fashioned about it, though Evie couldn't pick the style immediately. The face was thin, the nose long with a bump in the middle, the neck was long and thin and the dark eyes were narrow and slanty. The mouth was wide, but the lips were thin. The face looked pale and a bit sickly in the streetlight. But the most noticeable thing was the boy's hair. It was dark, and grew right down to his shoulders; and it was fuzzy on the ends and a bit greasy on top. One long strand kept flopping over his left eye as he laughed.

He pulled his head back from round the partition, then leaned perilously far over the balcony and pointed the rifle down into the street. 'Bang-bang-bang-bang-bang...' he yelled as he mowed down the cars.

'Of course, it should be a machine-gun,' the boy said when he'd finished. 'That's what they use in the movie.'

'What movie?'

'*If*, of course.' The boy stared at her as if she was stupid. 'Didn't you see it? They had it on TV again last week. That's the third time on TV. The seventh time I've seen it. It's my favourite movie.'

He stopped and corrected himself, in a pedantic way that Evie would grow used to over the weeks to come. 'No,' he said, 'it's not my favourite movie, it's the only movie I really like at all.'

Evie was confused. 'I don't know what you're talking about.' Evie usually wouldn't admit ignorance to a stranger, certainly not to a male one, but you could see from this person's looks that he didn't count. He was weird. And, despite the partition, Evie could see that he was shorter than her.

'*If*,' he said again. 'That scene at the end where the kids are up on top of the building and they mow down all the enemy on the ground with machine-guns. Whenever I see it I always get a funny feeling that it's *me* up there, shooting down – as if I've done it all before, in real life. What's your name?'

'Evie.'

'Yeah, I'm Noel. Mum will be collecting the rent from you, I suppose. Though it's not her house, it's the despot's. The despot stays in bed nearly all the time, though she can get out, and she speaks too sometimes. That's a secret.

17

What's she charging?'

'Eighty, I think.' More than for their nice house in Campbelltown; but then, rents were high in the inner city.

'Of course, she has to cut the price, they reckon it's haunted.' Noel burst out laughing. A wild, violent laugh.

How stupid, to try to scare her. 'I've got to go now,' Evie said, but he was rattling on and on.

'That's your father, I suppose, the guy with the beer gut. Your mother looks like Loretta Young in a midday movie, but spunkier. How old are you?'

'Sixteen.'

'Yeah, I'm fifteen.'

He didn't look it. Or rather, his body didn't, for he was a little shorter than Evie. And he was thin, like a primary-school kid. His face though could be old when he wasn't laughing.

'What music do you like best?' He fired questions like bullets.

'Oh, most things. Everything. I don't know. Nothing in particular.' That was part of the trouble with Evie. As far as music went, and food, and people, and possible jobs, and everything else, Evie had no particular opinions. She neither hated things nor loved things. She was just middle-ey Evie. Middle-ey-muddle-ey-piddle-ey-puddle-ey-fuddle-ey-Evie-Peevie. That was one of Maria's songs. Evie hated being asked what she thought of things, or what she wanted to do, because everything seemed as grey and floppy as everything else. Perhaps the strongest feelings she had were of disliking Ted, and liking Mum and Sammy; but even

18

then it didn't seem very strong. It wasn't like love or hate. Or not like love or hate seemed when you saw them in movies. And so people got annoyed with Evie because she was always so uncaring and undecided; and Evie thought less of herself too, because other people thought she was boring, and because it was very frustrating for Evie herself, never knowing what she liked or she wanted.

'The only music I like is Bob Dylan,' Noel said. 'But only his early stuff, not the stuff he's into these days.'

One thing about Noel, Evie thought, is that he's so full of his own opinions that he doesn't seem to mind that I don't have any. Evie knew that the guys she talked to in Campbelltown thought she was boring.

'What I wish,' Noel went on, 'is that I'd been around in the sixties, when Dylan was good and people fought if they felt things, like the kids in *If.* That's why I look like I do.'

Evie was confused again. The sixties were as far away as Ancient History. But she could now sort of recognize Noel's looks as being like those people with messy hair and black jumpers and duffle-coats that you see on old record covers. Evie looked, and sure enough, Noel had a black polo-neck jumper on, though it wasn't all that cold.

'People think I'm a creep,' Noel said.

Evie didn't say anything.

'It always kills a conversation,' Noel said, 'to let people know you know what they're thinking of you. Adios amigo.' Noel handed her the rifle. 'I found this in your front yard this afternoon. Sweet dreams.' And Noel's face disappeared around the partition and then Evie heard the mouth-organ in the room.

Evie's watch had stopped and she didn't know where she'd packed the radio, so she couldn't find out the time. It was dark and lonely upstairs now that Noel was gone, so she felt her way down the stairwell. Tripped at the bottom. Went through the dark diningroom and into the lounge, looked at the divan and decided: I might as well sleep out there, right from the first night. Evie rarely had such a positive feeling about something.

She made her way back through the diningroom, through the half-lit kitchen, and unlocked the back door. There was the empty, narrow breezeway, and then the scullery...

It seemed odd to Evie, the wasted space of the breezeway, but Mrs Cavendish next door had explained it to Mum and Mum had told Evie: In the old days, about a hundred years ago when these houses had been built, the scullery was where people had a fuel copper for the washing, and to boil up water for baths. They used to use the scullery too for washing up, and for peeling the vegetables, plucking chooks, and other messy things. In lots of houses they'd built a narrow passage called a breezeway in between the kitchen and the scullery to stop the scullery smells and heat from getting into the house. The scullery at 203 had been used as a combined laundry-bathroom until ten years ago, when they'd converted the tiny upstairs storeroom next to Sammy's room into a bathroom. But at the end of World War I, Mrs Cavendish had said, they'd got the gas on, and they'd got new gas coppers and had stopped using the old fuel ones in both houses. Mrs Cavendish knew all these things because her mother, who owned the two houses, had lived in 201 all her life. Mum said Mrs Cavendish's mother was evidently bedridden, poor old thing, but Mum hadn't met her yet…

Evie found a box of matches and went in. She'd had a good look by daylight, but just wanted to make sure.

It was a small room – small and square. The walls were unplastered brick, cracking a bit, painted grey. She could repaint them. The floor was concrete, covered with yellow lino; not too old, not too bad. There was a window looking out onto the side passage and 205's fence.

On the other side of the room, the back corner was completely filled in with a big diagonal cupboard. Evie had looked in there that afternoon, and that was where the old fuel copper was. It was a tall, brick structure, with the copper set right into it. Under the copper was a space that came up to Evie's knee; that was where the fire used to go. You could still see the fire-marks on the bricks, and on the floor too – for when they'd cemented the room they'd stopped at the cupboard, and under the copper there were still the old flagging stones. In the farthest bit of the corner was a rusty tin chimney pipe. No attempt had been made to turn the cupboard into a proper cupboard, with shelves and things: it was just a big, dirty, triangular, closed-in space, containing some broken odds and ends like an old push-mower and bike tyres and old paint tins and some old flagon bottles containing little bits of sedimented, noxious-looking liquids. Mrs Cavendish had told Mum that the cupboard had been built in 1920, and it sure looked it.

Evie glanced a bit dubiously at the cupboard now,

struck a match, and had a quick look inside just to make sure no one was hiding in it, or anything. One day soon she'd clear out all the junk, and then she'd get Ted to put some shelves up in there. Ted was good about things like building shelves, and got wood cheap because he worked for a builder.

Evie dragged a mattress through from the dining-room, psyching herself into liking this room.

...It'll be good down here. A place to be private. I can play the radio at night, and if I put up some thick curtains I can lock the door and sleep in the daytime and no one will know...

The last few months, Evie had been sleeping a lot. She'd get up and help Mum, and then as soon as Mum had gone to work and Evie had taken Sammy to the play centre, Evie would come home and go to bed again. Then she'd get up and do some housework, and then she'd go back to sleep again. Sometimes she was late picking Sammy up because she'd been fast asleep. Ted worked odd hours, and some-times he'd come home in the afternoon and find her asleep.

'Lazy bloody kid,' he'd rave at Mum. 'You'd think she'd be out looking for a job. I only wish *I* could have a kip in the afternoon.' When he was really vicious, he'd call her Sleeping Beauty, or Wee Willie Winkie...

But down here, no one will know if I'm in here asleep, or out looking for work...

Evie went in and got a couple of blankets and a pillow, snapped off the kitchen light, stepped into the breezeway, and pulled the kitchen door hard shut behind her.

She heard the lock click, tested the door with her

shoulder just to be sure, then crossed into the scullery and locked her own door too against the Newtown night.

2

Evie always went to sleep the instant her head touched the pillow. If she had dreams, they disappeared completely before she woke. Maria and Sammy sometimes screamed themselves awake with nightmares, and Jodie dreamed a lot that she was a fish, but Evie couldn't remember ever having had a dream in her life.

This night, though, something happened.

It was the sound of the footstep first, treading stealthily across the roof above her, only one foot, then two feet, more feet; and more feet too, a new set of feet, six more feet, lots more feet, running fast down the side passage in rhythm with the feet above. But only the sounds; she couldn't see anything.

Then it stopped, then it happened again.

But visually this second time, and soundlessly, she saw the shape of a foot plant itself silverly above her. Not a naked foot, with toes, but a boot-shape, rounded at the front, a heavy heel at the back, heavy though soundless the footstep now grew above her till it seemed to cover the ceiling, silver first then changing to black.

Then outside, in the passage that ran along beside her mattress, she could see feet in black boots planting down fast. One after the other, rhythmically running, a sort of running march-at-the-double; she could see them though she was inside and they were outside and there was a wall

23

of bricks between her and them. She could see them, though not hear them this time, and nor did she see bodies growing up from the feet but just felt the feet.

Then maybe she awoke, if really she'd been asleep (for it hadn't felt like sleep) because it stopped again.

Evie concentrated, listened, there was nothing. Got up and peered out the window, and there was nothing. Evie lay down. Mum and Ted would have to be home soon. Maybe they were already, maybe they'd come home and were lying on the double mattress upstairs in their room. Evie felt nearly half-inclined to go into the house and see; but more inclined just to stay fast in her room behind the locked door. A private sanctuary.

Time passed then; time that was so shapeless that Evie might as well have been asleep. Time that wasn't negative, and wasn't positive, time like most of Evie's time, that seemed just to exist as part of her life, moving Evie from one day to the next, time that made her hair grow by the month, that made her body grow by the year, but that didn't ever do anything more eventful.

Time that didn't press on her, that didn't impinge.

Not like this new time that had her again now, gripping her blood in its urgency, sending its feet pounding along her veins in boots as it ran up-and-over on-the-double through her head. Time that pressed now, meaning something, happening too fast, drawn out like ages; time that pressed just as space pressed, for the room now had shrunk to the size of the diagonal cupboard and Evie was in it, standing up, balancing on top of the copper, wanting desperately to cough but holding her breath for dear life.

Noel's face swam through her mind, the pale colour, the believer's eyes, the flame of his smile as he bang-banged and laughed down into the street.

Balancing, the face threw her off balance, and might have tipped her off the copper if she'd really been standing on it instead of lying down on the mattress as she had been all the time. She could feel the button-things beneath her hand, for she had no sheet.

Evie shifted, and shuddered with the memory, now that it was over.

Though it wasn't over, for it happened again.

This fourth time, the state Evie was in while it happened was more like a regular dream. Or rather, when she thought back over everything the next day, and again for days afterwards, the fourth time seemed more like other people's descriptions of dreams.

The fourth time, things came together, sound and seeing, and the things she couldn't see.

There is the cupboard, the closed air inside it, the sight of the wooden door as I look at it from inside. Then sounds of footsteps, first one, two, three, then lots running left-right, on-the-double, down the side there, overhead.

Shouts and crashing. The gang of thugs, trying to crash through into the kitchen; crashing over the roof into the upstairs back room.

Sammy! Evie thought. But she couldn't move.

And screaming more then, and more crashing, a sound like the kitchen door crashing open from inside, and bangs echoing over everything like a car backfiring.

25

No one's voice that I can pick.

Legs stiff, feet stuck to the top of the copper, eyes fixed in the darkness to the slatted wood of the cupboard door. Too scared to step out and look. Fear cold, like time all around. A hurry and slowness. And suddenly his face. Thin and white, too white and too thin, the dark eyes of his fear and hurry as he hands me the gun and disappears.

3

It was dawn when Evie got up. She could see the light then, coming in the window. She could hear sounds, coming from the kitchen. But okay sounds, this time.

She unlocked the scullery door, and went in.

'What a night!' Mum was making tea and toast and scrambled eggs. Ted was sitting at the table, waiting with his plate.

'*We're* up early!' Ted said. By 'we' meaning Evie.

'Yeah, that'll do me for a night and a half.' Mum had a habit of repeating herself.

'Why? What?' It flashed through Evie's mind that if Mum had had a bad night too, then it could've been something real, like burglars maybe, or maybe people having a fight next door.

'The car broke down,' Mum said. 'Just out of Liverpool. It took poor Ted ages to fix it, we only just got here.'

'It took poor Ted ages to fix it,' Ted mimicked, 'because poor Ted didn't have the right tools, did he, because someone who'd unpacked the boot had gone and unpacked the

26

toolbox too, instead of leaving it there, as anyone with a grain of sense would've done, as anyone with a grain of sense knows that the toolbox never comes out of the boot.'

'Oh,' Evie said. She was the someone who had unpacked the boot. As Ted well knew.

'Please knock it off, darl...' Mum piled food onto Ted's plate. 'What's done's done. All's well that ends well. We're home now and none the worse.'

'None the worse, except that we were up all night with no bloody sleep and I've gotta start on the new job today and you've gotta go to work too, while Miss Brilliant here twiddles her thumbs.'

Evie said nothing. Began to make herself a piece of toast. Evie-Peevie. She knew she had her peeved look on.

'Seeing as you're up, love,' Mum said, 'you might go and unpack the trailer, and then Ted can go straight to work when he's through with his breakfast.'

Evie pointedly took her half-cooked toast off the griller. She'd starve.

'Is there anything, Ted,' Evie said too politely as she retreated into the diningroom, 'is there anything that's in the trailer that shouldn't be unpacked?'

Ted ate on and said nothing.

'I was just asking, because after all *you* said last night to get *everything* out of the boot, and...'

'Skoot!' Mum slammed the diningroom door after Evie.

'You have to understand, darl,' Evie heard Mum say, 'she's a very young sixteen.'

'Better than being a fat, old forty-three-year-old,' Evie muttered to herself.

27

A couple of hours later, after Ted had gone, Mum thanked Evie for arranging the photos so nicely on the mantelpiece. Mum always did that sort of thing. Stuck with Ted when he was there, and then was specially nice to Evie behind his back. Mum had always been like that, ever since she'd got Ted, when Evie was five. It was as if she was so scared of losing Ted that she'd put herself down, and put Evie down, just to keep him.

'You'll be okay today, love, with the girls,' Mum said. 'You might find out where a park is, and take them there, but don't let Jodie or Ree go off on the bike, not till they know the roads round here, and careful with Sammy, with all the traffic.'

'What were you planning to do today?' Mum added as an afterthought.

'Oh, I thought I might find out where the CES is, see if there are any jobs going.' Evie had no intention. Not today. She was exhausted after last night. But it sounded good to say that, to butter Mum up. 'Or go right into town, to the Youth Job Centre.' Piling it on now, with jam and cream.

'Oh well. Leave it go till Monday. The kids will be at school then. One day won't hurt.'

(As if a million days would hurt!)

'By the way, love…' Mum was nearly out the door now, on her way to work, looking groomed and smart despite no sleep. 'Do be careful about doors. It's not like Campbelltown here, you know. When we came home this morning, you'd left the kitchen door wide open.'

Oh really? Evie thought.

28

4

It being Friday, Noel thought he might go to school. He tended to do that on Mondays and Fridays. He lay there in bed a while, thinking he might skip it, and go investigate those new people next door. But considering seriously, there'd be all weekend for that. And presumably six months, for it must be a six-month lease. Unless they got scared, and broke the lease.

Noel laughed, then stopped laughing, considered it seriously, then laughed again.

He sometimes wondered. It was true that tenants didn't tend to last long next door. Six months, a year maybe, and one lot had broken their lease. But how much it was due to something weird, and how much to the odd bits of weirdness that Noel sometimes put on; and how much it was due to the house being cruddy, and how much to the despot being a shit of a landlady, Noel just didn't know. Plus there were factors such as general high mobility in inner-city areas.

The weirdness, though, had started seriously. Or at least seriously in Noel's mind. When he was about six, Noel had overheard tenants in the despot's room, complaining. They were a young couple, with no kids, just starting out.

A bell rang. Ring-ring.

Run and run, Noel.

Fetch and carry.

Run in and see, Noel.

You might be needed.

29

Run and run, Noel.
The bell has rung.

Noel climbed out of bed, making himself take his time, forcing himself to relinquish the speed he'd been trained to; then put on his duffle-coat as a dressing gown and obeyed the despot's call.

The first thing Noel noticed as he walked into the room was the light. There was a lot more of it than usual. It poured in through the window, illuminating the despot on her bed. The blind was right up. Usually she only had it up a fraction. Sometimes days would go by when she wouldn't allow it up at all. Noel couldn't remember ever seeing it right up.

'Good morning, Nanna,' Noel addressed the despot. 'We've got the blind up so we can perve on the new neighbours, have we? It's a shame we can't see more…"Backyard Glimpses", I think that's how they'd describe it in a real-estate ad. Like "Harbour Glimpses". Though I must say there's a panoramic view of the scullery roofs.'

The despot had the back bedroom, the room that Sammy had in the house next door. Her high, hard, narrow bed was pushed up against the window so that she could peer out if she wanted to and check that no one was coming in her back gate and down the side passage. Though she could see a bit of her own yard, and a bit of 203's, most of the view was of the flat corrugated-iron roofs of the two adjoining sculleries, a metre and a bit below her.

'But what did you wish, oh Grandmother mine?' Noel continued, looking curiously at the despot. There was something about her this morning.

The despot said nothing, but kept her eyes fixed on Noel. She was as Mum would have left her before going to work: propped up on her three pillows, fully dressed and lying on top of the neat counterpane. Fully dressed right down to stockings and shoes, though she wouldn't move all day except to go to the toilet. The toilet was right next to this room, and the despot officially hadn't gone further than that since the last stroke, five years ago. *Officially* hadn't, according to what Mum and the doctors believed, but Noel had surprised her a couple of times when he'd lobbed into the house unexpectedly.

Once he'd found her downstairs, pottering on her two sticks through the gloom and junk of the scullery.

Once he'd found her up on the balcony, staring down into the street.

He hadn't told Mum: what was the point? If Mum knew she sometimes wandered, Mum would spend all day every day at work imagining broken legs or a stroke on the stairs.

Similarly, he didn't tell Mum that she could talk. If Mum knew about the little conversations, the whisperings with the despot's mates, Mum might think she was going loopy, and worry more. Of course, she wasn't just *going* loopy, in Noel's opinion: she was over the hills and far away. In Noel's opinion too, she'd always been like that, even back before the stroke. But she always presented a very sane aspect to Mum and the doctors. Grumpy, but sane. Perhaps afraid they'd put her away. As if Mum ever would!

'Oh, she's cunning, isn't she,' Noel murmured too softly for her to hear, 'the old Lucrezia Borgia.'

The despot fixed her eyes hard on Noel now, and pointed to her writing stuff on the bedside table. She could easily reach it herself, but Noel handed it to her. It was a thing called a magic-pad, that kids use: a sort of soft slate that you write on with a special pen, and then you lift up the transparent cover-sheet and all the writing disappears.

'THE BLIND,' the despot wrote in big capitals, like someone writing an anonymous hate-letter. She showed it to Noel, then lifted the transparent page and erased it. She always erased immediately. Before Noel got her the magic-pad she used to use ordinary pen and paper, and then as soon as the notes were read she'd tear them into tiny shreds and Noel would have to spend ages picking up all the confetti from the floor.

Noel smiled, and took the pad from her. Though she could hear perfectly well, he sometimes conversed back with her by notes. Just for fun. A dose of her own medicine.

'THERE'S NONE SO BLIND,' Noel wrote, 'AS THOSE WHO WILL NOT SEE.' He gave it to her.

'Nor so dumb,' Noel said, 'as those who refuse to speak.'

The despot erased angrily.

'IMPERTINENCE!' she wrote. Showed it, erased, then wrote: 'FIX THE BLIND.'

Noel looked up, and realized that not only was the blind all the way up, but that it was caught there, stuck there because the cord had got cobbled round and round the roller. She must have yanked it up so hard that it flew away from her.

'Scuzey-moi,' Noel said.

32

He climbed onto the bed, up over her, then stood on tiptoe on the window-sill to reach up and untangle it. It was difficult, he was so short.

'I wonder when we did this.'

Noel strained and grunted, nearly toppled onto her, then did it.

'There we are.'

Noel was back on the ground. 'Any more little services? We're only too willing to oblige.'

'WASH YOUR HAIR,' the despot wrote.

Noel smiled, erased it for her.

'REMOVE THE BREAKFAST,' the despot wrote. She waved her ring-hand at the electric food-warmer beside her bed. Mum always made her a good breakfast and left it there before she went to work. It would be eaten by the time Noel got up, and one of his before-school duties was to take the empty plates down and wash them. His midday duty was to come home from school and warm up her dinner and take it up and put it in the food-warmer. His first after-school duty was to remove the empty dinner plates and take up the afternoon tea. The despot loved her food.

Noel opened the food-warmer for the empty plates. But the porridge bowl was full under its silver lid and there were two eggs and bacon under another lid and four slices of toast under a third. That was a new one on Noel: the despot off her tucker.

Noel put them on the tray without comment. The cup had been used but the teapot was nearly full: only one cup instead of her standard three, and she'd drunk it without milk.

As Noel headed for the door, there was a croak behind him.

'*Noh!*'

The sound the despot made for his name. She had a different, two-syllable croak for Mum.

Noel turned. The despot was holding up her pad.

'THE NEIGHBOURS.

WHAT ARE THEY LIKE?'

'I dunno.' Noel wasn't a spy for her.

The despot shook her head and impatiently erased.

'THE GIRL.

HOW OLD?

DESCRIBE HER.'

'Ravishingly lovely. Spunky as hell. Just the right age. I'm head over heels already.'

The despot gave him a look. Those narrow dark eyes, like Noel's own, impenetrable. Noel waited, balancing the loaded tray. Till the angry erase, the next message.

'TELL YOUR MOTHER

I COULDN'T EAT.'

'Have a nice day.' Noel beamed and was out the door.

Of course Noel wouldn't tell Mum. The old girl was just bunging on an act. 'There's a little surprise though, waiting for you, my lady.' Noel ate the bacon, but put the porridge in the fridge instead of the bin.

Next door, Maria and Jodie were moving from the Weeties stage to the toast stage and Sammy wouldn't eat her Weet Bix with cold milk.

Evie put some milk on to warm, and the night came

34

back to her. That feeling in the cupboard. Evie wasn't used to something so sharp.

The milk boiled over, burnt and stank.

Damn Sammy and her hot milk.

Evie put some more on. Felt her mind drifting off, burnt the toast but caught the milk just in time.

'It's too hot!'

Evie poured some cold in.

'I only like it how Mummy makes it!'

'Stiff!' Evie put some more toast on.

'Evie, you said a rude word,' Sammy complained, delighted.

'I did not!'

'You did too!' Maria said, just to make Sammy worse.

'I did not too.' Being with the kids, Evie found she went down to *their* level. One day, she'd leave. As far as Evie had an ambition, that was it. She peanut-buttered some toast for Sammy. She could hear Maria now, clunking around in the scullery.

'Get out of my room!'

'*You* go in *my* room!'

'Come and do the washing up!'

'Do it yourself!'

Maria raced off and out the back gate. Well, that had got rid of Maria for the morning, anyway. And Jodie was getting ready to go, pumping up Ree's bike in the dining-room. Ree's bike used to be Evie's. It wasn't a BMX, and Ree despised it.

'Jodie, Mum says you're not to ride the bike, no one's

to ride the bike, not till you know the roads around here.'

'Yes,' Jodie said pleasantly, wheeling the bike out into the hall, out the front door.

So it was just down to Evie and Sammy. That was better. Unless Sammy was in one of her tough moods. She was far more strong-willed than Evie.

'Evie-Peevie,' Sammy said happily, 'this is lovely toast. I love my toast like this. I love it when you make my toast like this. This is lovely breakfast.'

When Sammy was in this mood, she made Evie happy too.

'We'll find a park this morning,' Evie said.

'With swings?'

'With everything!'

That morning Evie felt like a sightseer in a foreign city. It was lovely, plodding slowly because of Sammy, looking at new things, like someone in a documentary. She didn't even know where the main street was.

Evie could see the boy Noel in the distance, in his school trousers and his black polo-neck jumper. She could've caught him up but didn't bother. Then he turned down a lane.

Right at the end of the street Sammy and Evie passed a porch that had a thin old man sitting in the sun on the gas-meter box.

'Mornin',' he said. He had a parrot in a big wire cage and was poking lettuce in to it.

'Good morning,' Evie said. At Campbelltown you didn't see many old people. And you never saw someone just sitting outside their house. And strangers usually didn't talk to you.

'Hello,' said Sammy. 'I'm Sammy.'

He was still sitting there when they came back. 'Afternoon,' he said.

'Hi,' said Evie.

'We went to the park,' said Sammy. 'We had to ask a lady where it was, cause Evie didn't know and we were lost.'

'New in the street?' the old man said.

'We only moved in last night.'

'What number?'

'203.'

'Ah,' said the old man. 'The house that was Eureka.' He looked up and Evie felt him watching her.

'What's *your* name?' Sammy said, but Evie took her hand and walked more quickly now down the street. It was a bad habit for the kid to get into, Evie thought, talking to strange old men.

Lunch-time now and Noel came home from school. He felt a bit more cheerful about despot-duty today.

'Surprise-surprise.' Noel chanted to himself.

When Noel was a tiny kid and couldn't eat his porridge, the despot would serve it up to him again cold at midday.

'You should count yourself lucky to have anything, boy.'

And at tea-time again if Noel didn't eat it at midday. If he didn't eat it then, he went to bed with nothing. That was in the days when the despot was in charge of Noel, instead of vice versa. Right from when he was a baby Mum had had to work because Noel's father was dead, and so Mum had been out all day and hadn't known what went on. Sometimes the despot was okay and played games with him, but on her bad days she used to lock him in his room for just about anything. And Noel could still taste the glug of her cold porridge.

Noel got the bowl out of the fridge. A cold crusty skin had formed on the top. Lovely. Noel pushed aside the rhubarb pie that was meant to be the despot's sweets.

'Mummy, I'm hungry...'

Noel used to tittletat to Mum when she got home; but the despot always told Mum that the boy was a can't-help-himself-liar.

'Oh dear, Noel. Nanna says you wouldn't eat your tea....Maybe a jam sandwich wouldn't hurt.'

'Eating between meals,' the despot warned. 'That's what makes him sleepwalk, you know.'

'I suppose you're right, Mummy.'

As Mum always seemed to believe the despot, Noel just gave up. Mum was totally under the despot's thumb. She was a small woman, always tense, ready to flee, like a little lizard.

Noel could still taste the porridge. And hear the speech that always accompanied it.

'...If you'd been here, boy, when one in three was out of work, you'd know what it is to tighten your belt. Cruel it was then. Four days I once went, with nothing to sustain me save a little black tea.'

...The taste of that speech over the porridge. The stories of joining up slivers of soap, of boiling up the one lamb shank all week, of thinking it Christmas to get a choko. Noel had been brought up on Depression tales the same way other kids have Cinderella.

'Well, my lady.' Noel put the porridge on the tray. 'You may just find the Depression days returning.' There was macaroni cheese in the oven to be warmed up, but bugger her. '*Cruel it was then...*' Noel chanted.

Noel knew he was vicious, the way he was acting to an eighty-seven-year-old woman. But what about the way *she'd* acted when it was *him* that was weak?

Noel heard voices from the kitchen next door, was distracted, lost some of his anger.

'Oh bugger it.' He relented, and warmed up the macaroni. But she could still have the porridge for her sweets.

A scream came through the kitchen wall.

It was that girl, yelling full blast at the other kids. Noel had quite liked her. She looked ordinary, and listened to him. Noel decided to skip school that afternoon and go in there; then changed his mind and decided to go up the music shop instead. Plenty of time.

5

There was plenty of time. By that Friday fortnight Evie still hadn't got around to fixing her room properly. She had her bed and stuff from Campbelltown now, but she hadn't painted the walls or made any curtains. She'd just stuck an old blanket of Sammy's up over the window.

'What you find to do all day beats me,' Ted always said. 'But whatever it is, it must keep you flat out. Christ knows, it's not as if you're much help to your mother with the housework.'

Ted was wrong about the housework: Evie thought she did lots. But he was right, in a way, about the rest. Whatever it was that Evie did with her days, Evie didn't know either.

Evie should have had lots of spare time, but she didn't. She'd walk Sammy to the play centre. Then she'd go home and clean up for an hour or so. But then she should be free from about half-past ten till she had to pick Sammy up at two-thirty. Four hours each day to do something in. To fix up her room, or maybe do something proper about looking for a job. But the days just wandered past Evie, the time in them disappearing on things she had to do before she could do anything.

'I do so do things,' Evie told Ted that third Friday night, after tea.

'Like for example what!' Ted had been worse than usual, this last week. Really moody. Even snapping at the girls.

'Like the Monday after we moved in, for instance, I had to go to the dole office, to get my file transferred over from Campbelltown.'

That had taken so long she'd run the risk of being late picking Sammy up on Sammy's first day.

...Finding her way to the post office, looking up the phone book to find out where the local dole office was, going home to get the street directory, remembering when she got home that of course the directory was in the car, finding her way to the Newtown library, looking up the street directory there to find out how to get to

Parramatta Road, Camperdown...

By that time it had been half-past one and there wasn't time to get there and then back in time for Sammy.

'Okay,' Ted said. 'So you fixed all that up. Then what?'

'But I didn't fix it up.' Evie didn't bother with the details because Ted hated details. 'I did it on Tuesday.'

Again not bothering to explain that you walk about four kilometres to get down there and then you get a number and then you sit down and wait an hour or two till it's your number's turn, and then you talk at the desk and fill in forms. So it was half-past one again when she finished and there was no time to go all the way up to the Commonwealth Employment Service at Newtown to fill in the other set of forms that had to be transferred.

'Okay, so after two days Miss Brilliant had her form filled in. And on Wednesday?'

'No,' said Evie, 'on Wednesday I did the other form. Up at the other office.' Admittedly that only took an hour, and then she'd spent half an hour wandering around the noticeboards, reading ads for qualified plumbers and couriers with their own vans and à la carte chefs and factory hands with seventy-nine years experience and well-groomed temps with refs. Then she'd gone home and slept.

(Slept. Or maybe not slept. It hadn't *felt* like sleep, to feel like a flame; it felt more awake than most of Evie's time.)

'And on Thursday,' Evie went on (skipping over the sleeping), 'I went down the Newtown CYSS centre, to see what was going on.'

Mum knew that CYSS was some sort of government thing, so it was always a good alibi, when talking to her.

41

Back at Campbelltown, Evie used to go to CYSS sometimes with Roseanne; Ted called it the Dolebludgers' Club. Like going down the Catholic Club, or the RSL.

'Going down the Dolebludgers'?' he'd say, his eyes sarcastic on her. 'Be sure to tell me, when you get a good win on the pokies.'

Ha ha. Very funny. The real joke was the CYSS itself. Commonwealth Youth Support Scheme. As if a fancy name would work some sort of magic. Mum thought it was something about training you, or teaching you how to get a job. Ha, ha, Evie laughed to herself.

Ted snorted now at the mention of CYSS, but Mum said, 'Oh good, love' – encouraging but vague. She was taking up the curtains from the old place to fit the windows here. 'Anything useful?' Mum sometimes tried to feed Evie lines, to get Ted off Evie's back. (Off Mum's back too.)

'Oh. Yes. No. Maybe.' Keep it vague. Evie had screwed up her courage and gone down there. She felt shy, going somewhere full of strangers. She went in, and there was a guy running around with a video camera, and a fattish-sort-of girl running after him with a sound-thing. The girl was like a dog on a leash, connected to him via the sound-cord. They looked about twenty-five and you could tell they were in charge of the place. The guy was good-looking.

Evie had looked at the noticeboards to see what was going on. Macrame, yoga, the usual sort of stuff. Training you for all the yoga and macrame factories out there in the world.

'G'day,' the good-looking guy smiled.

But Evie felt shy and said nothing; she went home and had a little sleep.

(A little sleep; a little nightmare. A little nightmare, not a big one this time. More like an angry dream.

Bang bang.

Evie was hammering. Hammering at a piece of board.

But the nails were going in crooked, getting stuck, and as soon as she got one in one side, a nail would drop out of the other side and her board would still be swinging down.

Evie was in foul temper.

Bang.

Ted was there, but in the dream he was her father.

Bang.

Noel was there, but he wasn't quite Noel.

Bang.

Evie flamed with hatred.

Bang bang.)

Evie looked at Ted. That look on his red face as he took a swig from his can of KB. Yet she didn't hate him. She bucked against him a lot, out of habit more than anything else, for when he'd first married Mum he'd tried to be nice to Evie and she'd been jealous of him, and started to fight. Yet in real life she didn't hate him like she had in that dream. It was as if real life was more like dreaming.

'And then Friday I went back to the CES, to look at the noticeboards.' To get ideas for what to write on her form when the time came to lodge it on Monday. Evie had been on the dole well over a year now, and had been knocked back so often that she no longer bothered applying for jobs much, but she had to show ambition to work on her form.

'Okay, okay,' said Ted, walking out. Something more interesting than Evie had just come on TV.

'And then the next Monday,' Evie muttered on regardless, just feeling like a gripe, 'I went down to lodge my form and they hadn't got the stuff transferred and said my cheque would be late, I'd do better to lodge it back in Campbelltown, so on Tuesday I went out there and lodged it a day late so the cheque'll be late anyway and Thursday I went up to the CES and asked about a job and they got me an interview for next Monday, so I spent all day today getting my clothes ready for that.' (Leaving out Wednesday when Evie had slept. She really needed to sleep in the daytime now, after dreams and footsteps running through the night.)

'Did you go and see Roseanne, love, while you were out there?' Mum just asked that to keep the conversation flowing. Her mouth was full of pins.

'Yeah.'

'How was she?'

'Good.' Roseanne had spent the whole time talking about some guy Evie didn't know, and she hadn't wanted to know anything about Evie. Evie never had any guy to rave about, whenever Roseanne raved.

'That's good, love.'

'By the way, love,' mum added. 'What's the job you're going for Monday, that you're fixing some clothes for?'

'Nude bar-work,' Evie said, making a casual exit.

'Smart alec!' From outside, Evie heard Mum laughing at her.

Evie laughed back. Mum was all right.

*

Evie went into her room, shut the door, hurled herself on her bed, lay there a while in the quiet and privacy. She might go to sleep. It was still too early for bed even for Jodie and Maria, but Evie felt kind of sleepy and there was nothing else to do. Watching TV meant sitting with Ted and Maria and Jodie, and the alternative was going out, which she couldn't do. Firstly because she knew nowhere to go and no one to go with, and secondly because she had no money, her dole cheque hadn't come.

Evie dozed off, woke a couple of hours later. Shook her head to try to remember, but no, there didn't seem to have been anything this time. Not anything in her sleep that made her wake up, stuck tight to the bed, wanting to cough, desperate for something cold to ease her throat. Not anything like the terrible loneliness as his white face disappeared.

Evie got up and went around to the old outside toilet, behind the scullery. She could hear Noel and his mouth-organ in the toilet next door. The now-familiar whining melancholy of his Dylan songs. Evie sometimes faintly heard him in the daytime, playing in his kitchen.

Evie climbed up on the paling fence and leaned over.

'What do people do around here, Friday nights?' she asked when finally he came out.

'I dunno. Go into town and play Space Invaders. Go to some place if they've got money and listen to music. Stay home.' Noel never asked anyone at school what they did because, whatever it was, he wouldn't be interested in doing it with them. Music was the only thing, but Noel didn't like the same sort of music, and also the music places were mainly pubs and Noel was far too short to pretend to be eighteen. (Noel never asked anyone at school what they did because, whatever it was, they wouldn't want to do it with him. They thought he was a creep.)

'Do you feel like going for a walk?' Noel said.

'Not particularly,' Evie said. 'Hang on.'

She ran back and put on a jumper, then quietly locked the door, leaving the light on and the radio going. Let them think she was still in there. Not that Mum would mind her going out, but Evie felt like being secretive. She got fed up, having five people around her all the time, knowing every time she blew her nose. When she got a job she'd be able to leave.

'Come on then!' Noel's words came out like a yelp through the darkness. His voice had broken a while ago but it still occasionally went high.

'Come on yourself!'

From her room, the despot watched them as they sped out the back way, along the narrow lane that had been built between the fences so the dunny-can man could come along and collect the cans. The lane ran along behind a few sets of palings, then turned down into Liberty Street.

'This way...Left here...Now up here...' Noel muttered as he headed Evie along his special back route to Newtown Bridge.

'Not that way,' he cut in fast as Evie went to cross over past a corner deli. There were a couple of guys outside, big, a bit older probably than Evie.

(*Matt*, Noel thought. Matt Dunkley and Tasso Politis. When he was a little kid they used to shove him in the gutter

46

and steal the notes the despot would write to the shop-keeper, Tasso's father.

'Nanny's boy!' they'd yodel. 'Sookabubba, Sobbaguts!'

'Cowardy-Cowardy-Custard,' they'd yell, because he was too scared to take the both of them on.

Then he'd go home without the things the despot had sent him for, and he'd be in trouble again.)

Noel pulled at Evie's sleeve and got her past and into a lane without Matt seeing. 'This way's much longer,' Noel admitted. 'But much nicer.'

Nicer! This wasn't at all what Evie had had in mind. The idea of a walk had sounded boring enough, but she'd presumed they'd at least walk along the King Street main drag, looking in the shops, listening to the music floating out of the pubs. Back in Campbelltown, Roseanne and Evie had often walked around the shopping plaza when they were broke on a Friday night. Looking in the shops, deciding what lounge suites they'd buy when they got married, Roseanne laughing and chatting back to the guys who were walking around.

Whereas Noel's idea involved dark back streets and darker lanes, and finally when they got to Newtown Bridge and the main bit of King Street, Noel turned down past Uncle George's Greek souvlaki stall and led Evie through a dingy sort of empty car park that looked over the station.

'Here!' Noel said suddenly. They'd arrived at the front facade of a derelict, roofless building. A set of brick steps overgrown with grass led up to a gaping doorway.

Noel headed up the steps.

Evie followed.

Quite unprotesting, Evie followed, though she wasn't in the mood for this at all. Evie followed, though, because Evie was a follower. She wasn't in the mood for this, but she wasn't in the mood for anything else in particular. So she followed Noel, who did everything he did with the fervour of a fanatic.

The building was an old hall, with a stage, and Noel was on the stage already, lit up by moonlight, swaying as he played his mouth-organ.

Evie was down in the audience section, looking around for a comparatively clean bit of rubble to sit down on. Still unprotesting, she'd be Noel's audience, though she didn't think much of him either as a person or a performer.

'No, sit up here,' Noel interrupted himself and sat down. Though what he liked about Evie was the way she listened, she should be able to see the landscape too.

The landscape was rooftops, thousands upon thousands of them, four or five suburbs worth of rooftops laid out before them, dissected by a criss-cross of streets with street-lights. This was the landscape you saw from this strange high cliff of a stage that was left there without its back wall or side wall. Evie sat, dangling her legs over the suburbs. She could hear the intermittent roar of the trains pounding down the tracks over there, cutting over Noel's music.

'Sad-eyed Lady of the Lowlands', Noel played, thinking that though this girl wasn't at all suitable for the part of the heroine of the song, at least it was unfamiliarly pleasant to be sitting here beside a girl on a Friday night instead of playing down to the suburbs there alone.

While Evie was thinking that, though Noel didn't

count as a guy to go out with, at least it was unfamiliarly pleasant to be sitting on a Friday night beside someone who didn't make her feel stupid and boring and shy. When Roseanne and Evie sat on Friday nights with guys they ran into around the shopping plaza, Evie would try to think of things to say and would seem to have too many fingers to smoke as casually as Roseanne did.

After a long time of playing and not talking, Noel said, 'I feel like a chew.' He disappeared, then was back again a quarter of an hour later with two cans of Coke and two bulging Greek souvlaki-things with meat and salad inside huge round flaps of bread.

'Uncle George feeds me for free,' Noel said, 'if I play a few songs for him.'

So they both sat there, munching slowly without talking, licking off the meat and tomato-juice that tended to run out the bottoms of the souvlaki-things and down their arms.

'You're very quiet tonight,' Evie finally said.

'I'd noticed that too,' Noel said.

It was good there, peaceful and happy. A change from the tension of the two houses in Liberty Street. Evie and Noel sat for a long time dangling their legs over the suburbs, comfortable for once at simply being who they were, where they were, that Friday night in the middle of May 1981.

6

Nobby and Lizzie had been together since the Cruises moved in next door, when Nobby was seven, when Lizzie was six. That was ten years ago. Nobby had virtually moved in next door too that day, for from that day he'd spent every free possible minute there, with Mick and Lizzie, and also Colleen and Maire; and later with Bridget and Kathleen and Maudie and Fiona too, as one by one more daughters were born and the house grew more crowded.

'Bog Irish,' Nobby's mother always said. 'Breed like pigs.'

Nobby wouldn't say anything. He'd just kiss his mother on the cheek and slip in to 203 through the hidey-hole, and play with Lizzie. Then when the games were finished, he'd slip home again to roast dinner and piano music, while next door they'd be having a stew. Sometimes he'd feel like a traitor to both sides. But then he'd slip off fast again, to play with Lizzie.

Lizzie was always the closest, even closer than Mick. Mick was sometimes Nobby's mate, and sometimes he wasn't. Mick was older, and much solider than Nobby and Lizzie, and it used to take the two of them together to lick him. Lizzie could fight like a bag of cats, but by herself she didn't have the weight. And at the beginning Nobby had been a lousy fighter, because of having been brought up by his mother alone.

Lizzie still fought like a bag of cats. She was on the edge of the crowd now, on the other side from Nobby; standing there tense, obviously only half-listening to the speech, watching the road across Newtown Bridge, the road that the cop waggon would come from, if it came. The cops sometimes came and broke up the Friday-night street meetings. Arrested the speaker and anyone else who got in their way. Last week here they'd arrested Jack Sylvester, the bloke who was up speaking now. And then Mick and big Paddy Cruise had tried to grab Jack back, and they'd been lumbered too.

Lizzie was angry tonight, Nobby could see. Her face clenched in anger. Spoiling for a fight. Nobby grinned: Lizzie would love to get arrested. It would satisfy her Irish martyr-blood. Her Bolshevik daydreams.

'I wish I was Alexandra Kollontai,' Lizzie often said, imagining herself greeting Lenin at the Finland Station in 1917, fighting on the barricades.

And four times now when there'd been a brawl with the cops, Lizzie had wormed her way into the middle, flailing out with tight fists. Despite which, each time the cops had simply picked her up and tossed her out. Like a fish you catch that's not worthwhile.

'It's not fair,' Lizzie complained. 'It's just because I'm a girl. If I was *you*, they'd let me fight.'

If Lizzie was Nobby.

If Lizzie was a bloke, like Nobby.

But if Lizzie was a bloke like Nobby then she wouldn't be in there fighting, because when Nobby saw a brawl with the cops starting, something inside Nobby froze. He couldn't act.

He felt his blood as something thin.

He felt Lizzie felt he was weak.

Maybe she didn't know? Probably she did. She'd never understand.

Lizzie with her wildness flying.

Lizzie with her flaming soul.

51

Lizzie with her anger tonight, clearly busting for another go.

Nobby tried to get around closer to her, but the crowd was too big. About five hundred head, he calculated. Of course, people always got drawn like moths to light when Sylvester was speaking. Silver-tongued Sylvester, they called him. He was National Secretary of the Unemployed Workers' Movement.

'*...And so, fellow workers*,' Sylvester's voice flowed out easily over the crowd, '*I'll wind up now by reminding you of the main demands of our movement. One, that the dole be doubled. Two, the dole to be in cash instead of these lousy coupons. How can we pay rent, when we've got no cash to pay with? Three, any government relief work to be paid at full trade-union rates. And four, the end to evictions...*'

The crowd broke in and cheered. By this year, 1931, Australia was fully in the hold of the Depression, and it was common to see families thrown onto the street for not paying their rent. It was the middle of May now, and with winter approaching it was all the more urgent to force the government to stop landlords evicting people. Nobby was in the Anti-Eviction Committee of the Newtown UWM.

'*No more evictions! Down with the filthy landlords!*'

Nobby found his voice bellowing on after the rest of the crowd had hushed. He hoped Lizzie hadn't noticed.

'Oh yeah? We've finally seen your true colours, Sunshine.' It was Mick at Nobby's side. He spat on the ground at Nobby's feet, and walked off.

The crowd was dwindling fast now Sylvester was

finished. Lizzie was still in the same place, still tense as a cat, but she was turned around looking across straight at Nobby. Her face still spoiling for a fight.

Nobby wondered what he'd done.

'Here, Pa, want a hand?' He went over to help Lizzie's father roll up the banners.

'I can manage m'self.'

So Nobby collected up pamphlets that had fallen on the ground, working his way around to Lizzie.

'Sorry I didn't make it for tea.' Nobby always ate with the Cruises before Friday-night meetings. 'Didn't get back till just now.'

'And what makes you think you'd have got tea? You've a hide, Nobby Weston.'

Lizzie walked off fast after the half a dozen or so others who were carrying the gear to the Railway Workers' Hall overlooking Newtown Station. Her shoes had been issued by the Lady Mayoress's Relief Fund and were three sizes too big. They clattered fiercely on the pavement.

Nobby stared. In ten years Lizzie and he had never had a row. He trailed after her, then sat on the stage and waited while the others stowed the stuff. It wasn't just the Cruises. No one was speaking to him. He swung his legs off the edge of the stage and waited.

'Hey, Lizzie!'

The others had gone. Lizzie was up at the door, about to turn out the light.

'You can stay there long as you like, Nobby Weston. Just shut the door properly when you leave.'

She flipped the light out, leaving him in darkness.

'Whadda you think you're playing at?' Nobby was wild

himself now. Jumped off the stage and twisted his leg. Then ran through, hurdling chairs, knocking a bench flying, as he chased the shape he couldn't see, chased the sound of her quick running breathing. Out on the gravel, over to the fence, then down through the lantana bushes to the back of the hall, and up the stairs of the fire escape. Grabbed her at last on the landing, a thin wild shape panting as it tried to open the door that led backstage.

Lizzie still didn't give in. Fought him hard with her fists now, pushing him back against the landing railing. Down there glowed the lights of Redfern and Mascot and Alexandria, and Nobby felt the rusted iron of the rail wobble against his weight.

'For Christ sake, stop girl! We'll both be gonners!'

But she wouldn't stop. Nobby felt the depth of that distance drag them down. Both falling, two bodies clasping stick-arms, both spinning down to death. (Like one day, years before, when the world went whirley and they slipped off a shed.)

He slapped her then and grabbed her fists, pulling them round behind her back, pushing her down onto her knees. Winning. It was Lizzie who'd taught Nobby to fight. Then let his own body sink down to sit on the landing, holding her fast in case she started again.

But she was done. Her breath coming out noisily in coughs.

'Give in?'

'Just wait till I get me breath back.'

But she didn't try again. The coughing built up and up till she felt her whole body taken over by the huge coughs that started way down in her lungs and skipped their way up her windpipe.

'Hey girl, girl.' Nobby slapped her back to try to stop it. Sometimes these attacks of hers would go on for half an hour or more. At last it finished.

'I hate you, Nobby Weston,' Lizzie said. 'Bloody bronchitis.' She'd had it on and off since she was a kid, and it always came on specially bad when she was upset.

'Sorry. But I had to find out.'

'What?'

'Why you were sour on me. Why all of you were.'

'You know. You dirty traitor. You and your mother. Turning on your own class. Kicking kids out into the street. And then you have the hide to come tonight and cheer your scabby guts out, Big Comrade Nobby Weston from the Anti-Eviction Committee!'

Nobby looked out over the lights. Alexandria, Redfern, the back of Newtown, Macdonaldtown. Workers' suburbs full of houses that the workers couldn't afford to rent. There were strings and strings of houses there, whole terrace blocks in some streets, sitting empty now that their previous tenants had lost their jobs and had to move out. Hundreds of empty houses, and for every empty house there was a family now homeless, or near enough as made no difference. If they were lucky, they'd have squashed themselves into a relative's house; if unlucky, they'd be out living under bags and bits of tin in the unemployed camp at La Perouse. Families who'd had to move when their landlords kicked them out.

That was what Lizzie was talking about now. For

Nobby's mother had gone to Court today and obtained an order from the magistrate giving Lizzie's father a week to pay the back-rent. If he didn't pay it by next Friday, a warrant would be issued on Monday, 25 May, ordering the bailiffs to evict the Cruises.

'Pay the back-rent!' Lizzie said. 'She's off her head. It's twenty-five quid.'

It was five months since the Cruises had paid rent: for it was five months ago that Lizzie lost her job, and for two years Lizzie's earnings had been the only cash coming regularly into the Cruise household. Paddy and Mick had only had the odd day's work since 1929.

'No!' said Nobby. The old girl had done this secretly, without a word to him. 'I'll stop her,' Nobby said.

He was the light of the old girl's life, her darling treasure. She was tough as they come, but she'd never denied Nobby anything. 'She'll only be threatening, just to get at your pa.'

'To get at me, you mean.' Everyone in Liberty Street knew that Mrs Weston couldn't stand a bar of Lizzie. Mrs Weston, who played piano, the widow of a bank teller . . .

Sucks to you, Ma Weston, Lizzie thought. I don't want your sweet Sunshine anyway. Not in that way.

'The stuck-up cow,' Lizzie said.

'You're not wrong there,' Nobby agreed. Then felt dirty inside because he'd said it. There were still things about his mother he couldn't help liking.

One day when he was little, Nobby had seen her on the roof, fighting a southerly buster to pull a tarp over while the slates flew off around her head. She was shouting down into the street to stop the neighbourhood men from coming up to help her.

'I don't take charity!' She didn't give it either.

And she could be funny too sometimes. Like when she played the piano and made up songs about all the neighbours. But she only ever showed her wit to Nobby.

'I'll get round her, no risk,' Nobby said.

'And if you can't?'

'I will.'

'But just if you can't?'

'Then I'll stick with your side. Our side.'

Nobby looked down over the houses. One day he and Lizzie would live out there in a house, he said.

'You know I hate it when you go like this,' Lizzie cut him short.

I'm a pure red flame, burning only for the struggle.

The thought of a husband, and love, and kids, and doing the mopping to keep it all clean, made Lizzie feel as if someone had locked her up inside somewhere tiny and airless.

7

Evie flunked the job interview she went to that next Monday. It was for a sandwich hand, in a place in the city, and they had other girls with letters saying they'd worked in other sandwich places, so they didn't even try Evie out. Evie didn't mind, except for the money. Slap-slop, putting curried egg onto buttered squares, it wasn't thrilling. Not that anything was.

As she was all dressed up it was a pity to waste it, so she walked around Centrepoint a bit, then dropped into the local CYSS place on the way to pick up Sammy.

'G'day, I'm Roger,' said the friendly guy who was good-looking. He still had a video portapak on his shoulder, and the solid girl with glasses was still trailing after him on the end of the sound-lead. There was macrame in one room, and tap-dancing in another, and in the kitchen a whole lot of guys were eating rice and cooking more rice and talking a foreign language and laughing.

'Haven't seen you here before,' Roger said.

(*He doesn't remember me.*)

Evie couldn't think of anything to say. He looked exactly like someone she'd love to go out with. Really clean hair, thick and the right length and the right colour; a suntan (despite winter!) and blue eyes and clean faded jeans that fitted well and a yellow sweatshirt that said 'Make The Ruling Class Crumble'. Evie read it and couldn't understand it. It sounded like apple crumble, that they used to make in Home Science. The girl was obviously his girlfriend. She had on a black T-shirt with the same sort of writing. It said 'Eat The Rich'. Cannibalism made Evie feel sick.

'Were you looking for something in particular?' Roger had a really warm voice.

'No.' Evie felt silly in her best respectable dress and tights and Mum's shoes.

'There's things on the noticeboards,' Roger said. 'Or come again. Or Di's probably in the kitchen, go in and meet her. We've got to get down and film the demo.' He smiled again on his way out the door.

'Or come along,' the girl said, hurrying to keep up with him or the cord might break. 'We need numbers.'

'What?' Evie trailed out after them.

'Down at the CES headquarters. The unemployed demo.'

Evie watched them dump the gear in an old Volkswagen. There were banners on top, and boxes of pamphlets on the back seat.

'There's room,' the girl yelled to her. 'You can sit on my lap.'

'Oh no thanks.' Evie went to the play centre and picked up Sammy, then went home. Maria and Jodie were already there, because the school holidays had just started.

'You two can look after Sammy today.'

'I can't,' Maria said. 'I've got to go somewhere.'

'Where?'

'It's a secret.'

'*Tell* me!' Jodie demanded.

'It's a *secret*!'

Maria liked secrets for their own sake. Secret friends, secret places, secret money, secret food. Morning secrets and afternoon secrets and dark night secrets. Out at Campbelltown, she'd had lots of secrets, but now they'd moved here she'd have to start all over again.

A few days ago, she'd found her first one. It was an afternoon secret, a food secret, a friend secret, a money secret, a place secret, but mainly a food secret. Like most secrets, it'd started by itself.

One afternoon around the middle of last week, Maria had been mooching around the street thinking about getting a secret pile of money and secretly buying a BMX bike: *that'd* show Dad. For all she had now was Evie's crumby old hand-me-down ancient-history dinosaur, and Dad reckoned she didn't need a new one.

So she was wandering along the far end of the street when she spotted a fat foreign lady dressed all in black, sweeping and hosing her neat concrete front yard.

'Would you like me to do that for you?' Maria asked.

The lady looked up, smiling a wide smile, but with a blank look in her eyes. 'Excuse me?' she said.

'Would you like me to do that? I could do it for you, and you could pay me, and then you wouldn't have to get your slippers wet.'

The lady didn't seem to get the point. She looked back to an old man sitting on the porch.

'Bob-a-job is it, love?' He smiled too.

'No,' said Maria. 'I just want lots of money, that's all.'

'Ah,' the old man grinned. 'Sheer capitalist free enterprise, is it?'

Maria didn't know what his big words meant. She didn't say anything. The lady wasn't there now anyway, she'd disappeared inside her door.

But was back again a second later, with little white crescent-shaped biscuits on a plate.

'Eat, eat,' she urged. Then fast words in a foreign language. '*Einai orea, i koritzei!*' With one hand she stroked Maria's white-blonde hair, while with the other she held the plate right up to Maria's nose. She smiled, and there were teeth missing, and some of the teeth that were there were gold. It was like a witch story, Maria thought. The biscuits were poison; the lady was doing a spell on her head; propped up against the fence was her *broom*. Maria looked around for a cat, but could only see a bird in a cage.

Maria wasn't scared. She'd always longed to meet a witch. She took a biscuit, and it was covered in white icing-sugar that powdered down all over Maria's jumper. Arsenic, she thought, biting in. Quite delicious.

'*Einai orea ta mallia tou koritzei!*' The lady was gushing fast in foreign as she gently pulled and stroked at Maria's hair.

Maria looked towards the old man, whose eyes were on her, curious, amused.

'It seems she thinks your hair's pretty,' the old man said drily.

'Yes, pretty, very pretty hair,' the lady knew the words now. 'Very pretty girl.'

That was nice. The biscuits were nice (Maria took another one) and the lady was nice, and it was so nice to hear you were pretty. The lady was so nice, she couldn't be a witch, that was a pity, but the compliments and biscuits made up for it. I'll find a witch somewhere else, Maria thought.

Then the man explained to the lady about the money, and the lady let Maria sweep and gave her twenty cents.

'You come back, eh?' grinned the lady when Maria finished. 'Tomorrow. Next day. We have cake. You come back to Mrs Maria.'

'Maria,' said Maria. 'That's *my* name.'

61

'Is my name too,' said the lady. 'So we friends, eh?'

That was how the afternoon secret started. The next day and the next day and on Saturday and Sunday too, Maria slipped off away from Jodie and Sammy and Evie and sat in the kitchen with Mrs Maria and the old man, and ate strange Greek honey cakes and nut pastries and preserved fruit, and the old man talked a bit about the olden days when he was a boy, and Mrs Maria beamed and told Maria she was pretty and let her sweep for twenty cents, and the parrot chattered in its cage and picked up the crumbs that Maria dropped in to it. It beat afternoon tea at home with Evie hands down. At Evie's afternoon tea you got a choice between peanut butter on bread and peanut butter on toast, and Jodie or Sammy was always grabbing the jar away.

'Look, just make Sammy and yourselves a sandwich,' Evie said this Monday. 'Then go and watch TV or something.' She didn't care what they did, as long as she could be alone.

'*You* look after her, Jodie,' Maria said. 'I told you, I've got to do something.'

'We're coming too,' said Jodie.

Evie went into her room.

'No you're not,' Maria said.

'Yes we are.'

'Oh, okay, but don't tell Evie but.' The main point about secrets was to keep them secret from Evie.

As if *I* want to know, Evie thought in her room. She heard them traipse out the front door, one two three. Evie didn't care what they did that day, as long as she could be alone. She felt tired, and miserable, and caught in a knot inside, so she locked herself in her room and had a sleep.

Scrabbling, Evie felt these days. Scrabbling inside the cupboard. But *she* was inside the cupboard. She was Evie, a girl scratching on the door with her fingernail. Too scared to go out. Too scared to go and see. Stuck in the dark. The door swung back and open. Then there was the white face of the despot. Looking at her fearful-eyed before it disappeared.

8

The row they'd had that Friday night had been a good'un. Hammer and tongs they'd gone, Nobby and his mother, till nearly dawn. Lizzie had heard them through the wall.

The next day there was a deputation by the Anti-Eviction Committee on behalf of the Cruises. They tried pleading, they tried reason. They presented a petition signed by a hundred residents of Liberty Street, and two hundred other locals. Mrs Weston threatened to call the police if the committee didn't get off her doorstep.

'And when you've finished wasting your time with your no-good friends,' she added, pushing Nobby down the steps with her broom, 'you might deign to come in like a civilized son and unblock the drain for me.'

Nobby fixed the drain, then cleaned the silver. That was his regular Saturday morning chore.

The smell of the silver polish, the feel of the clean white rag, the sight of all the cutlery and the vegetable dishes and the dish-covers and the eggcups and the vases and the roast-plate and the teapot and the sugar bowl and the milk jugs and the two serviette rings laid out there before him on newspaper on the kitchen table – all this had been going on for Saturday morning upon Saturday morning for as long as he could remember. This wasn't man's work, he thought viciously, finishing a vase, moving on to a serviette ring.

N, he thought, idly running his finger over the engraving on the ring. *N* for his name, *N* for no one.

In the old days, Lizzie used to come in on Saturday mornings and help him, so he could get through it fast and they could go out and play. His mother hadn't liked it, but hadn't known how to object.

Lizzie's wide green eyes would lift to her as she opened the door. 'Good morning,' Lizzie would say, all prim in her pinafore. 'May I please help Nobby with the silver?'

'We don't need help.'

'Oh, but I like to, we don't have silver at home.'

Never sure if the child was mocking her, Nobby's mother would let her in, and there she'd sit singing and chattering in the kitchen as if she had a right, making Nobby be noisy and laugh.

They used to play Crusaders.

'This roast plate's the king, and the teapot's the queen, and the dishes and stuff are knights, and the vases are the squires, and all the cuttle-ry is the swords and lances . . . And these two rings,' Lizzie would reckon, 'they're our crowns.' Balancing Nobby's mother's serviette ring on her head as she polished, she'd giggle at Nobby whose head was too flat or something, and Nobby's crown would fall off with a dull clunking sound.

Nobby smeared polish over the ring, turning the silver to dull white, obliterating the *N*.

Or they'd be invading armies sometimes, sitting at opposite ends with equal battalions, and as each soldier's armour was cleaned he could advance on the enemy's camp. The serviette rings were the cannon balls, and the trick was to flick them down the table when the other commissar wasn't looking, and kill him dead.

One day, Lizzie had had this ring of Nobby's, and she'd flicked too hard, and it'd gone spinning off in a helix of flashing silver and apparently disappeared into thin air. They'd searched and searched, and hadn't found it, and Nobby's mother had muttered about light fingers and said Lizzie couldn't come and do the silver any more.

Six months later, Nobby had found it, in a dark corner beneath the dresser, but by then it was too late to get Lizzie back, for she'd turned fourteen and started work and she didn't get off till after dinner-time on Saturdays.

Nobby rubbed hard at the ring, wondering as he often did why the white polish turned to black upon the rag. A phrase of his mother's came into his mind: *'Too late!' she cried, as she waved her wooden leg!* Too late. Even if she could come now, they were too old to play Crusaders.

Rubbing at the ring now white turned to black and Nobby's mother came in and the row continued.

…And continued through the night and every night for eight more nights till the morning of the 25th came, and Mrs Weston put on her velour hat and went up to the courthouse and informed the magistrate that her tenant Padraic Fergus Cruise had not paid the back-rent, and so the magistrate ordered an ejectment warrant to be issued at any time between that day and June 22nd.

9

That first week of the school holidays was bad for Evie. Sammy still went to the play centre, because it was an all-year-round place for working mothers to leave their kids at; but Maria and Jodie were home all day, dropping crumbs where Evie had just vacuumed, slopping drinks when Evie had just cleaned the kitchen, following after Evie if she tried to go up the CYSS place, sneaking into Evie's room if she forgot to lock it, and taking her hairbrush and using up the battery in her radio and looking in her drawers. The only time she got any peace was around four o'clock, when the three of them would usually creep off somewhere, but by then it was too late.

By Friday Evie had had it. She washed her hair and put on some faded jeans that fitted well and a yellow sweatshirt that was like Roger's, but without the writing, and sneaked out the back way.

Noel was up in the despot's room delivering lunch and heard the slight creak of the gate, saw the despot immediately go tense and look – a cat and its prey – and Noel looked out too.

'Where are you going?' he yelled.

'For a walk!' Honestly. Wasn't there such a thing as privacy? She tried to yell quietly so the girls wouldn't hear.

'Hang on. I'll come too.'

'I'm okay, thanks.' What a stupid thing to say. Why wouldn't I be okay?

'I've got to go out anyway!' (You're pushing it, Noel.)

'Look, I want to be by myself.' Stormy then, but not quite knowing why, Evie ran along the lane and off down the street. He's a schoolkid, she told herself. It was beneath her dignity to be seen on the street with him in broad daylight. That Friday night, that'd been okay, off in that place where no one could see them, but imagine if everyone saw her coming into CYSS with Noel.

But when she got to CYSS, there was no one there who could have seen her. There was just a piece of paper flapping on the door:

Because we've been
running demos they've
threatened to cut the
funds and close this place.
So we're having a
picket down at CYSS
Headquarters.
11–2
Come along!!!

It was all double dutch. Evie didn't know what a picket was. Except for a picket fence. They'd had one of them in Campbelltown, painted white, out the front. In between the wide neat green lawn and the wide neat green nature strip. Evie suddenly felt homesick, and wished she could talk to Roseanne. Roseanne made her feel stupid sometimes, but she lived next door and was always there to talk to. Evie was lonely. An emptiness inside her.

Evie caught the bus back to Newtown Bridge and instead of going straight home she cut down past Uncle George's and sat by herself for a long time on the stage above the suburbs, till it was time to go and get Sammy.

When she got home she realized she'd forgotten to lock her room.

'I did not!' Maria screamed.

'I did not!' screamed Jodie.

(Noel heard the shouts from next door. He was in the kitchen, getting the despot's afternoon tea.)

They did not go in there, Maria and Jodie reckoned.

'Then how come the bloody cupboard's open, how come the top drawer's open, how come you've got my hairbrush in your hand, Jodie?'

'I did go in there but only just a minute ago, I didn't open the cupboard, I just got your hairbrush,' Jodie agreed.

Jodie was a round kid, placid as a fish, and usually Evie didn't mind her. It was Maria that drove Evie mental. Skinny, spiky, secretive Maria.

But this day Evie grabbed the brush off Jodie and shook her.

'Liar! You've been in there all afternoon, the both of you!'

Just as Jodie burst into tears Ted came home, then Ted yelled at Evie, then Evie burst into tears just as Mum came home.

'They get in my room! They hang around and follow me and use my brush on their nitty hair.'

68

'We do not!' Maria screamed.

Mum sighed, and took her shoes off. 'Why can't you two just leave Evie alone?'

'But there's nothing else to do,' Jodie said reasonably.

('You could go and see Mr Man,' Sammy said; but Maria grabbed her and dragged her into the loungeroom.)

'I'm just an unpaid babysitter!' Evie complained.

'Unpaid!' Ted yelled. 'Are we meant to pay you, as well as keep you?'

'I pay my board!' Evie gave Mum twenty dollars each week, out of her thirty-six dollars dole.

'It's the rent that's the worry,' Ted muttered.

Then Evie slammed into her room and locked her door while Mum burst into tears.

Rows, Noel thought, hearing the noise from next door. Rows.

On Sunday night he heard another one. Not the words, just the voices. This one was in the room next to his: Evie's parents' bedroom.

'*You did what?*' said Ted.

'I bought a trampoline,' said Evie's mum. 'That's why I went out yesterday morning. They'll be delivering it tomorrow.'

It was late, too late for a row, but she hadn't been game enough to tell him till now.

'Just think, darl, how much the girls will get out of it, Jodie and Ree and Sammy, I mean. It'll fit in the backyard . . .' (That was about all that *would* fit in the backyard; you couldn't swing a cat in this place!) 'And it'll give them something to do in the holidays. And Evie can teach them...'

Evie had been in the A-grade trampoline team at school; it was the one thing she'd been really good at. She could do somersaults, and everything. But better keep off the subject of Evie, her mum thought.

'...And the girls will love it,' Evie's mum repeated. By 'the girls' meaning his girls; or meaning him to think she meant his girls. For really, the trampoline was for Evie.

Evie had been looking pale since they'd moved here . . . she must be lonely without Roseanne...the trampoline would give her something to do when she was home alone all day...That was how Evie's mum's mind was working.

Evie's mum didn't know that Evie really had no urge any more to jump up and down on a trampoline.

Plus, Evie's mum thought, it would keep those other two out of Evie's hair...

Ted hit the roof. How much and take it back and where'd she get the money from, and so on.

'Three hundred and fifty,' Evie's mum admitted. 'But it'll last forever, darl. And it's okay, I got it on Bankcard.'

'Bankcard! But you can't use Bankcard!'

Evie's mum laughed. 'We've never used it since the day they issued it, darl. There's a thousand dollars, just sitting there.'

'Hardly sitting there,' Ted muttered. 'It's going back tomorrow.'

'No, darl.'

Rows, Noel thought next door. Family rows. They never had them in his family: at least, not yelling ones.

Mum didn't yell, she was as quiet as a little lizard, and the despot didn't yell, she wrote angry notes, and then made them disappear.

10

On the night of Monday 25 May, Nobby packed a few clothes in a sugar-bag and went in next door.

'Emigrating is it, son?' Paddy Cruise smirked at him.

'I thought I'd move here.'

'Well have another think.'

'And a mug of tea while you're doing it.' Mrs Cruise pushed the pot to him. This boy was the second son she'd never had. She'd patched him up dozens of times when he'd been in a scrap and was too scared to get some iodine from that mother of his.

'And when you've finished, you'll kindly take your little swag and go back in to your mam,' Paddy said.

'She's no mother of mine.'

Paddy gave it to him then. Full and strong. How his mother had given her life to bringing him up and how the poor woman could trip maybe, fall upon the stairs, and her be lying moaning in her blood and no son to hear her.

'I hate her,' Nobby said.

'That's as may be,' said Paddy. 'I do too, m'self. But things aren't desperate yet. They never execute the warrant straight away. There's still time for her to change her mind. With perhaps a little gentle persuasion. And till things get desperate, you'll kindly stay and protect her. Life might soon be a bit of a strain for your good lady mother.'

So Nobby took his sugar-bag home, and then began to lead a split life as the gentle persuasion that Paddy had referred to was exerted upon Nobby's mother.

For the UWM began to picket.

Every day that week, from morning till sundown, Nobby and Lizzie and Mick and Paddy and twenty or thirty more stood outside in the street with banners and placards.

NO EVICTIONS
UNITE, FELLOW-WORKERS
DON'T LET THE BAILIFFS SHIFT THE CRUISES!

The little Cruise girls and the other kids from the street ran and played around the picket line, cheering the pickets, yelling things up at the heavily curtained windows of Nobby's mother's place. And they skipped to the rhythm of the new skipping songs that had grown out of the occasion.

> *One two three four*
> *Mrs Scab come out your door*
> *Five six seven eight*
> *Pa is waiting at your gate*
> *Nine ten start again*
> *Lock her up in a dingo's den*
> *One two three four...*

At tea-time Nobby would eat with the rest of the pickets at the Cruises. And then go in next door to sleep in his own bed in a dark house completely silent. Nobby wasn't talking to his mother.

'Well, is she coming round d'you reckon, son?' Mrs Cruise said on the Friday night.

72

'She won't ever,' Nobby said, drying and drying a tin plate.

'Here, give me that, you'll wipe off the enamel.'

It was wearing the boy out. His face was pale and strained. It was like the Civil War all over again, Mrs Cruise thought. And this lad split like Ireland and her Lizzie going on like a great stupid and not helping at all.

For Lizzie was all for trouble. Jumping around on the picket line till her skirt near fell off, skipping and singing up at the windows like young Maudie and Fee, pushing Nobby further and further.

'Come on, Nobby, get me a paint brush. It's one side or the other. If you reckon you're on our side, you will.'

So Nobby had taken out his latch-key and gone into his mother's house, had got his mother's paint brush and taken it back so Lizzie could write in whitewash on the footpath outside his mother's gate:

DOWN WITH SCABS AND CLASS-TRAITORS.
NO EVICTIONS FOR THE UNEMPLOYED.

It'd be funny if it wasn't desperate, Mrs Cruise thought. That poor woman all alone in there, acting like stone to her own son, and all because she fears my larrikin of a Lizzie who's too young in the head to care. For Lizzie might be sixteen, she might have done grown women's work for two years, but her mother always reckoned she was a very young sixteen. Whereas Nobby was betwixt and between.

Mrs Cruise put a stop on her sympathy. That poor woman was to be the cause of her own children sleeping God-knows-where.

73

'Leave that. Go and give Lizzie a hand out the back if you're so restless you must do something.' Mrs Cruise often wished Nobby had taken the other side and stayed with his mother. It got on her nerves when he mooned around beneath her feet. As if she didn't have enough worries. She was edgy with her backache for she was pregnant again. It'd be another girl, with her luck that's for sure.

Nobby crossed the breezeway, looked cautiously into the scullery. Lizzie had been scratchy lately, jumping down his throat at the slightest. She was mopping up the floor now after bathing Fee and Maudie. Making as many puddles as she mopped, for there was something about the way Lizzie mopped that was completely hopeless.

'The dear knows, you're a lousy mopper,' her mother was always saying.

'And proud of it!' Lizzie would reply.

'Proud of it!'

'It's far from being my aim in this life to be a dab hand with a mop!'

'Well, what is it that you aim to be?'

'A flame.'

'Really, child, when do you intend to grow up!'

Lizzie slopped a puddle sideways as Nobby stepped in.

'Sit down and pull your feet up,' she threatened, 'or I'll mop you.'

'I'm sorry.'

'Stop saying sorry!'

'I'm sorry.' Nobby knew she thought he was weak.

Lizzie dumped the mop and sat down with Nobby on the green wash-stand. Said nothing for a while, then she

74

said it. 'I keep thinking you're going to run out on us.'

Nobby stared down at the puddles.

'Lay off me, girl. It's hard enough.'

'Stop calling me *girl!*'

'I'm sorry.'

'*Stop* saying you're *sorry!*'

Lizzie swung her legs as she sat on the green wash stand. You get a feeling of power, having someone in love with you. This is the first time it's happened to Lizzie.

(If he didn't love me, then I might love him.)

(If he wasn't like this, I'd be nice and not horrible.)

It's just that it can make you feel that you're locked up, when someone gives you love.

But it's wonderful too, having someone think your hair isn't messy and your words aren't stupid.

But if *they* think *you're* not stupid, then *they* must be stupid.

If Nobby didn't love me, then he'd be strong enough for me to love.

Lizzie's legs swung and her eyes saw all the water on the floor that her mop had missed. But it was up in her eyes that the puddles were. I have to stop this.

'I keep thinking of the trouble coming,' Lizzie Cruise said. 'What's going to happen, what it's going to be like.'

Nobby couldn't understand the tension in her voice. 'What trouble?' Wasn't this enough for her? 'We'll just keep picketing, day after day, and after a while she'll get fed up, and give in.' God knows, there was enough reason for her to be fed up already. Every time she stepped out to do her shopping she had to walk through a double picket line of sour-faced, jeering people. And the kids had started throwing mud at night at her windows, and dead birds and things over her back fence.

'D'you reckon?'

'Why, what do you think'll happen?'

'I dunno. But something. I reckon the cops will get into the act soon. Maybe not here, maybe at one of the other houses the UWM's picketing. Look, it stands to reason. We've won over two hundred cases in Sydney since February. Just by picketing, threatening the landlords, that sort of thing. So d'you reckon the State is going to let us get away with it?'

Nobby shrugged. He didn't think like Lizzie, in political words, he didn't look to the future. He hadn't had much time for politics at all till six months back, when the boss had turfed him out of his job. But when that had happened, all the things the Cruises had been spouting for years suddenly seemed right.

'I dunno. So what're you going to do?'

Lizzie was quiet. She plaited a long strand of hair, then unplaited it. She liked it messy, around her face.

'If you swear not to tell anyone,' Lizzie said, 'I'll show you something. Something Mick doesn't know about, even Ma doesn't know about. Swear?'

Nobby nodded. Held his hand out. Lizzie spat in it. Held out her own hand and Nobby spat. Then they clasped hands. That was the way they'd always sworn.

Lizzie pulled free then and closed and bolted the scullery door, checked that the curtain was right over the window, then pulled a big, old tin trunk out from the bottom of a pile of other trunks and tea-chests and suitcases.

'It's Pa's. He brought it when we came from Ireland.' She fiddled with the lock, pressed it upwards a special way, then sideways, and it opened. 'I worked that out years ago.'

Inside the trunk were books, old photos, a moth-eaten black coat, and something in an old, soft, brown bag that Lizzie now pulled out gently, as if it was a baby.

'Here.'

It was in two parts, the rifle and the bolt. Sparkling like new though clearly as old as the hills.

'Every six months or so when he gets drunk,' Lizzie said, 'he locks himself in here and sings to himself and greases it. I've watched him through the door-crack. It goes like this.'

She slipped the bolt in, fitted it together. Then pulled out an old tobacco tin of bullets, slipped one of them into the magazine.

Lizzie's face was soft as she stroked the rifle. She was far away, caught in a lovely jumble of the Easter Rising and the Russian Revolution...

And at the forefront of the barricades is Lizzie Kollontai...or is it Lizzie Connolly...her long black hair streaming back from the face that glows like a flame beneath the fires of the burning buildings...at the forefront of the barricades stands Lizzie, the inspiration of the struggle, the fierce fighter for freedom who works tirelessly, day and night, even now reloading to fire upon the enemies of the workers' revolution...

Lizzie took the bullet out, took the bolt out, packed the gun back in its bag.

'So now you know too.' It made Lizzie feel close to Nobby, sharing her secret.

But Nobby was shocked. Despite the years spent knocking around Mick and Lizzie, Nobby's mind was still linked to lace doilies, camomile tea, Job the parrot, the sound of the piano, and Saturday mornings spent polishing the silver. He'd never seen a gun before; except of course for policemen's guns, but they were always closed away in leather holsters, bouncing on the cops' behinds.

'Feel how heavy it is.'

But Nobby didn't want to touch it, even when it was asleep inside its bag.

'It won't come to that,' Nobby said, feeling cold in his stomach, feeling fear in his blood. *It won't come to guns.*

'No, of course it won't,' Lizzie agreed a bit sadly. Apart from Eureka, it never *had* come to guns in Australia. Or not as far as Lizzie knew. She dumped the rifle in the trunk, locked the trunk, rammed it right in at the bottom of the pile. 'Still, it's a good secret just to know.'

Lizzie burst out laughing. Nobby took everything so seriously. She'd only shown him as something mad, to cheer him up.

'C'mon, let's run down the railway track and nick some coal.' Lizzie grabbed his hand and hauled him up. 'I need to do something to warm meself up. Me bum's all wet from the puddles.' She surveyed the floor. 'Jeez I'm a lousy mopper.'

'Like a pair of ruddy six-year-olds,' Paddy Cruise said, hearing them yelling down the dunny-can lane.

'Need their sit-upons smacked, the both of them,' Lizzie's ma agreed.

Next door, at a back window, Nobby's mother watched them run, hand in hand.

The next day was the occasion of the first big eviction battle, at Redfern.

11

Noel stands on the balcony.

Bang-bang-bang-bang, down into the street.

I've been doing this for years, here on my balcony.

Line up that truck there, along the barrel.

One clean line.

The shortest distance between two points.

A to B.

Blast it down.

The last scene in *If*. When I saw that movie the first time, and saw those kids up on top of the building, blasting down...

Why have I had that in my knowledge since I was born?

Noel lines up the mouth-organ. Is crouching down behind the balcony railing, for cover.

Four men jump out of the truck, two from the front, two from the back. One of them goes up to the door of Evie's place and knocks. The others are at the back, hauling out a monster in brown paper. And with my mouth-organ that I poke through balcony railing I shoot them down.

They are men out there in uniforms that I shoot down.

'Jump,' Evie yells.

'Jump/jump.'

Out in the backyard in May afternoon sun, life hasn't been too bad this Monday since she came home after lodging her fortnightly dole form and found the Grace Bros men arriving with the trampoline.

It's a good, big, solid one and it takes up nearly all the backyard.

'One/two/three/*Jump!*/One/two/three/*Jump!*/Bounce/two/three/*Jump! Jump*, Jodie, *jump!*'

Evie's teaching Maria and Jodie. Jodie's surprisingly neat in her movements for such a round kid. Maria's all over the place, arms flying out in spikes, but she's gamer than Jodie, a higher jumper. Neither of them can quite get the rhythm of it.

'One/two/three…When I yell *jump*, Ree, you have to go right up in a big star jump. Three little bounces then a big jump with your legs and arms out in a star. Sing it like a song.'

'One/two/three/*Jump!*/One/two/three…'

Sammy's here now, so Evie makes Maria get off and takes Sammy by the hand and walks her up and down till she gets the balance of it, then jumps with her.

'One/two/three/Jump!/One/two/three/*Jump!*/One/two/three/JUMP! What a good girl!'

'…One/two/three/*Jump!*/One/two/three/*four*/

Mrs Scab come out your door…'

Next door, the despot hears from behind her blind. It's been going on for days now.

Next door, Noel crouches down on his balcony. I've been doing this for years.

It's Friday afternoon and the Kingswood parks and out gets Ted whose beer gut Noel lines up along the barrel of his mouth-organ, A to B. A distance between two points growing shorter by the second as B comes right up through Noel's gate intending to knock on Noel's door. Rent Day, Noel thinks. Noel crouches down and aims.

There's something about Ted, his bigness, his red-blondness, that reminds Noel of Matt Dunkley who used to bash Noel up.

'Sookablubber. Mumma's bubba. Cowardy-powdery-custard.'

As if it was *his* fault that he didn't have a father or brothers or even uncles or anything to back him up, as if it was his choice that he lived with Mum and Nanna who wouldn't let him play on the street, wouldn't let him have a bike, kept him home on wet days...

Bang.

But no sound comes out.

But B down below stops anyway, still upon the step, arm in mid-air towards the door, arm freezing now then dropping to B's side, and B turns and goes.

'All power, said Chairman Mao,' Noel laughs, 'comes out of the barrel of a gun!'

'Bang', says Noel.

But no sound comes out.

12

Nobby walked into the pub near Newtown railway station. It was Saturday afternoon. He ordered a lemon squash.

He didn't drink. Then he changed his mind and asked for a beer. He'd mown someone's lawn that morning so for once he had a bit of cash on him. He shouldn't spend it, should give it to mother, or put it in the picket fund, but bugger it. Whichever one he gave it to he'd feel he should have given it to the other. Nobby sipped at his beer. He didn't like the taste of the stuff, it was sour. I'm sick of feeling guilty.

Mother sour, Lizzie sour, once upon a time I was happy.

Nobby drank a bigger mouthful, looked around. He shouldn't be in here by rights, but he'd shot up so much this last year he doubted if anyone would question him. Five-foot-four one year, five-foot-nine the next, it was exhausting being a beanstalk...

Nobby felt his gut growl. There hadn't been any dinner.

...Whereas it looked like Lizzie would always be little. *Thin-as-a-pin/and-sharp-as-tin/I'm-Lizzie...*Lizzie used to skip to that when she was a kid. Lizzie was always a great skipper. One New Year's Day she'd done a thousand without faltering up on top of the Kennets' chook-shed roof. Whereas Nobby's feet couldn't do more than half a dozen jumps before they'd tangled in the rope.

> *Scab scab dirty scab*
> *Scratch her eyes*
> *And give her a stab. . .*

That was one of the new rhymes the Liberty Street kids were skipping to. Not just the kids. Lizzie with her flying hair that her mother was always rousing about.

'Holy Mother of God, child, tie your hair back,

plait it, something!'

'And don't you go telling her it's nice, because it's not, son!'

Son. Son.

'Sonny Boy,' Mick sometimes called him. 'Ma's Little Sunshine.' Though which ma he meant wasn't always clear.

Nobby was sick of being a son.

'You old enough to be in here, Sonny?' the barmaid asked.

Nobby nodded. Sonny. He ordered another beer. She could hardly be of legal age herself, that barmaid.

This beer was even sourer.

Lizzie. Her black hair flying out from her face like a witch-broom. He thought she thought he was weak. To be like Lenin, Nobby thought, to know things, and lead things, and do things, then Lizzie would love him.

Whereas now she thought he was weak. Nobby sometimes thought he could feel his father's bank-teller blood creeping in his veins. Blood made from melted pianos, and water left over from washing lace doilies, and silver polish and bank ink and stamp glue.

(Silver polish. He'd fled that morning without doing his chores. The first Saturday morning he could remember that hadn't been spent cleaning silver. Silver wasn't man's work.)

'Got the price of one spare, Comrade?' An oldish bloke Nobby recognized from the International Unemployed Day march sat down beside him. It was nice not to be called Sonny. Nobby pushed over a coin.

'A turn-up for the books in Redfern today,' the bloke said.

'What?'

'Redfern. That house we been picketing in Douglas Street. I was there.'

'Yeah?' said Nobby. Not real eager for knowledge today. He wanted a holiday from even the thought of picketing.

'Yeah, about half-past nine this morning it is, see? Only the poor cove and his missus there and about ten of us from the UWM. Not enough of us, see? We've got some tables and that pushed against the door but nothing much, see? and we're not expecting nothing, just having a cuppa and a bit of a chinwag when out of the blue there's this belting at the door – bang bang bang, see?'

The bloke rapped hard on the bar counter.

'And it's the cops there and the agent, just a few of the blighters at this stage.'

'*Cops!*' Nobby said. That was new.

'Yeah...Well the poor cove's missus yells out, see? "Yous can't come in. This house is in the hands of the UWM."' But that's just red flag to a bull, see?'

'Before you've time to say boo there's more of the beggars there, and more belting at the door – bang, bang, bang, see?'

More rapping on the bar.

'Only this time it's a dirty great sledgehammer they're knocking with and so before you've time to say boo they're in here, see? Knock back the table and stuff and we try to shove the door shut, see? but they're into the house and into us too, batons coming down like hail they are, they get me on the side of the head, crack me a whopper on the back, red and blue all over I am, like a ruddy Union Jack. Well then, see, we fight and that too, don't get me wrong, and I grab the leg off a chair they smashed getting in – I'm in the kitchen now, see? We're split up, with the other blokes in the lounge, but to cut a long story short, we're not strong enough, see? So they herd us out the back way, and out the front there's a dirty great crowd of people that have come running when they heard the blue was on, and they're cheering us and booing at the cops and there's all manner of carry-on, but to cut a long story short they've won and we've lost and the agent's men go in and get the poor cove's furniture and load it in the agent's van – reckon they'll take it to where the poor cove's going to live, but as he hasn't got nowhere to live, what's the point of that, you tell me! – and the crowd sort of drifts off, see? and only two larrupers stop to keep guard over the van, and the poor cove's cheese-and-kisses is there crying in the empty rooms – I go back in, see? cause I've left me hat and coat there, and she tells me something – I'll tell you in a minute...'

The bloke took a long swig of his beer.

Nobby felt cold. That was new, cops going in. It was only ever the bailiffs. It was new too, the UWM losing.

Nobby looked at the bloke, and there was sticking plaster on the side of his scalp and two big cuts on his forehead and the beginning of a black eye that Nobby had missed before in the gloom of the bar.

'So that was it,' Nobby said. He felt hopeless now about the Cruises. The cops would come and break their picket and Lizzie would live at La Perouse, under bags and bits of tin.

'Oy-oy, we don't give up that easy, Comrade,' said the bloke. 'I'm only up to interval. Hang on to your Minties for the second show. Here, have a read for yourself.' He handed Nobby that afternoon's *Sun*.

REVOLVERS AND BATONS IN EVICTION RIOT.

It was page one, headline news. Nobby felt vaguely important just looking at it, even though he hadn't been there. It was as if he were somehow part of history. Then a word in the headline took on meaning.

'Revolvers!' Nobby said.

'I told you there was more to it,' the bloke said smugly.

Nobby read through the first bit. It was all more or less as the bloke had said. Except that the bloke knew more, because he'd been in the house and the reporter hadn't. '*But there was a further development…*' Nobby read.

> *But there was a further development at 11 o'clock when a motor lorry on which there were about forty cheering men, drove up to the house. Several of the men jumped onto the furniture van and started to throw the furniture into the lorry. About twenty others, armed with iron bars, rushed threateningly towards the two policemen.*
>
> *When one of the policemen climbed onto the van in an endeavour to drive the raiders away, the other policeman stood facing the crowd, protecting his companion. One man then emerged from the crowd with an iron bar in his hand, and, sneaking behind the constable, made a blow at him. The policeman on the waggon, however, saw the move, shouted out*

a warning and his mate had just time to jump aside before the blow fell.

Both policemen then drew their revolvers and warned the crowd to stand back.

In the meantime, the alarm had been sent to the Redfern police station and thirty constables dashed to the scene, flourishing their batons as they raced down Douglas Street.

It was lucky for their companions that the journey from the police station was only two hundred yards.

The police singled out two men who were arrested . . .

'*The crowd,*' Nobby read out loud, '*which almost completely filled the street, was driven away by the police, and the furniture was replaced on the van...*'

'*Driven away!*' The bloke interrupted, angry. 'Makes us sound like a mob of flaming tame sheep. You can bet those reporter-johnnies would be the first to get the hell out if there was a big pack of larrupers running at *them* with their batons flying and some with revolvers waving in their mitts.'

There was no demonstration as the van was driven away, and soon the thoroughfare...

Iron bars, Nobby thought. They were new too. If the men hadn't come with the iron bars, then the cops...

'What I was going to tell you,' the bloke said. 'What the poor cove's missus told me, see? was that the cops had their pistols out *in* the house, not in the kitchen where I was, in the lounge, see? It's when she tells me that that I race up the UWM hall – they're having a meeting, don't know nothing about the blue – and right, they say what's sauce for the goose is sauce for the gander, see?'

'That's new in the eviction struggle,' Nobby said slowly, 'cops and guns.'

Lizzie's face last night as she held the gun.

'We ain't seen nothing yet,' the bloke said. 'They reckon there's a house they're picketing around here somewhere, due for the bailiffs any time.'

'Yeah,' said Nobby, 'I'm in it.' Not saying how he was in it. 'In the thick of it.' Not saying how thick he was into it.

'Barricades,' the bloke said. 'Sandbags and plurry barbed wire like we had at Gallipoli, that's what yous need. I been thinking: get a big group of yous – more than what we had, but yous can't have too many, not enough room, see? and get right into the house, dig yourselves in, make your defences strong, and the johns'll never get yous out, see?'

'Never!' Nobby agreed. Feeling himself getting strong now, a tree not a beanstalk, a comrade not a sonny-boy, looking forward to an act, the blood in his veins not silver-polish and ink but man's blood made of beer and wire and glory.

13

On Monday 1 June, Evie started a job; though it was hardly what you'd call a job. Ted got it for her.

'I've got you a job, Sleeping Beauty,' Ted had said the night before, over tea. 'Doesn't pay much. In fact it doesn't pay at all. But at least it'll be a change from the club.' Ted meant the Dolebludgers' Club. Tequila Sunrises and jackpots down the CYSS centre. This joke was getting worn.

The job was to go in next door and get the despot's midday dinner for her, Monday to Friday. Ted had been talking to Noel's mother that afternoon when he went in about the rent, and she'd mentioned how Noel had to come home from school and do it, and so Ted had volunteered Evie. Mrs Cavendish was worried because second term was about to start, and Noel's last report had said he often missed afternoon classes. Mrs Cavendish thought it was because he came home at midday to do the despot's dinner; she didn't know he often worked up at the music shop in King Street.

'Oh Mum,' Evie wailed, 'do I have to?' It sounded dreadful. Evie hadn't met the despot, but from the little bit Noel had said on the balcony that first night she sounded revolting.

'It won't hurt you, love,' Mum said. 'Just till you get a job. And just think,' (speaking brightly) 'the quicker you do that, the sooner you can stop doing this, if you don't like it.'

Mum still deep down thought that Evie could go out and find work just like that, if she really wanted to. Mum had done door-to-door selling for a make-up company for years. They employed lots of working mothers like her, who dropped out every so often for a couple of years while they had a kid, and then dropped back into their old job again. She seemed to think Evie could just drop into a job too.

'And it really won't hurt you,' Mum repeated herself.

'What's she like?' Evie said.

'I've still never met her. Have you, darl?'

Ted said nothing. He was getting moodier and moodier. And that was that.

The next day at 12.30 Evie let herself in the back door with the key Mrs Cavendish had given Ted for her, and read the note on the kitchen table. 'Dear Evie,' said the tiny handwriting...

> *Dear Evie, There's a pie in the oven it should only take 10 mins to hot up. But after you turn it on go up and introduce yourself she knows your coming and turn on the electric food-warmer beside her bed. Then when you take her dinner up pop it in the warmer and don't wait for her to eat because she never eats in front of people not even Noel and me. Her sweets are in the fridge – apple sago and custard she likes them cold. Teapot should be on the shelf she likes it strong five teaspoons please dear. Milk in the little milkjug and PLEASE remember to pop the cover over it (Noel often forgets). I've set the tray and please remember to put the silver covers over the plates dear. I think that's all thank you again dear for you're kindness in doing this, Noel says your a good friend of his so I felt confident about you're managing to do this even though I've only seen you and haven't met you yet. You must come in one night this week and Noel can play you his Bob Dylan records or maybe the weekend. Thank you again dear, must fly to work,*
> *regards Rita Cavendish.*

Evie laughed when she reached the end. 'Must fly to

work dear.' What is she, a witch or something?

Seriously though, it was weird. Mum had said the old bat had had a stroke and couldn't speak or move. But Noel had said something...she couldn't quite remember.

Evie looked around. The kitchen was exactly the same as theirs, but neater and cleaner. There were no Weeties packets and soft animals and *Mr Men* books and make-up samples and bits of old homework and ashtrays on the bench, but there was a small black-and-white TV set in the corner, and a big poster of Bob Dylan on the chimney, underneath a huge, old, loudly ticking clock. The clock was the kind that you have to wind up and set each morning, the glass front opening up so you could move the hands around. At Evie's place, they had an electric digital radio one. The ticking of this clock got Evie down.

Evie read the note again, then for no reason turned it over. There was big scribbly writing on the back.

*P.S. Good Luck with the despot. Have fun. See ya –
Noel.*

Evie thought: He's the right age to be a friend for Jodie and Maria, not for me. It was a pity, it'd be good to have a friend around here.

She put the kettle on, opened the oven, looked at the shepherd's pie, lit the gas. The tray on the table was set, right down to a rose in a little cut-glass vase.

After you turn it on go up, she knows you're coming.

Evie walked noisily up the stairs. No one had even told her what room or anything: typical. Evie was concentrating on being peeved to put her fear down.

Evie got to the stair landing and stopped. Up that way,

to the two rooms at the front, or up to the back? Away from the clock, the house was silent. Evie looked at the yellowing wallpaper, the carpet worn so thin you could see parallel threads. Then she heard the breathing. Loud and arhythmic, almost like water bubbling, it came from the back room. Evie went up there. As she reached the door, the sound stopped.

Evie stepped into the back room and got her first sight of the face that was already in her dreams. The blind was down that day, and in the near-darkness of the room the face of the despot glowed out with its thick coating of white powder, glowed beneath the cracks like a whitewashed brick wall. It was Noel's face, gone fat and rotten. The long narrow nose, the excited eyes, the high cheekbones, the sharp chin, the wide mouth; all still there on her but with the angles obliterated by the fat. The hair fine and fuzzy on the ends like Noel's, thin on the top, flopping over her left eye as she laughed now, her hair just like Noel's, but grey-white instead of brown. And the laughter too was wild like Noel's, but vicious. Noel's laughs always included you.

Evie hated her on sight. This was the most positive feeling towards another human being that Evie had ever felt in all her life. *I hate you, despot.* And mixed in with the hatred was a strange feeling of recognition, as if Evie had hated her before, and only just met her.

So that it was a satisfying feeling, and also an exhilarating feeling. Evie felt on top of the world, to be feeling something so strong.

'I'm Evie,' Evie said. Smiled like a nurse on TV, and switched on the food-warmer.

92

She waited, but the despot just sat there propped up on her three pillows, fully dressed right down to lisle stockings and polished black shoes, her revoltingly fat body taking up the whole of the narrow bed. The despot said nothing, but her eyes were going up and down over Evie's jeans, her fresh-pressed blouse, her face, her shoulder-length in-betweenish-coloured hair.

Evie went down, fixed the lunch, then carried up the tray. Again the despot said nothing and Evie waited a while. This time she had a good look around the room. The most noticeable thing was that there was really nothing to look at. Just a big old wardrobe, a chest of drawers, the food-warmer, the bedside table, a stiff armchair. You'd expect the room of an old person (especially a *crazy* old person, Evie thought) to be jam-packed with stuff from the past: framed photos and unframed photos and china things and old paintings on the walls and other junk. But the atmo-sphere of this room was at the same time both crowded and bare. Crowded, simply because the room was small and the furniture was large and the body of the woman on the bed was huge and looming. But the room was bare of anything personal. There was nothing on the walls; nothing but a crocheted runner on the chest of drawers; and nothing on the bedside table but the tray Evie had just put down there, a powder compact, and one of those invisible-writing things that kids use.

The despot watched and Evie watched. The funny thing was, Evie thought, that the despot seemed to hate her too. And with the despot's hatred, as with Evie's, there was an element of familiarity to it, as if the despot had been hating Evie, and waiting for Evie, for a long long time.

Suddenly the despot moved her hand. This hand, her left hand, her ring-hand. Six rings weighed down the third finger – two wide gold bands, and four sparkly lumpy rings: a diamond set in rubies, a diamond set in sapphire, a diamond set in topaz, a diamond set in pearls. True, the diamonds themselves were small, and the flanking stones were little more than chips; they weren't millionaire rings, but the kind of ring that a working man would spend his savings on. However, the effect of them all, pushed one on top of each other up the fat finger, was obscene. The hand pointed imperiously at the pad-thing on the bedside table.

Evie moved nearer and handed it to her.

The old woman wrote, held the pad up for Evie to read. 'REMOVE THE ROSE.'

'Okay,' said Evie. She took the flower out of the vase, stuck it behind her ear like a hula-girl, wiggled her hips, and slipped out the door.

That was the pattern for the next couple of days. The despot would stare, Evie would stare back, right at the end there'd be one remark from the despot, and that would be it. Except that there was an increase in the tension between the two, an escalation of the hatred. And except that Evie's nights got worse each night.

The escalation was shown in the remarks. The despot got more personal.

'TUCK YOUR BLOUSE IN,' said the magic-pad the second day.

Evie disobeyed, said nothing.

'YOU'RE NOT PRETTY, YOU KNOW.'

The writing said that on the third day.

'Look who's talking,' Evie replied. It wasn't particularly smart, but it was better than saying nothing.

14

Ted stood in the phone booth down the end of Liberty Street. Wretched booths, they make them too small. Kids had gone and smashed the ledge, bloody vandals, so there was nowhere to put the letter he'd been sent. He read the number, held the letter between his teeth, dialled, and got a Telecom recording. Swore quietly, rang Directory Assistance, got another number, got through, asked for the Bankcard Collections Section.

A pert little girl took his name and put him through to a smart-voiced man. The man called him Ted, as though he knew him, what a hide.

'Well, Ted,' said the man, like a headmaster, like police, 'we still want to know why you haven't paid your account.'

On the porch over the road sat a thin, old man, watching the poor cove wrestling with his collar in the telephone box. It's the father of those kids, he observed. He often saw him, driving off in the morning, saw him often too other times in the day, when he'd drive the Kingswood back and park it here, down the end of the street, and sit in it.

Poor cove, the old man thought. There was a dejection in Ted that the old man recognized. He'd seen it in many blokes, that look. (Known it in meself, come to that.)

Thirteen hundred bucks, Ted thought, hanging up.

Evie's mum didn't know she'd pushed their Bankcard account $300 over the limit. Evie's mum didn't know that Ted had been making cash withdrawals.

15

On the night of her fifth day of despot duty, Evie went on strike.

'I'm not going to do it, Mum, ever again!'

'You bloody are, y'know.' Ted didn't even look up from his plate.

'Mum, I can't!'

'Give it a burl, love. Now here comes an aeroplane, where's it going to land?' Mum was flying fishfingers into Sammy's mouth.

'Mum, she's a shit!'

'Mummy, Evie said a rude word,' Sammy said happily.

'Don't talk like that in front of the kids, love. God knows, Maria's bad enough already, worse since we moved in here.'

'I am not!' Maria said.

'Yes you are,' Jodie said pleasantly. Jodie was always agreeable. That was how she annoyed you.

'You're a shit, Jodie.'

'Mummy, Maria said a rude word,' said Sammy, even more happily.

'Don't swear, Maria.'

'Evie did!'

'Well, Evie shouldn't.'

'Evie-Peevie,' Sammy chanted, 'Evie-Peevie, Evie-Peevie, Mummy, Evie's not eating up her aeroplanes.'

'Mum, I *can't* do it!'

'Give it a burl, love.'

'Mum, I won't. She's an old witch.'

'A *real* witch?' There was awe in Jodie's voice.

'You'll bloody do as your mother tells you.' Ted picked up his plate and slammed out to eat in front of the television.

'Mummy, Daddy said a rude word!'

'Just stick at it please love, for me.' That meant that if Evie didn't do it, Ted would get at Mum. 'Ted wants you to do it because, well, you know, it never hurts to keep in good with the landlord. Landlady, I mean. Here comes the aeroplane, look, it's a big jumbo, just one last mouthful, sweetie.'

'So I'm to suffer, because Ted wants to crawl up Mrs Oatley.'

'If you're *scared*, Evie, I'll go in with you.' The idea of a witch next door made a lovely shiver go right through Maria.

'Is that the old dear's name, love?' Mum said vaguely. 'Really, love, it can't be that bad.'

'I'm having nightmares!'

'No wonder, the amount you bloody sleep.' Ted was back in, dumping his plate in the sink.

16

Bang. Lizzie was hammering. Every time she got a nail in one side, the wood would splinter around the nail on the other side, and the other side would swing down. The nails were too big for this thin wood, or something.

Be buggered if she'd yell and ask Pa what to do. She could hear him sniggering inside the house, inside the hallway.

'That's me darlin',' he laughed, as another nail came out and she started again. 'If at first you don't succeed...'

Pa was watching her through the spy crack.

'What're you makin', me darlin'?'

'A wigwam for a goose's bridle.' Treat him like a child.

Pa treated *her* like a child. Just because she was a girl. Nobby was only a year older, and Pa let Nobby in the house. Pa let Nobby be the runner. Whereas she, Lizzie, a true Cruise and not a feeble-blooded Weston son-of-a-traitor, had been sent to stay around the corner at Mrs Kennet's with Ma and the girls. Even though she'd be much better at being the runner than Nobby, for she was a better size for squeezing through the gap.

Bang. She hated Pa for that.

Bang. Hated Nobby too.

Lizzie peered through the spy crack and saw Pa's face on the other side. Heard him grunting.

'Heave-ho!' she heard, and Pa's face and the spy crack disappeared. They must be building the sandbags higher. Five foot high they were already at the door, and six feet thick. No way the cops could get in the front. For the window to the loungeroom was boarded up too, with sandbags six feet thick behind it.

'Heave, me mates, one-two-three-up!'

Bang, Lizzie hammered.

Not that the cops would even get to the front door, for the front fence and gate and the little front yard were criss-crossed back and forth with roll upon roll of barbed wire, going up about six foot high.

'Even better, see? than we done it at Gallipoli,' reckoned Mr Dacey, who'd come to lend his Redfern experience to the Newtown pickets.

'It bloody better be!' Pa reckoned.

'Whadda you mean! We done it great at Gallipoli.' Mr Dacey was a fervent old digger, for all he was a Communist.

'So great you lost!'

'Maybe,' Ex-Sergeant Dacey grunted. 'But we won't lose this one, see?'

'That's for certain-sure,' Paddy Cruise agreed, though deep-down he had his worries. They could make the house a fortress, and he and the other twenty-odd blokes who'd decided to picket inside the house could barricade themselves in, could wait there for the cops...and the dear knows, the barricades were strong. Strong enough to sustain an attack by twenty cops, forty cops, coming in front and back. For there were towers of sandbags against the back door too, and against the kitchen window that looked into the breezeway, and against the kitchen side window...and all these doors and windows had been boarded up with stout palings, layer upon layer of palings first, before the sandbags were piled up and up. The only way in or out of the house now was via the diningroom window at the end of the side passage. They needed that free so the runner could come and go. Even that window, though, was three-quarters boarded and sandbagged – leaving just enough of a gap for Nobby's skinny body – and they kept the gap sandbagged unless Nobby was actually coming through.

'One-two-three-*up*!' Another sandbag landed on top of the front-door pile.

'They'll never get in,' said Mick Cruise.

'That's for certain-sure,' agreed Paddy, as he agreed night and day. But though twenty cops couldn't get in, and maybe forty of the beggars couldn't get in, maybe sixty, maybe even eighty, Paddy had been in enough trouble in his life to know that if the cops were really determined they could just keep upping the numbers, and in the end no amount of sandbags could prevail. Paddy had been in the Easter Rising: had been barricaded in the post office in Dublin in 1916...where they'd been beaten.

Still, you had no choice but to make a stand. Out at Bankstown, at the edge of the suburbs, the UWM was barricading itself into another house. No one knew how that'd go either. This was all a new tactic. They were all in the dark. Still, you had to be in it to win it.

Bang, went Lizzie outside. She wished she was in it. It was barricades, like Russia and Kollontai.

'Me darlin's fierce with me,' Paddy muttered to no one in particular. 'The girl is ravin' mad.' To think he'd let her stay in here.

Paddy's mind ran over the arsenal of weapons that the pickets had collected: over the piles of blue metal and broken bricks for throwing down from the balcony, for throwing out the half-boarded upstairs back windows if the cops came up the side passage; over the stockpile of sturdy saplings and axe-handles for defending themselves if

100

the cops did somehow manage to shove back the sandbags and get in...

And it was only by pushing through the bags, Paddy reckoned, that the cops could get in. They couldn't climb up the outside dunny and onto the scullery roof and into the upstairs that way, for Mr Dacey had covered the dunny and scullery walls with enough barbed wire even to stop the Turks.

...Maybe we *can* stop them...

...But if we can't...

'Me darlin's mad.'

Even Nobby was only let in on sufferance. Only because he was skinny enough for the gap. So Paddy let him run messages, trot in with news and food, trot out to empty the piss-buckets, but at the first hint of trouble Nobby Weston was going to be out on his pink ear and the gap sandbagged up, Paddy was determined on that.

Bang bang three four
Mrs Scab come out your door...

Lizzie had the rhythm right now: hammering, it seemed, was like skipping. Once you got it nice and steady, the nails just slipped in straight and stayed there. Happy for a moment now despite pa, despite Nobby, Lizzie hammered in time with Maudie and Bridget and Kathleen and Fee out there in the street.

Bang ten
Start again
Lock her up in a dingo's den.

There, Lizzie's sign was up.

Up too was Mrs Weston, right up at the loungeroom velvet curtain, peering out through a chink into the street, pressing her forehead against the cold glass to ease it. The pounding sound went on for ever now, the rhythm of the children's feet tapping on the pavement like a wicked metronome, the small feet of the little girls, the banging of the hammer, the big shoes of Elizabeth, who ran out now, clambering through barbed wire to join them, her too-big shoes pounding out her hatred now upon the pavement.

Over the rope
And under again...

The rhythm of the skipping made the pain in Mrs Weston's head, but it eased the pain in Lizzie's. She was just a body, keeping time, ticking off the seconds till the trouble came, jumping off the energy that stored up in her soul without release.

Jumping, she hated less, for she was hating more these days, hating Pa now for her exile, hating Nobby for his luck, hating Nobby too because she'd shared with him her secret. But hating most that thing in that house. That was the cause of the trouble with Pa, the trouble with Nobby.

Nobby turned into the far end of the street, running full pelt down. His mother watched him from the window, Lizzie watched him from the pavement: his face on fire, his eyes shining, the effort of the run making two bright spots on his pale cheeks. They both noticed how tall he'd become as he ran straight past the both of them without a glance, past and off up the dunny-can lane, round to the back to get into the house and men's business.

17

A man sits with the despot. He's a big man, tough, but he's not tough tonight. He pulls at his collar, to make it looser; his shirt seems too tight under the arms. He's scared and ashamed. He's out of work, and trying to get work. He has no savings, and he can't pay the rent. Once again he pleads with the despot.

'I'll pay it all, soon as I get work. If you can just bear with me a bit...'

The despot's eyes don't warm to him. She has thin lips, and a wide mouth that is set into a straight, unrelenting line.

He's never begged in his life before.

'It's the kids,' he says, 'they're my worry.' He'd be all right himself, if she threw him out. He'd move, go interstate or somewhere, and look for work. But you can't have kids without a roof over their heads.

There's no discussion. She won't budge.

18

Next door, Evie sings 'Jump!' on the trampoline in the backyard in the dark. She's out there every spare minute she's home these days.

One/two/three/Jump!/One/two/three/Jump!

'As I skip and I jump!'

Ted and Mum and the kids are getting her down. Making lunch every day for that old bag is getting her down. Having to think about Roger at CYSS and wonder if ever he might like her, is getting her down. The sound of Noel and his music is getting her down. Not having a job and money is getting her down. Stopping herself from thinking about lots of weird things is getting her down. (The trampoline at least gets me up.)

The other day, Evie found long black hair in her hairbrush. Jodie and Maria go into her room and brush their nitty hair with her brush, but this was black hair, and their hair is blonde, that white-blonde colour with a trace of green from chlorine swimming pools. Mum's the only person in the family with dark hair, but mum's the last person to go into her room and use her hairbrush, and anyway, Mum's hair is short.

Evie goes right up into the air and over in a somersault, then down, jump, jump. It eases Evie's head, somehow, the rhythm of the jumping. She's just a body keeping time.

Next door in her room in the dark the despot watches from her window the girl who's neatly jumping, beating out the time.

Evie sings:
Over the rope
And under again
She lives in that house
And she gives me a pain
I wish she'd go off
And fall under a train
As I skip and I jump...

BOOK TWO
Fusion

At Bankstown and at Newtown
We made the cops feel sore.
We fought well
And they got hell
As we met them at the door.
We met them at the door, boys,
We met them at the door.
At Bankstown and at Newtown
We made the cops feel sore.

ANON,
TRADITIONAL VERSE, 1930S

1

Noel woke from the gun dream, and it was morning. He'd had that dream since he was a kid, but it was getting more urgent. These days he often woke with the memory of the cold metal against his chest, but today he could still feel it sticking into his ribs.

Noel moved, and his mouth-organ clattered to the floor. He reached over for it and lay there playing Dylan for a while, then got up and was about to go in to morning despot-duty but changed his mind and ran a bath. If he was to have a bath and wash his hair, he had to do it before he saw the despot. Otherwise the despot would *order* him to wash his hair, and then of course he'd have to let it stay dirty.

Noel lay in the bath a long time, playing the mouth-organ. If he stopped, he could hear the despot mumbling in the next room. She was well away today, the old Mumble-whine-rhubarb-rhubarb. Noel listened for a second.

'Mumble-whine-rhubarb-rhubarb,' the despot's voice said.

'And mumble-wine to you too,' Noel said. 'Sounds like

you've had a drop too much of the old mumble-wine, if you ask me.'

He played a tune to drown her out. Made lots of mistakes. Very tricky it is, to play a mouth-organ while washing your hair. Especially when you have to duck under for the rinsing.

'Still, as the man says, Life's meant to be impossible.' Noel read lots of newspapers. Not just the normal daily ones, but also the left-wing weeklies that people sold outside Coles Newtown on Saturday mornings. Noel sometimes played his mouth-organ up there, busking, and people gave him free copies. Noel liked reading them but they didn't seem enough. There was sometimes a wildness in him that wanted action, any action, but he wanted quick, complete action like those kids in *If*; not marches and meetings like those weekly papers advertised.

'*No more tears, dooble-ey-doo...*'

Noel lathered up his hair a second time. Mum still bought baby shampoo, she hadn't realized yet that he was fifteen.

'*No more tears, dooble-ey-doo, no more tears, baby shampoo...*' Noel tried to play the shampoo ad underwater.

He heard tap sounds next door. Then Evie's voice and Sammy crying.

'*No more tears, dooble-ey-doo, no more tears Baby Blue,*' Noel sang as he surfaced. He thought he might go in after despot-duty and have a yarn to Evie. He hadn't done more than say hello to her in passing since the night up on the stage. It was funny, that: the way you could feel really close to someone, and then just *because* you'd felt so close, you felt sort of embarrassed the next time you saw them. Noel sometimes even found himself feeling hatred for Evie, because she knew about his secret landscape.

'Mumble-mumble-rhubarb-*Noh!*' The despot's voice loudly croaked out the sound she made for Noel's name and Noel jumped out of the water, hurled on his duffle-coat and raced in still wet. She might have fallen out of bed.

False alarm. She was lying there like Lady Muck, like usual.

'You okay?'

The despot just looked, then sighed. Wrote.

'I DIDN'T KNOW IF YOU WERE THERE.'

'Of course I am, Nanna. Or I was. I'm not there now, I'm here. Do you want something?'

The despot shook her head. A 'No' shake.

So Noel just got the breakfast stuff out of the food-warmer and packed up the tray. Once again, she hadn't eaten. She hardly ever ate in the mornings any more.

'Would you like me to leave it? You might feel like a pick a little later.' It was steamed kipper and grilled tomato, the despot's favourite.

The despot shook her head. Another 'No' shake.

Despite himself, Noel felt uncomfortable. This had been going on a bit long, even for a performance by the despot. He felt bad about the cold porridge the first time.

'How about the blind? Is that how you want it?' It was halfway up, as it always was in the mornings now.

The despot shook her head: No. But yanked it down herself. Noel could hear the voices of Evie and Sammy as they trampolined.

109

Up in the air
And down again
She lives in that house
And she gives me a pain...

Noel laughed. The despot reached for her powder compact and puffed more white powder over her face.

'TELL YOUR MOTHER I HAD ANOTHER BAD NIGHT.'

'Sure, Nanna.'

But Noel wouldn't. She'd been complaining of that a bit too, the last fortnight or so; but then she'd used that trick in the past to get her own way.

The bad nights she'd had when Noel was six, and wanted a birthday party. She'd had them again when Noel was eight, and wanted a bike. They were the same nights she'd had when Noel was ten, and wanted to play football. And of course there was the whole string of them that had come to stop Mum going to dressmaking classes, and to Saturday-morning flower arranging, and even to church.

Noel didn't believe any more in the despot's bad nights: 'She's a can't-help-herself-liar.'

Though, looking at her today, maybe she did look a bit strained beneath the powder. Serves you right if it's true and I don't believe you, Noel thought. The despot had brought him up on the tale of the little boy who cried 'Wolf!'

That day, it was earlier than usual when Evie went in to do the despot. That day was a Wednesday, the middle day in the third week of Evie's despot-duty. If she got it over and done with early, she could go to CYSS on the way to pick up Sammy. She'd been dropping in there a bit lately, and Roger was teaching her to use the video camera.

Evie let herself in the back, turned the gas on under the braised steak, frowned at the ticking clock that always made her feel hemmed in, put the kettle on, and found the teapot missing. Noel must've left it up there.

She walked up the stairs, silent in her sandshoes.

'Noel. Don't go, Noel. Noel. Don't leave me.'

The voice coming from the despot's room was quite distinct. It must be Noel's mother. But Noel's mother's voice was apologetic and thin, and this…was a bit thin, but hardly the whisper-sorry tone of Mrs Cavendish.

'*She speaks too, sometimes. That's a secret.*'

Noel had said that the first night. That was the only time he'd ever talked about the despot to Evie.

Noel must be in there now, and the despot talking to him.

Evie made her feet make a noise as she took the last few steps: knocked, and walked into the despot's room. Noel wasn't there. Just the despot, on the bed, her mouth clamped shut, her eyes bright and watery, fixed hard on Evie. Evie felt frightened in her stomach, though why she should feel afraid, she didn't know. Evie said nothing.

'Hussy!' The despot communicated with her voice.

COMMUNISTS FIGHT POLICE

Riot at Bankstown

INSPECTOR SERIOUSLY INJURED

Barricades and Barbed Wire Entanglements

One of the most serious disturbances ever dealt with by the police in New South Wales occurred at Bankstown this morning, when 40 policemen, in carrying out an eviction order, fought a pitched battle with 16 men defending a barricaded house.

Nearly every combatant was injured, some seriously. The most serious injury was that received by Inspector White, of Regent-street, whose skull was fractured by a piece of blue metal flung from one of the windows of the house. One of the occupants, Richard Eatock, was shot in the thigh by a policeman.

The police had to force their way into the house – a weatherboard cottage in Brancourt-avenue – which was barricaded in an amazing fashion with sandbags and barbed wire entanglements.

HAND-TO-HAND BATTLE

When the police approached, and surrounded the house, the occupants, who were mostly Communists, showered them with big pieces of blue metal. To cut their way through the barbed wire entanglements, the police had to expose themselves to the full force of the shower of stones. Although many of them were hit, the police succeeded in cutting their way through. Rushing the front verandah, they drew their batons and fought hand-to-hand with the defenders, who used axe handles, garden forks, saplings, and iron piping.

The raid was the result of a disorderly campaign which has been conducted by anti-evictionists in the Bankstown districts for many weeks.

A volley of revolver shots was released by the police, nine bullet holes later being found in the woodwork of the cottage.

One of the defenders, Richard Eatock, fell back suffering from a bullet wound.

The police eventually entered the house from the side as well as from the front and back. The occupants put up a short but fierce resistance, but at last, realising that they were hopelessly beaten, they surrendered.

Some of the men were treated on the spot by the Canterbury-Bankstown District Ambulance, others were taken to hospital and treated, but only two were admitted to hospital. The 14 men not admitted to hospital were eventually taken to Bankstown police station.

Two more men were detained at the station, and later 16 men were charged.

Several waggons were despatched by the Canterbury-Bankstown Ambulance, and the following were treated for various injuries:—

Richard Eatock, of The Mall, Bankstown, bullet wound in the right thigh; Alex Makaroff, of Chiswick-street, Chullora, injuries to the hands and probably a fracture of the skull; Douglas Kendell, of East-street, Lidcombe, incised wound of the head; John Arthur Terry, of Nelson-avenue, Belmore, cuts on the head; John Boles, of Liverpool-road, Bankstown, lacerated jaw; George Hill, of Crown-street, Surry Hills, lacerated scalp; Harold Woolfe, of Boronia-road, Bankstown, lacerated scalp; Jack Hansen of Cornelia-street, Punchbowl, incised wounds on the head; and Daniel Sammon, of Clyde-street, Clyde, lacerated scalp.

CROWD WATCHES BATTLE

A large crowd watched the battle from a safe distance. News of the encounter spread round the neighbourhood like wild-fire. The noise of the conflict could be heard a quarter of a mile distant. Glass in the windows was smashed by the flying missiles hurled by the besieged and returned by the police vanguard. After the battle, the cottage presented a battered appearance. Not a window was left intact, and a side door had been smashed in during the conflict. Inside there was devastation. Scarcely a piece of furniture remained. The floors of what had once been bedrooms and living rooms were littered with dirt, blue metal, broken glass, and the crude weapons which the occupants had used. Bloodstains marked the floor, and the sandbags on the front verandah.

MEETING OF COMMUNISTS

More than 300 Communists attended a meeting at Bankstown to protest against the actions of the police during the riot in that suburb later this morning. Wild speeches were delivered, one speaker declaring that what had happened today was only the beginning of a revolution, and that further developments would take place at Newtown.

Wednesday 17 June 1931. The Liberty Street pickets are crowded around Nobby in the kitchen, reading the afternoon paper that Nobby-the-runner has just brought them.

'I was there!' Nobby is saying. 'I was out there!'

A picket called Isaacs slaps him on the back.

'Good on yer, lad,' says Mr Dacey. So glowingly that Nobby doesn't mind being called 'lad'.

Mick Cruise envies him.

A young bloke called Williams asks him how much blood there was.

'I saw the pistols. I heard the bullets. It was like the war, so many guns. And then I saw Eatock limp out with that bullet in him. They were all handcuffed.'

To be a hero, Nobby feels. *To know things and do things and lead things.* Everyone is slapping him on the back, though all he did was stand in the crowd and yell.

'All right, comrades,' Paddy's voice is booming over. 'We've all had our read now and there's nothing we can do about what happened today, so I vote we have our tea and bag up the gap and settle down for a good night's sleep in case Lang's Larruppers pay us a visit tomorrow.'

The pickets drift off from Nobby's newspaper. Isaacs and Murchison and Nicholls and Johnnie Kennet sit down on the floor and play euchre. Mr Dacey pulls out his tin whistle. Murphy lights the two kerosine lamps – for the electricity has been cut off and the pickets live by candlelight and lamplight at night. Paddy gets out his penknife, sticks his feet up on the table, and starts to cut his toenails.

'Aren't we going to do something?' Nobby says.

Paddy moves onto the second foot. Says nothing. He's

114

got enough trouble keeping all the pickets nice and steady without this lad with his nerves strung tight like piano wire.

'I was out there!'

Nobby saw blood drawn, and he feels he'll never be the same. For Nobby, it was like the Russian Revolution or the Easter Rising, that Lizzie is always spouting about. The police use bullets, so shouldn't the people use bullets back? It seems only fair. Tit for tat. The way Mick and Lizzie had taught him to fight, you never let no one beat you. If a kid gets the better of you in a scrap one day, then you go back the next and do *him*. If he moves on from knuckles to rocks, then you pelt rocks back.

Nobby can't stop saying it: 'I was out there!'

'And out *there*,' Paddy nods towards the backyard, 'you'll be in a minute, soon as you've run up and got us our tea. Ask Ma to give you all the bread and jam she's got, we'll eat cold tomorrow, because from now on I want you out there all the time.' Paddy's got a feeling the cops may come tomorrow, and there's no way he wants Nobby in the house.

Nobby protests. But you can't budge Paddy. Paddy is sweeping his toenail clippings off the table.

2

That evening, Roseanne came down from Campbelltown. Her father was going to some club in town, and Roseanne had nothing to do so she said: 'Drop me off and I'll have a look at Evie's new place, and pick me up on your way home.'

Evie was pretty boring, but she was better than sitting

out at Campbelltown and doing nothing.

Ugh, Roseanne thought when she arrived. The house-paint outside was coming off in strips, like peeling sunburn, and the little front yard was just weeds. Roseanne didn't like to imagine how many people must've died here over the years.

From his balcony, Noel shot her. Then stood up to watch her live body go up to knock at Evie's door. Roseanne looked up and saw a creep of a boy looking down a mouth-organ at her from the next-door balcony. Noel hated girls who looked like that, in smart-coloured jeans.

'Gee it's dark and pokey,' Roseanne said when she got inside.

Evie didn't say anything. When Roseanne arrived, Evie was feeling funny.

She'd just had a fight with Ted, and for once she'd fought.

Not sitting in her Evie-Peevie sleep but alive and fighting.

'*You* reckon...the way *you* talk...anyone can just go off and get a job, easy as that!'

Ted sat there with his can of KB. He didn't say anything, but Evie knew what he must be thinking. There was fight and anger then in Evie. A redness flying behind her eyes. Better to be awake and struggling than the nothing she'd always felt before.

Bang, I hate you, Ted.

Hate, a feeling. Like what we've got next door, you and me, Mrs Oatley.

'I think I'd like to have a baby,' Roseanne says. She and

Evie are in the scullery. Mum and Ted are out.

Roseanne smokes, and drinks some beer from one of Ted's cans that Evie has got her from the fridge. Evie doesn't care if Ted notices.

'If I can't get a job I might as well do something,' Roseanne says.

It's still all airy-fairy in Roseanne's mind but Evie doesn't know that. It all seems too old for Evie, full of things she can't work out.

Evie talks about Roger. He's her boyfriend. Not in real life maybe, but in the mind of Evie these days the thin membrane between real life and some other world is disappearing.

'He's got lovely hair,' says Evie. 'Really clean, and a really good suntan. He goes surfing a lot. He often takes me, weekends.'

'What sort of car's he got?'

Evie falters. They don't travel by car. They're just suddenly there, alone on a beach with no other people, sitting high up on a rock, dangling their legs down over waves and waves of bright blue freedom; feeling good. 'A Kingswood. Same model as Ted's.'

'Yeah?' Roseanne is impressed if it's true, but she's not sure it is. How would someone like Evie get someone like this? 'What's he do?'

'He makes movies,' says Evie. 'Only little ones so far,' she swings back closer to the truth. 'On, you know, video, and I help him, and do the sound.' Evie's ambition: to supplant that fattish girl with glasses and trail around after Roger like a puppy on a lead.

'One night we took a camera to the beach and made a film of all the lights.' It didn't sound so exciting, when you said it like that.

'Chris doesn't like movies,' Roseanne interrupts. Roseanne doesn't like it when Evie talks: the point of Evie is to listen. 'Chris is into music.'

'Yeah?' Evie leaps in quickly. 'Noel's into music too.'

'Who's Noel?'

'The guy I'm telling you about.' Evie hasn't yet realized her mistake.

'I thought his name was meant to be Rod or something.' Roseanne doesn't care. Rod or something, or Noel, he doesn't exist anyway.

'What did I say?'

'You just said Noel.'

Jump jump. Evie's mind keeps making sudden jumps these days and she gets muddled.

She'll have to keep calling him Noel now, when she talks to Roseanne, to cover her mistake.

'He plays mouth-organ,' Evie says. 'Real well.' Making in her mind a picture of Roger playing mouth-organ.

'One night he was playing in this big place up at Newtown and he got me this free ticket to go and watch.'

3

Lizzie's out in the street when Nobby runs past down to Kennets' to get the tucker. She's not talking to Nobby. Hasn't spoken to him for over a week.

Thinks he's smart, Nobby Weston. Hanging around in

118

the house all day while she's stuck out on the street, keeping the picket going. Her and baby Fee all day, her and the other girls when school gets out, her and a couple of dozen grown-ups too in the daytime, but the grown-ups change, come for a few hours and then go. Only Lizzie is there all the time, making the signs, leading the chants, making it tough for the scab to walk through if she wants to walk into the street.

Lizzie's lonely, split from Nobby. He's been there, always beside her, for ten years now, her best friend. Her only friend. Following her lead, doing what she does, doing what Mick does too but only if Lizzie does it first.

But now it's just Nobby doing what Mick does, or even doing things first.

Sometimes now, it's as if she's at war with Nobby. Lined up against each other, like Saturday mornings with the invading armies. She much preferred it when they were both Crusaders together. Lizzie shivers. I'm cold as silver.

For some reason, there flashes into Lizzie's mind the bright memory of that helix of a spinning silver serviette ring that disappeared that Saturday morning into thin dark air. That last free silver-Saturday morning, long ago now. That morning was the first time she realized Nobby's mother's hatred for her. And now the hatred had led to this. In Lizzie's memory now the silver spins faster and faster till the spin of the movement turns red as a flame. I'm warm, I'm a flame. No I'm not, I'm cold as silver.

Lizzie gets cold out on the June street, so she skips to keep warm. Skips to get Fee to skip with her, to keep Fee warm.

Fee Fee
Here with me...

Fee, my baby sister, only four. You shouldn't have favourites, but I do.

Lizzie grabs Fee's hand with the automatic action of a big sister and skips her up and down, *Fee with me...*It makes the loneliness sometimes warmer, holding Fee.

Lizzie's out on the street with Fee when Nobby runs past down to Kennets' to get the tucker.

'Hey Nobby!' she yells. She's not talking to him, but her voice yells out to him.

Nobby runs past. Lizzie with her brigade of kids. They throw old tins over his mother's fence at night, and Nobby hears them through the night as he and his mother lie in their beds, not sleeping in the silent house.

Mother, Mother, Lizzie, Girl, don't split me like a piece of firewood.

Lizzie yells out, but she's been playing not speaking. Nobby can play that too.

Nobby runs past; Lizzie skips and chants. Secretly Nobby feels that Lizzie's being a bit childish. Lizzie playing revolutions. Nobby saw one today.

4

Noel was playing his mouth-organ in the outside dunny. It was a nice private place to be. Lots of people would think he was a creep if they saw him sitting in here with his mouth-organ, with his new music propped up on the

120

toilet-roll holder, with his candle. Mum had given Evie's mum the bulb from here the night Evie moved in, and since then Noel has used a candle. People would think he was a creep, but they did anyway, and anyway they wouldn't see him here because it was a private place. A line of poetry from school went through his mind.

> The grave's a fine and private place,
> But none, I think, do there embrace.

Embrace. The word made Noel feel embarrassed somehow, and clumsy. He imagined putting his arms around someone and giving them a hug, and kissing them, but the kiss missing them and Noel feeling stupid. Noel had never tried that, and that was another reason why he never hung around with the guys at school.

He tried now to imagine embracing Evie. He could faintly hear her voice talking to the voice of that other girl that he'd shot from the balcony as she arrived. He'd been going to ask Evie tonight if she felt like going down the landscape again but he couldn't now because that other girl was there. Noel felt vaguely jealous of Roseanne. Noel hadn't been down the landscape since the time he took Evie. And Evie was really cold to him now, ever since she'd started doing despot-duty.

Noel went back to picking out a tune in the new music he'd got up the music shop today. He helped out there some-times in the afternoons, while the boss went out. The boss didn't pay him, but he let Noel play the instruments and he gave him things. Like this music book called *Dole Days* that went with some new record of old Depression songs that some group had just released. It wasn't Dylan, but maybe he was going off Dylan a bit: Dylan made him feel cold and lonely.

Noel couldn't imagine having his arms around Evie. She kept slipping out of them and went running off down the street.

So he sat there playing this stuff he'd been given for free. He had some vague idea that he might play it one day to torment the despot, if she started tormenting him again.

'*Cruel it was then...*' Noel quoted. The theme-song of his childhood.

Cruel it was, Evie's loneliness. She'd had something, and thrown it away, and now she missed it terribly, but she didn't know what it was she'd had. The not-knowing made her cranky, gave her headaches. She swung her legs in time to the music and didn't hear a thing Roseanne was saying.

Next door, the despot heard the music too. Lonely in her room she lay, looking out from her dark room onto the dark roofs, the dark backyards.

> *We belong to the doley-oh mob,*
> *The doley-oh mob are we!*
> *We never fight or quarrel,*
> *We never disagree...*

The sound of that tune floating through the long dark night, the sounds they made to mock her. Evie's laugh. The flicker-flicker shadows she saw, of Noel's candle.

The despot leaned out her window and rang her bell: loud.

Noel jumped. Evie jumped. They were trained to the despot's call.

5

Lizzie's out in the street when Nobby runs off to Kennets' to get the tucker.

Lizzie's heard by now about Bankstown, wants to ask him – 'What was it like?' – but he's in too much of a hurry for her as he goes down and as he comes back past with the hot stew going slap-slop inside two billycans, and a sugar-bag of bread and jam slung over one shoulder.

His mother watches from the window. Watches the billycans as well as her son. It's three days now since she's eaten, for she won't walk out the door now to go to the shop. Her son comes in late at night, never thinks to bring her a little food. Her son doesn't speak to her. He's no son of hers. She feels the hatred in the house at night, the coldness of her son lying awake in his room, she lying awake in hers, the hatred of the men who sing next door...

As I was walking down the street,
A copper said to me...

Nobby disappears into the lane. Lizzie wants to run after him. *But yer think yer smart, Nobby Weston.* They think they're smart, him and Pa, but she's got a plan.

After what happened at Bankstown today, Lizzie is more dead-set than ever not to miss the action here. Lizzie plans to hide in the cupboard in the scullery. The scullery isn't fortified, so she can creep in there later tonight and hide and wait.

Lizzie grabs Fee's hand and runs off down to Kennets' to bathe Fee and Maudie and have her tea.

Nobby's mother watches Elizabeth Cruise's too-big shoes thudding down the pavement, and she feels jealous, and she feels hungry, and she feels vengeful.

6

'Chris is really lovely,' Roseanne says again. 'A really lovely guy. Much nicer than Kim.' Kim was her last love.

The sound of a mouth-organ drifts in faintly from the next-door toilet and makes Evie lonely.

It makes her lonely, Lizzie's love, that thin white face makes Evie lonely. The face like Noel's, but older; and with his hair short instead of long like Noel's, the ears stick out a bit and the long thin white neck looks somehow vulnerable.

She wants to skip and jump, to cheer him up.

She wants to skip and jump, to cheer herself up.

The loneliness without him.

7

In the kitchen the pickets eat the stew. Only three shanks between the eighteen of them, but the broth's filled out with lots of spuds and chokoes and pumpkin. Better than a lot of them would get at home, for everyone from round about has been giving what they can for the pickets' rations.

'Don't wait for the billies, son,' Paddy says. 'We'll toss them down from the balcony in the morning.' The sooner this lad's out and the gap bagged up, the better.

'Righty-oh,' Nobby says cheerfully.

Too cheerfully, but Paddy's got too much on his mind to be suspicious.

Nobby shuts the kitchen door on the pickets.

Nobby has a plan too.

Nobby crawls through the gap in the diningroom window and creeps into the scullery, then pulls a big old tin trunk out from the bottom of a pile of other trunks and tea-chests and suitcases. He fiddles with the lock, presses it upwards, then sideways, carefully, holding his breath and praying, up and sideways, and it opens.

Inside are books, old photos, a moth-eaten coat, and the thing in the old soft brown bag, the thing that Nobby pulls out now as reverently as if it was a Bible. He pulls out the old tobacco tin too and sticks it in his pocket. Then Nobby locks the trunk and – quietly now – rams it right in again at the bottom of the pile, and creeps back in through the gap.

(To be someone and do something, then Lizzie will love him.)

Nobby slips up the stairs and hides himself under the big double bed in the upstairs front room. The counterpane hangs right down to the floor, so no one will see him. Looking up, he sees the criss-cross of the bed-wire, beneath the mattress. It might be a long wait. (What if it's days?) Nobby wishes he'd had time for tea. He's hungry already.

125

Downstairs, Mr Dacey plays his tin whistle. Mick and Williams and Paddy plug up the gap. The others sing.

8

Roseanne was still raving on. Evie swung her legs back and forth as she sat on the dressing-table, and blocked her mind off from Roseanne. Evie heard the music, but only faintly. It was a jolly sort of tune that only made her lonelier, she wished she had a love. The tune sort of bounced along in time to the scrabbling. Scrabble-scrabble. In the cupboard. Evie often heard it, but since that first night she hadn't looked in there. Hadn't even opened the door. It had been open, that day Jodie had been in her room, but Evie had slammed it shut, not even looking. The cupboard was probably connected with the weirdness, and Evie didn't want to know. A minute ago she'd even thought she'd heard the despot ringing, like the despot did all the time now when Evie went in to get her midday dinner.

Ring, ring, and Evie would go running up the stairs, only to find that white face staring at her. Occasionally there'd be something on the magic-pad.

'TELL'

But it wouldn't say what to tell, who to tell.

'WHAT'S THE DATE?'

It had said that on Monday.

'The fifteenth of June,' Evie had said.

Then the despot had just looked, and said nothing.

'I'M HUNGRY.'

It had said that yesterday.

126

'I'll bring it up in a minute.' But then when Evie had taken the food up, the despot had waved it away. That ring-hand ordering her. That bell ordering her, ring-ring.

'What's that scrabbling sound,' Roseanne said, 'in the cupboard?'

Roseanne shuddered: probably rats. Roseanne's dad had said something about Ted being down on his uppers. ('Don't breathe a word to Evie. I don't even think he's told his wife.') Roseanne's dad used to drink with Evie's Ted at the Campbelltown Catholic Club. 'You've even got *rats!*' Roseanne said.

Her shrill voice went through Evie, woke her up.

'What, d'you hear something?'

'In the cupboard.'

Evie almost hugged Roseanne. If Roseanne heard it too, it couldn't just be Evie off her brain.

'No, of course I don't.'

Of course I don't have rats.

Pushed like this, by Roseanne there in her new pastel jeans that her mother had just bought her, with her packet of cigarettes that she smoked so expertly, Evie leapt to the defence of 203 Liberty Street.

'Look, I'll show you.'

Evie flung open the cupboard door. Roseanne jumped onto the bed. Stood there precariously on the springy mattress in her high-heeled sandals, looking like the farmer's wife in Sammy's *Three Blind Mice* book.

Nothing ran out of the cupboard. Evie laughed to see Roseanne, then bent and looked under the old copper, looked in the big gap where the fire used to go. There were no rats there. The scrabbling sound had stopped as soon as she opened the door.

'It's just the boy next door,' Evie said, hearing the music a bit better now that Roseanne had stopped raving. 'He spends half his life in the dunny.'

> *As I was walking down the street*
> *A copper said to me:*
> *Do you belong to the doley-oh mob?*
> *Well come along with me...*

The music was coming easily to Noel, more easily than usual with new music he'd never seen before.

'What's that?' Roseanne said from the bed. She started giggling. Could giggle now, now there were no rats. Standing upon the bed in her shoes made her feel silly and giggly after drinking two cans of Ted's beer. She saw a heart that must be poor dumb Evie's, poor dumb Evie scratching out a big heart inside the cupboard door on the paint, it must've taken her hours. 'What's that?' said Roseanne.

'I've never seen it before,' said Evie.

On the inside of the slatted wooden door was a large heart, picked out with a fingernail.

Inside the heart was something that said:

I
Love
N
4
Ever
18/6/1981

'Hello, I'm Noel.'

A voice came in the door and addressed itself to a girl in pastel jeans bouncing giggling on a bed. A body accompanied the voice. Someone short and thin.

'Oh, you're *Noel*, are you?' the giggler giggled. It made a big deal of it. 'Evie, *Noel's* here!'

'What?'

Evie wanted to be alone with the heart.

To work the heart out.

To work out the date: for that was today.

Only just today, for it was only just Thursday. Just past midnight and becoming Thursday 18 June 1981.

'Noel,' said Roseanne.

I have to be alone with the heart, to work the heart out.

'Noel with the lovely hair, really clean, and a really good suntan,' said Roseanne.

I have to work this out.

'Your boyfriend,' Roseanne added. 'Remember?'

Evie remembered lots of things. Lights out there, criss-crossed neatly by the wire of the streets. That was one thing. *I'm a flame.* That was another.

But getting in the way of that was Noel there at the door, pale and stupid, and Roseanne still bouncing and laughing.

I love for ever, a feeling told Evie. A feeling that almost had a shape, it was so strong, a feeling that jumped through her mind, sharp as silver, bright as flame. Evie's mind kept making sudden jumps these days and she got muddled.

Roseanne laughed, and the flame flicked out, the feeling of the love was gone now, chased out of her mind by the embarrassment, the laughter.

Noel was embarrassed too. Embarrass/embrace, he thought, the two words coming together as he watched Evie standing in front of the cupboard door. Her shoulder was pushed against it, so he couldn't see the heart. The girl Noel had shot in the street was laughing on the bed in pink jeans. Noel was still carrying his mouth-organ, and it was real and comforting.

Bang, Noel blasted but it didn't stop anything. It didn't even make a sound.

'So you're Evie's love.' Roseanne stopped bouncing and climbed off the bed. She felt sick, a bit. 'Evie's told me all about you. I should've clicked, when I heard the mouth-organ, that you were just the boy next door. Evie told me about you playing up at Newtown.' Roseanne lit a cigarette.

Evie looked at Noel, whose face was particularly pale tonight. Evie felt very sick.

Noel felt sick. Evie had laughed with Roseanne about his secret landscape. He said nothing.

'Piss off,' said Evie. She screamed at him. 'I'm sick of you creeps next door. Will you just bloody piss off and leave me alone! For ever!'

Noel ran, and as he did, Maria came to the scullery door and said there was a man at the front door who'd been knocking and had woken her up.

'It's Roseanne's dad and he says she has to go now.'

9

Evie lay on her bed for a long time after Roseanne had gone. Lay with her eyes open, her face flushed still at first with the

130

shame of Noel, the fury; lay staring at the open cupboard door, concentrating her will upon the hatred so as to close her mind to the heart.

I love for ever.

Never never.

It's going to be a long hard night.

Evie lay very still to make the time pass, to make the feeling go, and as she lay she felt the edges of herself dissolve into the place, so that there was no longer any line between the night, the room, and Evie.

It was now she saw the girl with long black hair peer out from the triangle of the cupboard, then snap shut the wooden door.

Oh, you, Evie thought, as if the face was someone she knew from primary school perhaps, from way back anyway.

I remember lots of things. But can't now, can't quite remember how Evie was seven weeks ago when I felt nothing in me.

I know I know hate now, but I don't know where it should go; know I know love, but that was gone before I ever had it. I know Evie's changed since she moved to Newtown.

Yet Evie still is Evie.

So when Evie saw a face in her cupboard late that night she decided to clean the cupboard out. She'd been meaning to do it for ages.

Getting up then, pulling the edges of her body back out of the night, Evie opened the cupboard again, and it was just a big, dirty, triangular closed-in space, containing only an old fuel copper and a broken push-mower and bike tyres and rusted paint tins and flagon bottles encrusted with sediments of poisonous-looking liquids.

Turning her back on the heart, closing her mind to the heart, Evie started pulling all the junk out.

10

Crouching in darkness, for some reason underneath a bed, Noel heard singing.

> ...*A copper said to me:*
> *Do you belong to the doley-oh mob?*
> *Well come along with me!*
> *And he grabbed me by the collar,*
> *And tried to run me in.*
> *So I upped me fist*
> *And I knocked him stiff*
> *And we all began to sing...*

Then Noel heard silence, and it was the silence of hatred.

An echo of the words Evie had screamed at him floated for a second, but as Noel lay there hearing his own breathing, hearing the despot's breathing, he knew it was the hatred given out by the old woman and himself that made this silence that seemed to last for hours.

Then suddenly there came the bullet bangs, and the voices, that even in this dream he recognized as being those customary bullet sounds and voices he was always dreaming. He could never make out what the voices yelled.

Noel climbed out from under the bed. That was odd,

because usually the dream stopped at this point: Noel in this dream knew he was dreaming, so expected his dream to end but it didn't. He climbed out from under the bed, and that part, though dream, was also true this time, for earlier in the nightmare Noel had fallen out of his bed and rolled under it. Noel climbed out, and recognized his own room, and that was a shock, for he felt he should be in some other, but similar, room. That poster of Bob Dylan shouldn't be there.

As a child, Noel used to sleepwalk. He hadn't done it for years, but this night he did.

Noel was scared. His dream was full of running men but he was alone. They were out on the balcony, here in the room, he could hear them in the back room, hear them on the stairs, but Noel was scared stiff and quite alone.

He ran to the balcony and crouched down, and there were men down there in blue uniforms shooting up at him; and so he pulled out his gun and shot down into the street at the men who were shooting at him. Only he didn't shoot: he tried to, and the blood inside him became a thin tepid trickle that wasn't strong enough to hold his arm up, to hold the gun up, but the trouble was it wasn't a gun it was only his arm.

Panic then seized Noel, wild panic, he was frozen inside this lump of noise and movement that surged around him and he jerked now, struggled, freed himself from the lump and on all fours he crawled through his bedroom, through running legs, past Mum's room, down the stairs, through the legs of the others running up and down, blue legs suddenly as well as brown legs and bare legs, legs in long white underpants and blue serge legs too, past a bullet that flew past him hitting plaster that sprayed upon his hair, white chalk flying in clouds inside the darkness; pausing now, on the landing, he heard the despot breathing through the noise.

'Noh!' The sound the despot made for Noel's name.

'No!' screamed Noel. 'No!'

Refused the call and crawled on down on all fours like a cringing dog, still holding his gun, his gun that wasn't real, crawled down through the diningroom where men were hitting men and men were wrestling men and there were more blue men than other men and the blue men were winning easily now and Noel wanted to help one of the other men who was kneeling there, but Noel was terrified, and just a boy.

In the kitchen a shadow loomed, thrown up by flickering candlelight, and the shadow went to snatch him but the boy scuttled now, fast, maybe a cockroach, close to the floor as low as a beast he scuttled out of the grab and through the half-open kitchen door, stood up and opened the scullery door and slipped in there to escape.

In his scullery, Noel breathed, for the act of standing up had woken him. Noel stood there in his pyjamas, trembling from the effort, shaking still from the terror of the dream, from the fear that stayed in him still (that would stay in him for ever). And in him with the fear was a dirty feeling.

Noel saw the wide green eyes of the young man who'd been kneeling in the diningroom, forced to his knees beneath the blows from a pistol-butt that rained down upon his head. Kneeling, the young man was, but trying to stand, his hands crawling up the wall, trying to get a leverage; and there was blood running freely from the man's arm, and as the hands moved up they left their pawmarks, stamped in blood.

Noel had seen the young man, and not helped. Noel could have risen up, taken the blue man by surprise, smashed his fists into the pistol-butt, pulled out his own arm here that was a gun, pulled this gun out and shot the blue man, at least hit him with the gun, but Noel was a cockroach running this way and that, mad-scared between the legs, look-after-his-own-skin.

Noel stood, breathing. Taking in air to his lungs. Still only half-awake, shivering in June in pyjamas without his duffle-coat, hearing clunks next door that he didn't recognize as Evie clearing out junk, but which drew him.

Awake now but still a zombie, still stuck in his dream, Noel performed an action which made his arms and legs move in a familiar way, taking any mind that Noel had along with them.

Noel walked shivering over to the corner of his scullery and crouched down near the old fuel copper, there in the corner. He felt under it, pushed in under the gap, and pulled out all the bricks that were loose, not mortared in, they'd obviously been shifted before. Then Noel's body crept through the hidey-hole, till he was under 203's copper, and next his body slithered out, while Evie just watched.

Noel says nothing, he just gets up.

Evie says nothing either.

She's accustomed by now to Noel popping from

135

nowhere, and it's dawn, and Evie's exhausted, standing on the copper, keeping her balance despite tiredness as she tries to clean out this damned cupboard.

Noel shivers.

Evie has her arms up high, trying to straighten the rusting old tin chimney that Noel has dislodged in his crawling, and as she shoves the chimney, this thing falls out pat into her hands.

Legs stiff, feet stuck to the top of the copper, fear cold, like time all around. A hurry and slowness. And suddenly his face. Thin and white around the dark eyes of his fear and hurry as he grabs from her the gun.

'That's my gun,' Noel says, and disappears.

11

Evie lay down then, and didn't get up till she'd heard Ted and Mum leave. The girls were in the kitchen, and everything was so noisy and messy and normal that Evie wondered if the night had happened. Then, as she went to put the milk back in the fridge, something about the fridge door caught her eye, and her stomach turned over, as if she'd just gone too fast in a lift.

On the fridge door they had a set of those plastic magnetized letters, for Sammy to learn her alphabet with. Sammy played with them a lot, writing her name and everyone else's names, and Maria and Jodie would sometimes write four-letter words.

This morning there was a name there, but it wasn't anyone Evie knew.

noBby wesTOn

Evie read, and felt her stomach lift and drop fast. '*Who did that?*'

The girls giggled at her fierceness.

'Whose name's that?'

But the girls giggled more.

Evie shook Maria, for she was sure from her face that it was Ree that had done it, but Maria just laughed and pulled away, then grabbed her lunch and was off out the front door, Jodie at her heels.

Evie looked at Sammy. But Sammy couldn't know. Was just laughing because the others had, because Evie being so wild looked so funny. Evie didn't usually get wild like that.

Surprised herself at her wildness, Evie paused, tried to think why the letters upset her, and then suddenly anger gripped her again, anger at living in this bloody place where, ever since they'd come here, things had kept pulling at her, making her feel. Evie swiped her forearm across the fridge door, sending the bright-coloured letters flying off into air, and then they fell upon the floor, a scattered jumble, spelling no name.

'I'm going to tell on you!' Sammy said.

'Who'll you tell?'

'Mr Man!'

'You and your *Mr Men* books!'

12

After the battle was over, Mrs Weston stepped out onto the street. She could do it now for they were gone now, vanquished, the feet of the children that skipped out their two-four time in crotchets upon the pavement, skipped to steal her son, to stop her living.

She was hungry, it was four days now. Four days since anything but black tea. And hungry too was the boy in her house, a thin, white-cheeked boy who'd run in as a fugitive to lie upon her floor.

'Get in here, boy,' she'd said. Hiding him beneath her bed, knowing he'd be safe here because no police would question *her*, she was the policemen's accomplice.

'Scab, scab!' screeched Job the parrot, ever quick to pick up new tricks. 'Give her a stab!'

Stepping out through her gate onto the pavement, her neat black shoes had been polished that morning as they were every morning, come fire, come hail, come revolution, whether she was going to step out that day or not. In her dizziness from the hunger she wondered who the thin boy was, but whoever he was he was the cause of her stepping out now to buy food for she wouldn't have done it for herself.

For the first time in her life, for this fugitive beneath her bed, Mrs Weston is partaking of an act of charity, but it is too late.

'I don't take charity!' She didn't give it either.

Many years before this, standing on her roof under the bruised sky of a southerly buster, with all the slates flying off around her head, she'd defied the heavens who had given her a bank teller then taken him away, leaving her with just a sickly son and a piano and a parrot. 'I don't believe in you!' she'd screamed into the sky. Throwing off five generations of Methodism in one sentence, she'd defied her God to prove he was there by making her fall, taking her up to heaven to be with her bank teller, whom she'd loved. But nothing had happened.

After that, she expected nothing, gave nothing.

But wanted to give a soup now at least with the three shillings she'd hoarded in the piano stool (she was too much herself to keep it in the tea caddy like the rest of Liberty Street), wanted to buy with her last money in the world some food for the fugitive, whoever he was.

He looks a *nice* boy, Mrs Weston thinks.

Over the hills and far away in dizzy hunger.

Her mind sent far away too by the children's feet upon the street, by the effort of being a traitor.

(*'May we come through here?' the nice Police Inspector had said.*

'Oh, yes,' she'd said, making her first betrayal.)

'I must tell my son,' Mrs Weston stepping says, 'I must tell him that I'm hungry.'

But he's most unsympathetic these days, her son. Argues late through the night, tells her to get the widow's pension, then she won't need next door's rent. Take the pension. That's charity. And socialism too, brought in by that man Lang. She'd rather live off the rent from the Irish bog. He's no son of hers. This last week, he hasn't even spoken to argue.

Mrs Weston steps but her feet seem to take her nowhere, she still hasn't reached 203.

203, Lizzie, hussy. The way she jumps around the street with her safety pins flying. I'd rather see him dead than let her have him.

But my nice fugitive.

...'May we come through here?' the nice Police Inspector had said.

'Oh certainly,' had answered the betrayer.

...On her first night in Newtown, Evie had worked one thing out: if a gang wanted to break into 203, this is how they'd do it: in the kitchen door, but if they can't do that, over the scullery roof and/or through the balcony partition (though that would mean that they'd have had to break into 201 first; unless the owner of 201 was an accomplice of the gang)...

After the battle was over, Mrs Weston walked down the street that was dead quiet now the battle was over. 203 was a mess. Barbed wire, bits of sandbags, blue metal, bricks. Over the front door, half-swung-down, was a flimsy wooden sign.

THE EUREKA STOCKADE

Ah yes, remembered Mrs Weston stepping off to buy a lamb shank, that was in the past, the Eureka Stockade.

BOOK THREE

Facts

Have you ever been to Crazy Land
Down on the Loony Pike?
There are the queerest people there,
You never saw the like!
The ones who do the useful work
Are poor as poor can be,
And those who do no useful work
All live in luxury!

ANON, *THE TOCSIN*, 1930S

1

On the day after the gun-dawn, Evie went to CYSS. There were new big signs up on the wall:

FIGHT CUTS TO
CYSS FUNDING

STOP GOVT ATTACKS
ON NEWTOWN CYSS

The only person who seemed to be around was that project officer girl who wore glasses.

Sharnda watched Evie come in. It's that medium girl, she thought. The girl of medium height and medium build, with in-betweenish, brownish hair cut medium length with a fringe. Sharnda had noticed her a few times lately but had never got around to talking to her because Evie was always busy having the video camera explained to her by Roger.

('Another of Roger's little groupies,' Sharnda had grinned to Di.

'He can't help his looks,' Di defended him. 'He doesn't really lead them on.'

'I know,' Sharnda said. 'I only hope she keeps coming, that's all. The sooner he finds someone other than *me* to hang around after him with the sound stuff, the better.')

On this Friday, though, Sharnda did talk to Evie.

'G'day. Roger's around somewhere, out the back maybe. What's your name again?'

'Evie.'

'Hi, I'm Sharnda.'

'What?'

'Sharnda. It's sort of short for Alexandra.'

'Oh,' Evie said vaguely. 'Like Alexandra Kollontai.'

Sharnda stared at Evie. She would hardly have expected Evie to know of Alexandra Kollontai. Sharnda had noticed that except when Evie was with Roger and the camera she tended to look dull and blank, or even somehow peeved. Sharnda was suddenly interested: Kollontai was one of her heroes.

'Do you like Alexandra Kollontai?' Sharnda asked.

'Who?' Evie looked blank.

'Alexandra Kollontai.'

'Who's she?' Evie was looking past Sharnda: looking for Roger.

'The woman whose name you just said. You just said that my name was the same as Alexandra Kollontai's.'

'I've never heard of her.' Evie's bored look had changed to her peeved look. She felt that Sharnda was pestering her about something she didn't want to know about.

'But you just said her name.'

Then Evie looked straight at Sharnda, suddenly interested. 'Did I really?'

'Yes.'

'Oh.' Evie paused, confused. 'Well, who is she?'

'Was, not is. She's dead. She was one of the leaders of the Bolshevik Revolution. An early feminist. And she wrote stories too. She was around in Russia in 1917.'

'But *I* don't know anything about any of that!' Evie wailed. 'I hated history at school!'

Sharnda didn't say anything. She felt she'd upset Evie somehow, and the whole issue seemed to have blown completely out of proportion. Then Evie took her by surprise again. She looked at Sharnda very seriously and said, 'Do you ever think you're going mad?'

'Sometimes.'

'Is that true, or are you just bulling me to make me feel better?'

'Why would I tell you bull to make you feel better?'

'Because you're a social worker. Because that's your job.'

'Fair enough. But still, I do sometimes think I'm going mad.'

'I do too.' But Evie felt more cheerful now. It's nice to know you're not Robinson Crusoe. 'Just lately,' she added. 'Since we moved here.'

'What sort of mad?' Sharnda asked, because Evie seemed to want to talk. Underneath the sullen top layer of this kid, Sharnda thought, there was some sort of bright interesting spark.

'Oh, nothing much.' Evie was uneasy. 'Stuff like what happened just then. I think something, or I say something, or I do something, and it's like someone else did it,

145

or sometimes it's like *I* did it a long time ago.'

She was quiet, then abruptly talked again. 'Like, there's this old woman, a real old witch, I have to get her lunch for her, anyway, soon as I met her I really hated her, hated her guts, but it was like I'd known her for ages and knew why I hated her, but I *don't* know why I hate her.'

'There's other weird things, too,' Evie added; then clamped up.

'What, you only moved into Newtown lately?' Sharnda was just trying to keep the conversation going.

'Yeah.'

'Whereabouts?'

'Liberty Street.'

Sharnda was interested again. 'What number?'

'203.'

Sharnda did something then that, more than all her kind inquiry, made Evie feel comparatively sane. For she repeated '*203!*' at the top of her voice and gazed at Evie as if Evie had just said something really clever.

'Hey Roger!' (He'd just wandered in.) 'Evie lives in that house in Liberty Street, the one I told you about.'

'Good one.' Roger had a really warm, quiet voice that always made Evie feel as if he was listening to her. But when he said this, he sounded especially warm, and he too was looking at Evie as if she'd just won an Olympic medal or saved someone's life or something.

'When can I come round,' Sharnda said, excited, 'and have a look around your house?'

'What?' Evie said. 'What're you on about?'

Sharnda was bad at explaining things. She tended

146

to start in the middle, talk in a rush, and expect people to know what she meant. She collected herself now, and tried to go back to the beginning.

'When I was at uni,' (she was a bit embarrassed, felt she was sounding like a schoolteacher) 'I wrote a history thesis about how unemployed workers in the 1930s Depression got together and organized and fought for more dole and for jobs, and against evictions and stuff...It's what they're going to have to do again now,' she added, suddenly eager.

'Anyway, in 1931 there was this long campaign in Sydney against evictions, and as the unemployed kept winning, the authorities kept using more and more force against them. The biggest battle of all happened in your house...'

'There's even a song about it,' Roger cut in. ' "At Bankstown and at Newtown, we made the cops feel sore..."'

Evie felt her stomach turn over, as if she was going up too fast in a lift. It was as if Sharnda was telling her about some secret thing Evie had done, that she'd thought no one knew about. 'What happened?' she said, to make sure.

'Cops came with guns,' Sharnda said, feeling her voice straining a bit as it always did when she talked about the battle. 'They came with guns and they shot at the unemployed. One guy was hit in the arm. Cops came with guns with bullets in them, and people were shot, just like in the Eureka Stockade, except that Eureka has got into the history books because it happened long enough ago, and the Liberty Street battle has been left out of history books, because it's too recent, and the knowledge of such truth could be dangerous...'

147

'Danger...' Evie said slowly. Tasting the word like an ice cube that you take into your mouth: too large, too square, too cold to be comfortable, but you can't spit it out. 'I know what you're talking about.'

It was the sound of the footstep first, treading stealthily across the roof above her, only one foot, then two feet, more feet; and more feet too, a new set of feet, six more feet, ten more feet, running fast down the side passage in rhythm with the feet above. But only the sounds; she couldn't see anything.

Then it stopped; then it happened again.

But visually this time, and soundlessly, she saw the shape of a foot plant itself silver-ly above her. Not a naked foot, with toes, but a boot-shape, rounded at the front, a heavy heel at the back, heavy though soundless the footstep now grew above her till it seemed to cover the ceiling, silver first, then changing to black.

Then time pressed, meaning something, happening too fast, drawn out like ages; time that pressed, just as space pressed, as danger pressed, for the room now had shrunk to the size of the diagonal cupboard and Evie was in it, standing up, balancing on top of the copper, holding back her dreadful coughing, holding back her fear, trying to straighten the rusting old tin chimney that Noel has dislodged in his crawling and as she shoves the chimney, the thing falls out pat into her hands.

'Guns,' Evie said. Sharnda thought she seemed in a daze.

'So can I come round,' Sharnda said, 'and have a look?'

She wasn't sure what she wanted. Partly to look for evidence: old scrape marks of a ricochet along a wall. But mainly it was just that it'd be an honour for her, to go where her heroes had fought. Others feel the same way about the battlefields of Marathon, or Culloden, or Gallipoli. Or Eureka.

'Roger, you'll come too won't you?' Sharnda threw in a bone to draw Evie.

'Come?' Roger said sweetly. 'Sure. But we won't just come. We'll film it. We'll do a re-enactment: get all the kids from here, they can dress up as the cops and the pickets and the crowd and stuff…'

(Sharnda thought: Let Roger loose with a video portapak, and he thinks he's the guy that made *Gone with the Wind*…)

'Okay, Evie?' Roger said sweetly.

But the way Roger said it, there wasn't a question mark at the end.

'Okay,' Evie said. 'Okay.' Secretly worrying about Ted. About a lot of things.

2

Noel was sick. Must've caught flu or something, running around that gun-dawn in his pyjamas and no duffle-coat. Running? no, crawling, crawling down the stairs…

The other day upon the stair
I met a man who wasn't there…

Noel's head whirled. Spun him back to desperate green eyes that looked into his own as he crawled through the

149

diningroom, holding his terror close to him like something real to ward off night.

Then Evie's face yelling, *You're a creep, why can't you leave me alone*, Evie's face swam above him, way above; then she reached out a hand but he was quick through the hidey-hole. In the safety of his bed, Noel pulled the blankets right over. I'm not here, I don't exist. In his flu, his brain soared far above his forehead as if he was up high in an aeroplane.

Pelting down the stairs though in his mind like the other night, he encountered in half-darkness a beast that scuttled through the legs *quick*...a cowardy custard...no, a cowardy cockroach...

I'd rather be dead.

Dramatizing then, like an actor in a movie, he pulled the rifle out from beneath the bed and held it to his brain.

Playing games.

'Russian Roulette...'

Playing nothing.

'You are familiar with the rules?'

A jaded gentleman he was, in his white tropical pyjama suit, dying of dissipation; or perhaps thwarted in love...

'You're a creep!' yelled Scarlett O'Hara, words flying out her mouth as Roseanne in her pastel jeans giggled...

It was better before.

A jaded gentleman he was, in his white tropical pyjama suit, and he'd shamed the family honour; or perhaps been thwarted in love...

'*Piss off!*' Noel remembered.

Then the fever took him over.

So rolling again into dark as I scuttle through the hole,

but the hidey-hole now is down the barrel of the gun, and my finger here pulls the safety catch back, and as the trigger squeezes in the bullet moves up, and the coward that is me has bravery in me yet, for there's a bullet in the gun and I know it's certain death; and now the bullet comes out *Bang!* and lodges in my brain: 'I'm dead, real dead, got a bullet in me head! Look Mum, look Evie, look Nanna!'

Noel laughed. A wild violent laugh beneath the blankets that made him burst out of his warm hidey-hole, spluttering for air. Who're you kidding, Noley-Poley? For the gun was lying beneath the bed like it always was, his brain was lying in his head like it always was, and the bang of the bullet was a knock on the door that he nearly ignored but didn't, it might be Evie. Noel snuck out on the balcony in his dissipated pyjama suit but no such luck, it was only Ted down there, big Ted.

3

Evie picked Sammy up and took her home. It was only three o'clock but Ted was there already, sitting in the loungeroom with his eyes glued to *Sesame Street*.

Evie felt nervous, coming in the front door, seeing him there, knowing she had to ask him about the film.

'G'day Ted!' She was extra friendly.

'Hello Daddy!' Sammy threw herself at him. 'I made you a lovely pasting!' She presented Ted with a big bit of paper with old Christmas cards and bits of wool and coloured macaroni stuck all over it. 'A lovely lovely pasting. Lovely lovely,' Sammy smooched.

Ted said nothing. Ignored the lovely pasting. Ignored his lovely Sammy.

'Would you like me to get you a beer, Ted,' Evie said.

'No.'

'Are you sure? It's no trouble.' (It was a lot of trouble, being so nice to Ted.)

'No.'

'How come?'

'Look, if you must know, Miss Stickybeak, I'm off the grog, that's all.'

'Oh.' That was odd. Ted was hardly a drunk, but Evie had never known him to go off the grog. He had four cans of KB every night: two when he got home, one with tea, one after tea: regular as a clock.

'Shitty-beak!' Sammy giggled. 'Daddy, you said a rude word!' She tried to climb onto Ted's lap.

'Just get her out, will you!' Ted snapped at Evie. 'Feed her or something. Or take her out to your bloody trampoline!'

Evie hauled at Sammy, who started howling, and the pasting tore, and Sammy howled more. Ted jumped out of his arm-chair, slammed out the front door.

'Just think,' Evie told Sammy, 'now you've got *two* lovely pastings.' It didn't stop the tears. Evie hugged Sammy. 'Isn't Daddy mean!'

Sammy pulled out of Evie's arms. 'He is not. And he's not your daddy anyway. He's my daddy. My daddy and Jodie's daddy and Ree's daddy. You haven't got a daddy.'

Evie shrugged and let her go. That was one thing that didn't worry her. If fathers could be judged by Ted, and by

Roseanne's dad, and others that she'd met, the fact that hers had cleared out just after she was born didn't worry her in the slightest. She and Mum had managed all right, before Ted came along.

Evie heard Ted knocking next door. Friday: Rent Day, she thought. But he was being a bit eager, the old Ted. Mrs Cavendish wouldn't be home yet for him to pay her. Even Noel mightn't be home. Though he probably would be. Evie thought he probably hadn't gone to school again today. She'd heard a sound like him walking about this morning.

The last Evie had seen of Noel, early yesterday morning, he'd grabbed the gun from her and crawled back through the hole. Then she'd heard him being sick next door.

Evie hadn't done despot duty that Thursday or Friday. She hadn't felt up to it. Noel can do it. Or the old bag can starve, for all I care. Evie had simply slept all day Thursday, slept and dreamed and woken and slept and dreamed and woken, sleeping each time through questions and more questions, waking each time with a worse headache, the sleeping wore her out. She'd wanted to go in and talk to Noel; but the memory of Roseanne's voice still made her squirm: 'It's Noel. Your boyfriend. Remember?' Remember? I remember too much...

Ted came back in looking shitty. 'Wouldn't open the bloody door. Snuck out on the balcony in his pyjamas, yells down that he's sick, then snuck back in again, lazy little beggar. You're a good match, you two, I'll give you that. You and your boyfriend.'

My boyfriend. There it was again. Evie said nothing.

Was Evie-Peevie.

'Don't act dumb with me,' Ted said. 'You can fool your mother with your trampolining and your young-for-your-age act, but I know Lover Boy was in your room at sparrow's fart yesterday morning, I heard his voice in there when I come down to make a cup of tea because I can't sleep because he's kept me up half the night with his bashing around and his ruddy mouth-organ.'

Evie didn't try to explain. You couldn't explain things to Ted. Plus she couldn't say anything, because of the gun. Evie didn't know why, but she knew the gun had to be kept secret. In her dreams, the questions tormented her. 'Where is it? Where is he?' And Evie would shake herself awake, she was scared she'd tell them. Though tell them what, when she was awake, she didn't know. One of them was a policeman, big, who yelled at her, like Ted was doing now.

'But if you think I'm worried, you can have another think. Long as your mother doesn't know, I don't care what you do. I've got better things to worry about than you.'

'And I've got better things to worry about than you!' Evie ran, slammed the door behind her. She felt sick. Him suggesting that her and Noel...

4

That weekend, Evie put off telling Ted and Mum that people wanted to come around to their house and make a video. And she put off going in to see Noel too. She wanted to see Noel, to ask what he'd done with the gun, to tell him what Sharnda had told her, but she couldn't stand the thought of going in after what Ted had suggested.

That weekend, Noel lay in bed, with the gun hidden beneath it, lay there feeling sick. He *was* sick sometimes, into a white plastic icecream container that he'd brought up to his bed.

His grandmother, in her room, was restless. Writing interminable notes, that she erased. On Thursday and Friday, while Noel's mum had been at work, Noel had heard her mumble-whinning to her mates. On Saturday and Sunday she was silent, but all the time writing.

At one stage on Saturday he took pity on her. Went into her room and offered to play noughts and crosses. She liked games, the despot. That was about the only thing she'd done when he was a kid. She'd played games with him. Ludo and snakes and ladders and sometimes battleships and noughts and crosses, but more usually euchre and five hundred and solo and even poker. She'd played hard, making no concessions to his age, never faking it to let him win, and in the card games they'd played for cents; so that he'd spent his childhood being hundreds of dollars in debt to her and doing chores to work it off.

That was the one issue he'd ever heard his mother row with her over. 'You could let him win sometimes. Or you could forget the debt.'

But the despot wouldn't budge: 'No one ever let *me* win!' For the despot loved the power of victory as a child does, rubbing it in. 'I've won! I've won!'

I've won. She didn't say it that Saturday, but Noel could see it on her face, the greedy anticipation that Noel would put his nought *there*, and she would put her cross *here*, and make a line and beat him.

But in her haste the despot had slipped. Noel drew his nought here at the bottom and not there at the top and it was Noel who made a line.

The despot didn't even deign to look at him. Carefully lifted the bottom corner of the transparent magic sheet and erased Noel's nought, then filled one in for him up the top, put her own cross down the bottom, and slashed a line through her crosses and won.

'But that's wrong, Nanna. It isn't what happened.'

She looked then, fixed him with her eye, then wiped the whole page clean and wrote:

'IF I WRITE IT DIFFERENTLY, IT HAPPENED DIFFER-ENTLY.'

You're a cheating old woman, Nanna. Then Noel thought: No, not an old woman, just a kid. For that was how kids thought.

Once when Noel was about seven, Matt and Tasso and another kid called Billy had knocked him down and taken the shop note that Nanna had written. Too scared to go home yet again without anything, Noel had bought some random things, then written a note with those things on it.

When he'd got home, the despot had hit the roof. Peanut butter instead of sugar, jam doughnuts instead of cornflour, and what was this Donald Duck pencil sharpener? 'This isn't what's on the note, boy!'

'Yes it is, Nanna.' He'd proved it to her.

The despot hadn't been amused. Had sent Noel to his room. Where Noel had lain, sobbing at the injustice of the world, for in his seven-year-old mind the second note had

156

quite replaced the first and he couldn't see why he was being punished. If I write it differently, that's how it was...

'Okay, Nanna,' Noel said on the Saturday, but didn't ask her if she'd like another go. He'd learnt as a child: games to the despot weren't to be played with, they were real.

So that weekend, Evie sat in her room, putting off everything. She wanted to see Noel, but she couldn't go in.

That weekend, Noel and the despot were sick in their rooms, and Noel's mum scuttled around the house, popping through their doors like a nervy lizard from a crack, trying to wait on them both. Took food to the despot, which she waved away. Took food to Noel, who couldn't eat without being sick later into the white icecream container. She wanted to get the doctor, but they both baulked.

'I'm not sick!'

(Just dead I'm dead got a bullet in me head.)

'I'M NOT SICK!'

(Just alive, not dead, battling on a roof with an unwanted life while the children jump up around me like slates into the sky.)

So all Saturday and all Sunday morning, Evie didn't see Noel.

On the Sunday afternoon, Sharnda came around to show Evie some photocopies of some documents she'd used when she'd written her thesis. Ted answered the door.

'Hello, I'm Sharnda, is Evie home?'

Ted looked at her as if Evie had no right to have visitors. But let her in. Jodie and Maria stared and whispered, started to giggle, then hid their mouths behind their hands. Sammy

157

joined the game. Sharnda felt shy, tried to explain herself, talked loud over the television football.

'I work up at the CYSS centre.'

Ted really got going then. Raving on about dole-bludgers, like someone on talk-back radio. What you should do with people like that is turn the radio off. But Sharnda had to go and do her social worker bit.

'One of the problems of young unemployed workers is that their parents refuse to believe that they can't get work, whereas in actual fact...'

'How can *you* talk to *me!*' Ted exploded. 'Coming in here with your fat salary, telling me how to run my family. You *live off* the unemployed!'

You're half-right, Sharnda thought. But probably not for long, mate. 'The way things look, they'll cut off the funds for the centre and I'll be unemployed myself in a couple of weeks.'

Ted looked sharply at her, but said nothing.

All the time this was going on, Newtown battled Souths on TV. Maria took advantage of Ted's involvement and switched channels.

'Turn that back, miss.'

Sharnda's eyes were roving around the walls. But in fifty years the house had been painted and repainted, wall-papered and rewallpapered, and there were no marks that could be bullet holes in the plaster...This is all a far cry from '31, Sharnda thought, as she observed the pine-and-vinyl chairs, the roller skates, the white-tile coffee table, the bright professional photo of bright modern smiling people (though Evie wasn't smiling, she noticed), the TV set where

158

Newtown was just scoring a goal. Ted and Sharnda both let out a cheer.

'Looks like they've a chance this year, Newtown,' Sharnda said.

Ted looked at her dubiously. 'Why would you care?'

'Because I live here.'

'Evie's out the back,' Ted said. 'Go on through.'

'I never used to back Newtown,' he added, 'but now I'm here I reckon I might as well.'

As Sharnda went through the kitchen she heard his voice floating out after her. 'The people you should worry about is blokes who've worked all their lives and then lose their jobs. They don't have CYSS centres and social workers. Who gives a stuff about *them!*'

Sharnda knocked at Evie's door and heard 'Come in!' She stepped in uneasily, feeling shy with Evie too now, but not with Noel, who wandered in from the back way, white-faced and sick-looking, meandering in like he had a right to be there, a boy Sharnda recognized from when she'd been up outside Coles on a Saturday morning handing out pamphlets about an unemployed workers' rally and he'd been there, playing his mouth-organ.

Sharnda handed them the first of a stack of photo-copies.

SYDNEY MORNING NEWS

FRIDAY JUNE 19 1931

DESPERATE FIGHTING

Communists and Police

BARRICADED HOUSE STORMED

Barbed Wire Entanglements and Sandbags.

The most sensational eviction battle Sydney has ever known was fought between 40 policemen and 18 Communists at 203 Liberty Street, Newtown, yesterday morning. All the defenders were injured, some seriously, and at least 15 of the police were treated by ambulance officials.

Only one man was hit by bullets fired at the walls of the house by the police, and it is not known how the injury was inflicted. Probably the wounded man was struck by a bullet which had been deflected in its path.

Entrenched behind barbed wire and sandbags, the defenders rained stones weighing several pounds from the top floor of the building on to the heads of the attacking police, who were attempting to execute an eviction order.

After a desperate battle, in which iron bars, piping, rude bludgeons, and chairs were used by the defenders, and batons by the police, the defenders were dragged, almost insensible, to the waiting patrol waggons.

SHOWERS OF STONES

Shortly before dawn, 50 police and detectives approached the building.

The two-storied house, a terrace, was fantastically barricaded on the outside by barbed wire. All doors and windows on the ground floor were reinforced with towering stacks of sandbags which reached to the ceilings. Every stack was about 6 feet thick at the floor and weighed probably half a ton.

When police reached the pavement outside the front fence, a terrible shower of stones rained down on to their heads.

POLICE DRAW REVOLVERS

After a short consultation, the police drew their revolvers.

At a word of command they commenced firing steadily at the balcony railing behind which the men were crouched.

HELP FROM LANDLADY

Leaving one group to continue the barrage, another group of police led by the Inspector in charge knocked upon the door of the adjoining terrace at 201 and were admitted by a woman, who is the owner of both properties.

Shortly afterwards, five police climbed from the balcony of 201 to the balcony of the besieged house, and succeeded in driving the defenders inside.

Were it not for the help of the landlady, the inspector in charge stated later, the police task would have been extraordinarily more difficult, so well barricaded was the house.

ATTACK FROM REAR

Meanwhile, a further body of police approached the house from a back lane and made a concerted rush on the back door.

By this time, summoned by the frantic calls for help from the guards on the ground floor, most of the men on the top floor rushed down the staircase to the small dining-room. It was here, in near-darkness, that the terrible hand-to-hand combat occurred.

Diving one by one through the narrow breach in the sandbags, the police steadily met the terrific onslaught of the besieged men.

Wielding bludgeons improvised from iron bars, palings, and wooden batons pulled from wrecked furniture, the guards made frantic efforts to repel the invading police.

The room was absolutely bathed in blood. Practically every man was bleeding from one or more wounds. Insensible men lay on the floor, while comrades and foes alike trampled on them. The walls were spattered and daubed with blood stained hands.

One by one the defenders fell. Those who were still on their feet were overpowered, and handcuffed.

HOSTILE CROWD

From the moment of the police arrival, a crowd hostile to the police, numbering many thousands, began to gather in Liberty Street. They filled the street for a quarter of a mile on each side of the building until squads of police drove them back about 200 yards and police cordons were thrown across the roadway.

At times the huge crowd threatened to become out of hand. It was definitely antagonistic to the police. When constables emerged from the back of the building with their faces covered in blood, the crowd hooted and shouted insulting remarks. When the defenders were led out they were cheered. When one patrol waggon containing prisoners was being driven away, people standing well back in the crowd hurled stones at the police driver.

'THE EUREKA STOCKADE'

An examination of the house revealed a crude sign over the front door, re-naming the house 'The Eureka Stockade'.

This was an example, the Inspector in charge stated, of how foreign Communists would even pervert glorious moments in Australia's history for their own nefarious ends.

(In the Eureka Stockade of 1854, the foundation stones of Australian democracy were laid when miners gallantly fought against armed troopers).

TREATMENT OF INJURED

Practically every combatant was treated by the Newtown Ambulance at Newtown Police Station, after which the majority of the defenders were taken to Royal Prince Alfred Hospital.

Twelve police suffered injuries to practically every part of their bodies and 2 were taken to hospital in police motor cars.

Of the 18 defenders, the most seriously injured were: Michael Cruise, 18, shot wound in left arm, cerebral concussion and lacerations to head; Padraic Cruise, 41, head injuries; Lester Dacey, 54, head injuries; Joseph Isaacs, 30, fractured hand; John Murchison, 31, fractured skull; Brendan Riley, 43, head injuries; John Kennet, 19, head injuries; Cecil Kennet 21, head injuries; Gino Bellotti, 35, head injuries; Jack Finley, 26, head injuries; Reg Bly, 29, fractured skull.

ARRESTED MEN CHARGED WITH RIOT

The 18 men arrested were charged that, being armed with sticks, staves and other weapons, they riotously assembled to disturb the peace, and continued to riot for half an hour.

This is the first time a charge of Common Law Riot has been brought in Australia.

TENANT IN TROUBLE

It is believed that the tenant, Padraic Cruise, migrated to Australia in 1916 after being in trouble with the authorities in Ireland.

SEARCH FOR GUNMAN

It is alleged that after the police commenced to fire upon the front of the house and shortly before they made their way onto the balcony, a gunman was seen on the balcony, pointing a gun down at the police.

Police state that the gunman appeared to be a young man of pale complexion, and is not one of the pickets arrested.

'MYSTERY'

No gun has been found on the premises, despite careful police searches. The arrested men deny all knowledge of a nineteenth picket.

The alleged escape of the man despite the fact that the front entrance, the back yard and the back lane of the premises were completely surrounded by police is described by police as a 'mystery'.

YOUNG GIRL

In the search for the gunman police discovered a young girl cowering in a cupboard, but careful questioning revealed that she'd seen nothing of the battle.

The police are still conducting their enquiries.

Noel and Evie sat on the bed, reading together. Every so often, Noel would look quickly at Evie, or Evie would glance fast at Noel. '*Help from landlady*,' Noel read out loud, and they knew they were thinking the same thing. Then right at the end Noel began to hiccough badly. *Search for gunman*. He felt Evie tense, next to him.

'*Police discovered a young girl cowering in a cupboard*,' Evie read out loud and shuddered.

Neither of them spoke to Sharnda of the gun they'd found. Neither spoke of dreams, or the despot.

'Did they find him,' Noel spluttered through his hiccoughs, 'that gunman?'

'No,' said Sharnda. 'If he existed.'

'What do you mean?' Evie demanded.

Sharnda told them then that she'd scoured the papers for any account of police finding a gunman, but there was nothing. Over the next four days the Search for the Mystery Gunman had got three more mentions in the *Sydney Morning News* – all along the 'police-are-conducting-their-inquiries' line – a passionate but uninformational account in *Black's Weekly*, and an even more colourful editorial in the worst of the afternoon rags...

RED TROUBLE BREWING:
NEWTOWN RESIDENTS QUAKE

The search for the mysterious Communist Gunman, the nineteenth picket who according to police disappeared from the embattled house in Liberty Street Newtown last Thursday, is mystifying Sydney's police.

Meanwhile, residents of Newtown and neighbouring suburbs are unable to sleep at night for fear lest the gunman pay them a mysterious visit.

Sydney police report increased Communistic activity in Newtown lately, as these red rats of revolution capitalise upon the sad plight of our nation and attempt to stir up the Australian working man with their imported foreign lies.

Proof of their trouble-making is shown by the fact that in the recent eviction riot over a Newtown house police drew their revolvers to quell an unruly mob.

Sydneysiders might well ask themselves if they haven't a democratic right to sleep peacefully in their beds without attacks to property and possibly life and limb being perpetrated around them by mysterious gunmen and the rest of this red rubbish from the European sewers.

Despite sickness and hiccoughs, Noel laughed. Felt proud, too. That was him, the Mystery Gunman that made people write about him so funnily. That was Noel. He didn't know how it was him, but he knew it'd been him with the gun.

'And after that,' Sharnda said, 'there wasn't any more. No further mentions of a search, and no statement that the search had stopped either. The only thing that seems to me to make any sense of the whole thing is the denial that there'd ever been a gunman, that the Communist Party's *Workers' Voice* put out.'

'THE MYSTERY GUNMAN'

Since Thursday's violence by the armed forces of the state these same forces have not been content to leave well enough alone but have been harrassing the arrested men and also members of the UWM and the tenant's family in their so-called search for a so-called mystery gunman.

UWM leaders wish to make it clear that the mystery gunman is a mystery indeed, except in the minds of our so-called public protectors.

The UWM opposes the use of guns and the only guns present at Liberty Street were those in the hands of our so-called public protectors.

This search is a deliberate piece of intimidation, enabling police to obtain warrants to search the homes of UWM activists. It is also a deliberate attempt by police to put the blame for Thursday's violence upon UWM pickets, by suggesting to the public that police violence was necessary to quell the disturbance.

Yet even if the nineteenth

picket did exist, which he didn't, it is shown in the police's own account, published in the *Sydney Morning News*, that the alleged gunman only *pointed* a gun, and that he allegedly did this only *after* police fired their revolvers.

The fact that there was no gunman is proved by police failure to produce either gun or gunman despite the fact that they had the house in Liberty Street surrounded.

UWM leaders predict that police will allow the matter to drop because of the embarrassment that will be caused by their failure to find a man who does not exist.

In the meantime however the police interrogation has caused two female members of the tenant's family to require medical attention.

Noel held his nose, held his breath, did a headstand on the bed to stop his hiccoughs. He started to chant upside-down; 'The other day upon the stair I met a man who wasn't there...They're telling lies,' he added.

'Who?' Sharnda demanded.

'The UWM people, or whatever they're called.'

'I don't think so!' Sharnda was belligerent: defending her heroes. 'Why d'you reckon that?'

'Because...' Evie began, but Noel toppled down on her, and Evie shut up. They were tangled up there for a second, then both leapt to opposite ends of the bed.

'The back door,' Sharnda said, changing the subject because they looked embarrassed. 'Can I go out and look at it?' She stepped out of the scullery bedroom and stood in the breezeway, investigating the door for any marks around the architrave to show where the police had smashed.

'But they didn't smash it down,' Evie said in a dull voice, almost as if she was explaining something to a young child; as if Sharnda was Sammy and ignorant. 'They came over this roof, and got in through Sammy's room upstairs

– they'd got onto this roof through the window next door. And then they came down and opened the door from inside.'

'Shooting too inside the house,' Noel said, his hiccoughs starting again. 'Shooting up and down the staircase.'

'How did you know?' Sharnda said.

'Know what?' Noel was defensive. (Why have I had this in my knowledge since I was born?)

'It's just obvious,' Evie said in a flat voice. (That first morning in this house. 'By the way, love,' Mum had said, 'When we came home this morning, you'd left the kitchen door wide open.' Oh really, Evie had thought. Evie who'd known she'd locked it. Evie who knew it could only have been opened from inside.)

Sharnda looked at them: a thin, sick-looking boy; a medium, ordinary girl; and took Evie's statement on face-value. I guess it must be obvious. Sharnda silently handed them a statement that she'd found amongst the papers of the solicitor who defended the Newtown Eighteen.

STATEMENT OF THE PICKET MICHAEL CRUISE

I was in the front room upstairs when I heard someone
yell 'Here they are.' I ran out onto the balcony and it was
still dark but the streetlights were on and I saw a bus
roar up and police jump out and then the street was full of
police with revolvers firing up into the balcony at us and
we started throwing bricks in defence of ourselves. I was
on my knees to avoid the bullets and just then I stood up
to see how things were, and a bullet got me in the arm. I
bolted then with a couple of others into the back bedroom
and when I looked through a gap in the window I saw police
on the roof of the scullery, coming from the back bedroom
next door. They opened fire through the window and then
crashed through the boards and hunted us down the stairs,
still shooting. As I was halfway down three police ran down
over me and I heard them pulling back the sandbags at the
kitchen door. I bailed up there a second, and the police came
through the kitchen and started to shoot up the stairs.
So I jumped over the bannister and into the diningroom
and most of us were in there then, there was just a couple
of candles and the lamp to see by, and then all the police
came in, and started to batton us unmercifully whether we
showed fight or not, calling out 'I'll give you Red Russia,
you B's'. I was hollering for help but I was knocked to my
knees, and forced to stop down by a policeman who was
belting his pistol-butt into my head again and again. I tried
to stand up, but I couldn't, and one of our side crawled past
me then, and I had my hands up trying to get a grip on the
wall to get up, but I couldn't and fell. The policeman put

Blood everywhere I looked,

167

his foot on me and battoned me while I lay on the floor, and then put the handcuffs on me and punched me on the jaw. I was then taken outside and put in the patrol and taken to Newtown station. When we got there we had to walk from the patrol through a line of police to the charge room. They kicked and punched us all the way. We were then charged, some going to hospital, some to cells. I went to hospital where I was for three days. Signed: Mick Cruise

P.S. I wish to state that never at any time did I see any 19th picket or any man with a gun (I mean any of us with a gun) I want to make that clear in my statement, and I'd swear to it. Signed Mick Cruise

Evie slowly read out the bit that had been scribbled onto the bottom, in handwriting.

'Excuse me,' Noel said, and Sharnda watched him open an old wooden cupboard in the corner and crawl fast through under an old copper, and then she heard the sound of him being sick next door.

Evie slammed the cupboard shut fast in case Sharnda saw the heart.

With Noel gone, Evie felt vulnerable. Felt the weight of the gun-secret pressing heavily, felt the weight of knowing too much, but not enough, felt Sharnda's questions like the questions through her sleep.

('What did you see?' 'Where did he go?' 'Where's the gun?' Pa, Mick, Ma, all asking. And then the heavy asking of the police. Questions beating down like the Inspector's ruler on the table '…I'll tell you nothing,' Lizzie defied them. 'I don't know…')

'What's wrong with him?' Sharnda asked, but Evie cut in with her own questions.

Their questions, her questions, everything used to be so dull and simple but these days it was like the world swung around in circles.

'The girl in the cupboard,' Evie said. 'Do you know anything about her?'

'No. I've often wondered who she was.'

'Not was,' Evie said. 'Is.' Twisting Sharnda's words of Friday, seeing Sharnda looking at her oddly but unable to stop herself. 'Nobby Weston,' Evie added, 'Do you know what ended up happening to him?'

'Who's he?'

'Oh, just a guy I know.' Wondering herself who he was, why she'd said the name. The name that she'd seen upon the fridge. That name had just come out of her voice, like when she'd said Alexandra Kollontai the other day.

Sharnda was looking at the *Sydney Morning News* report. 'I've only just realized. Last Thursday was the battle's fiftieth anniversary.'

'Yeah.' It seemed obvious. On Thursday morning at dawn we found the gun. I love 4 ever, 18/6/1981.

Then Sharnda said it was funny, the dates ran parallel. It didn't seem funny to Evie. She wanted Sharnda to go so she could think. So told her that she'd talked to her parents and it was all okay about the video – she'd work out a good night for it.

'She must've been a shit, that landlady,' Sharnda

concluded. 'Not just evicting people, but actually helping the cops.'

'Sure,' Evie agreed, sick of Sharnda. (I *told* you the despot was dreadful! I'll tell you nothing.) 'Sure,' Evie said again, making up that she had to cook tea, letting Sharnda find her own way out, not telling her that Noel's grandmother must be the landlady, so that Sharnda left knowing nothing about Noel except that he was that boy who lived next door.

5

After he thought he'd finished being sick, Noel came back in through the hidey-hole. Evie was still sitting on the bed with the photocopies.

'Where's the gun?' she said.

'Safe.'

'Good.'

She didn't ask any more. Why I like Evie, Noel thought, is because she doesn't torment me with questions.

Evie went out, and Noel read through some of the photocopies, then Evie came back in with two mugs of tea. 'I don't know if you take sugar, but I put three spoons in because you need it for energy if you've been sick.' Evie was bossy sometimes, it came from being a big sister, but that evening Noel liked it: it's nice if you're feeling alone and sick.

Noel was reading through the stuff again, but Evie didn't want to. When Sharnda was here, she sort of made it far away like history, but it wasn't history to

Evie, it was too close to the bone.

It was somehow dangerous, Evie thought, what she knew. (Sharnda had said something: what was it? About danger). This feeling of knowing too much, but not enough. Like when you're a kid, and you half-know a secret, and you're scared you'll let it out accidentally because you're not sure what's *in* the secret, and what's out of it. These nights questions came into Evie's sleep like hooks. Evie didn't ask Noel where the gun was, because she didn't want to think about it, didn't want to know. If you think about a question mark, Evie thought, it's shaped like a scythe. And you're in its path, and you have to jump over it.

Nobby Weston, Evie thought. Who's he?

She looked at Noel, who was quiet and reading. It was strange, how he made her peaceful; and other times, this wild laugh that was in him made her happy; but most of the time, she couldn't just let him make her feel peaceful and happy because all these people and questions seemed to be searching them out, forcing them together, pulling them apart, never letting them just be Evie and Noel.

In his own way, Noel was thinking the same thing. Why me?

The other day upon the stair
I met a man who wasn't there
He wasn't there again today
Oh dear I wish he'd go away...

(Go away, Mick, Noel thought.)

Only he wasn't Mick, this man Noel had met on the stair. Mick was later. This man on the stair: that was Noel.

171

He'd met himself there, but not a man but a boy...

'*I was hollering for help and one of our side crawled past me then...*'

...Not a man but a boy, not a boy but a beast, not so much a beast but more a cockroach. Why me, Mick Cruise whoever you are, why me?

'The Cruise bloke,' Noel said. 'He must be related to this Padraic or however-you-say-it bloke who was the tenant of the place.'

'Yeah,' was all Evie said. She'd hated history at school. The police found a girl who was cowering in a cupboard. Leave it at that.

But Noel wouldn't. 'Who *was* she?'

'Who?'

'You know.'

Evie did and she didn't. She knew the face, for she'd seen the ghost, and she knew she was the girl and that the girl was she, or sometimes anyway. But didn't know her name, her own name, no, *her* name, oh god, things like this made Evie go in circles and she didn't want to.

'*You know,*' Noel said again, for *he* didn't, but Evie must. He fought his will against hers, like Sammy when she thought Evie had a secret; for a difference between Noel and Evie was that while Evie knew both people, the face of the girl, the face with the gun, Noel knew only himself, himself that was gutless. He knew the night, the gun, the running, knew it off by heart, but when he'd gone into the scullery maybe his mind had come back too fast to 1981: for he didn't know Lizzie; he only knew Evie.

Only Evie, and himself who-wasn't-there. Whoever I

am, this guy that I was, I'm gutless. Frozen like ice, I wish I could act.

Acting/act. Despite himself, Noel laughed. Sometimes you used the word to mean pretending, and sometimes you used it to mean doing.

Then he saw Evie watching him laugh. She must think I'm a creep, laughing at nothing. Noel stopped short.

I wish he'd keep laughing, Evie thought.

So Noel and Evie sat, uncomfortable with each other. It was a long time since the night over the suburbs, sitting together swinging their legs, away from the tension of their homes.

'Do you want to come up with me and see her?' Noel finally said.

'No,' Evie said. She didn't want ever again to see that fat rotten face.

'How do you think *I* feel?' Noel demanded. 'What if *your* grandmother had done what mine did?' Noel felt as if there was poison in his blood.

'C'mon then.' For on the other hand Evie had to know: who Nobby was, this mystery gunman. And who she was, the girl inside her.

Ted was sitting in the kitchen with the door open, waiting for them, a funny look on his face, as they opened Evie's door and walked out.

(*Lover Boy*, Evie thought, and wished Noel to the end of hell.)

'What's this I hear about you and all your Dolebludger Club wanting to play cops and robbers and make a film in my house!'

173

Sharnda must've gone and opened her big mouth.

Ted and Evie had a dingdong row then, Noel trying to stand invisible beside Evie. Evie felt Ted's eyes shifting over the bed that was all messed up from them sitting on it and Noel doing headstands. She felt cold inside and hateful.

6

Evie and Noel had both of course seen enough TV to know how to run an interrogation. There's the hard method, and the soft method. In the hard method, people on TV use torture, or they yell, like the Inspector in Evie's dreams, pounding a ruler on a table like surf crashing in a storm against a coast. In the soft method, they talk quietly, drawing the secret out of you like the Irish voices that tugged at Evie's mind in her dreams, pulling at her knowledge like the undertow of waves circling back. (No, Pa, no, Mick, no, Ma, I'll tell you nothing.) But never on TV (or even in dreams) had Evie or Noel seen the right method for interrogating a sick, eighty-seven-year-old woman.

As they climbed up the last steps, Noel's mother popped out of the bathroom and said, 'Oh you're feeling better, dear.' She added 'Hello, dear,' and a nervous smile at Evie.

'Could you go downstairs please, Mum.' Noel said gently, 'and make me some soup, please.'

'I don't think...' Mrs Cavendish began quietly to object, but Noel and Evie stepped past her.

The despot was in her night-gown, writing by the light of her bedside lamp. (If I write it differently, it happened differently.) Writing furiously, filling a page, then making it disappear, writing furiously again, her head bent down, ignoring them.

Mrs Cavendish popped in, worried, behind them. 'I just settled Nanna down for the night,' she whispered. Trying to edge them out of the room.

Evie and Noel stood there, hating. The despot still didn't appear to know there was anyone in the room.

'Tomato or chicken, dear?' Noel's mum whispered.

'I don't mind, Mum. Anything. Nothing.'

Nothing. Evie and Noel followed Noel's mum down to the kitchen.

'If you would, dear, you might remind Ted,' Mrs Cavendish murmured as she took a jar of jellied broth from the fridge, 'that he didn't pop in on Friday, if you don't mind dear.'

'Tell me, Mum,' Noel said, 'all you know about Nanna.'

Noel's mum was a little woman, light on her feet, but though her movements were swift she took a long time to do anything, she was so finicketty. Just for a bowl of soup she put down a spanking-clean tablecloth, and then a place-mat, pepper and salt in cut-glass shakers, and then poured milk into a jug, got out a glass, then another glass for Evie.

'Or would you prefer warm milo, dear?' she apologized to Evie. 'I'm afraid we have no cordial.'

Then she laid a bread-and-butter plate, a bread-and-butter knife, a soup spoon, then a dinner plate to put the soup bowl on. She stirred the soup, letting it come to the boil gently, and sliced bread, and made toast, and cut it in triangles, and then took butter from the fridge and cut a slice and put it on a clean flowery butter dish, then

175

got a little silver butter knife, then a clean white serviette in a shining old silver serviette ring that said *N* in twirley engraving.

Evie's mum just would have boiled up water in the jug and made a cup-a-soup from a packet. Would have slapped the mug down on the laminex then sat and had a cigarette and talked to you while you drank it. Evie felt uncomfortable in Noel's mum's kitchen. The clock up there looked as if its hands were frozen, the time ticked so slowly. Evie longed to reach up and shift them.

Noel's mum finally ladled soup into a bowl and placed it in front of Noel. 'I'm afraid I don't know anything, dear,' she said. She stood, while Noel and Evie sat. 'My father, your grandfather, died when I was little. So I grew up without a father, just as you did, dear.'

Noel nodded impatiently. 'The despot's a widow, tell me something I don't know.'

'But I'm afraid I can't tell you anything more, dear,' Noel's mum told him. 'She's never talked about the past, I've never liked to ask her. She's always been a quiet woman, kept herself to herself. Even when I was a little girl, she didn't talk to me much.'

Quiet, Noel thought. Hardly. If you heard her mumble-whining to her mates, old Mum.

Kept herself to herself, Evie thought. Then why doesn't she keep her temper to herself instead of taking it out on *me*. I've never done anything to *her*.

Evie felt uncomfortable, sat spinning the silver serviette ring around her thumb: they didn't have serviette rings in her family.

'It's funny, the only thing I remember, dear, was that we had a parrot, a noisy nasty thing that used to scream out a lot, in the night too sometimes, and then she'd yell back at it: "Keep quiet, persecutor, or you'll be dead too!" She talked to that parrot, I think more than she talked to me, but she'd mutter into its cage and I never heard. She called it Job, after that prophet in the Bible, the one that suffered so much, poor man, when God sent down all his afflictions. I always felt she sort of meant the name for herself. She's suffered a great deal in this life, your nanna, dear.'

Evie span the serviette ring slowly round, the action eased her tension. 'This is old,' she finally said, looking at the tiny craftsman's mark inside it.

'Yes, dear. Noel's nanna gave it to me for him when he was just a baby.'

'Older than that,' Evie said. After the mark it said 1914.

'Yes, dear. She had it in a drawer, wrapped in tissue paper. I dare say it must have belonged to someone else once.'

'Who?' Evie demanded, remembering the heart. I love N 4 ever.

'Who?' Noel demanded, feeling part of the ring.

But Noel's mum looked useless. She was the sort of person who never asked questions herself, and felt uneasy when other people asked them. 'Promise me, dear,' she said to Noel who sat silent, not eating his soup, 'promise me you'll never ask her anything that might bring back the past. And you too, dear,' she added to Evie. Noel's mum was a poor frightened woman, begging them.

Noel and Evie said nothing, but it was the same as if

177

they'd said they promised. That avenue was closed. Evie span the serviette ring angrily and it went flying off her thumb and rolling across the lino into darkness.

BOOK FOUR

Interim

We belong to the doley-oh mob,
The doley-oh mob are we!
We never fight or quarrel,
We never disagree.

ANON,
TRADITIONAL SONG, 1930S.

1

He'd left her, her nice fugitive. Had told her a tale about a girl he said he loved, made her swear on the Bible that if she came, the fugitive's love, she would pass on messages between them. Then he'd bundled a couple of things into a sugar-bag, asked her so polite if he might possibly take an old grey army blanket, refused her offer of her last shilling, and slipped out the back way in dead of night, last Thursday night. It was so lonely here without him.

First her husband left her, years ago, slipped off up into black heavens and left her here with a parrot that said things and a wicked piano that thumped day and night and a son that wouldn't speak (no son of hers); and then she got the fugitive, found him like a gift in the dawn, as if black heavens were trying to give her back a thing to replace the others. Gave a gift, only to take it away.

'I don't give charity.' The heavens gave no charity. So why should she?

She'd been going to keep him as a pet, a darling treasure. He could talk to her, to keep her company. It was lonely, having no voice speaking in her house but Job the

181

parrot since her son stopped speaking. Your voice gets so, you forget how to use it.

So she clung to his body as he left and she begged, the first and only time she'd begged in her life, but the begging did no good. He'd gone for ever, her lovely fugitive.

Noel's mother was right in intuiting that when she'd named the parrot, the despot had had in mind her own sufferings, though when she'd named the parrot, back around the middle of World War I, her sufferings were just beginning. She still had her husband, though he was a sick young man, dying of TB despite being a bank teller, dying through the night, unfit even for war. Noisy through the night too was her son, sickly too, waking screaming in the night as decades later her grandson was to do, her grandson who even as a just-born infant was so like her son that she'd insisted he be called after him, without telling his mother why. Rita, she was always so obedient (the despot despised her) and any questioning in Rita's soul had been taken away utterly by the sudden death of Noel's father who was a pedestrian run over by a hit-and-run car just before Noel was born.

Sudden death. Sudden deaths and lingering deaths: there were many in this story. Her own death lingering now, refusing to take her as it had refused before, one day upon the roof. When no thunderbolt came crashing down, and she was left there to battle with a heavy tarp and an unwanted life.

All she wanted now from life was to make some sort of change. If I write it differently, it happened differently. Ever since that dawn last Thursday (it's Monday now), ever since she heard the battle creeping down the stairs, she's been writing letters to make it change.

'Noh!' she'd yelled that dawn. But no one came. No one to tell.

But maybe, she thinks, tell Lizzie. This Lizzie who comes each day with my dinner. Write now, explain to Lizzie; but Lizzie, she hasn't come since that gun-dawn. She's run off with my nice fugitive. They all run and skip and go.

The parrot though (she returned full circle), the parrot had been given to her by her bank teller. 'He'll be a comfort to you,' he'd said, 'when I'm gone.' A comfort: a parrot: a stupid green and red thing with a vicious pecking beak! She'd thought of Job's Comforters, those vile men whose visits to Job only seemed to mock his woes, and so that was what she'd called the thing: Job's Comforter. But it shortened very quickly just to Job.

Yes, she was Job early on, an innocent victim, tormented till she threw defiance at the clouds: she'd go it on her own. Expecting nothing, giving nothing, except of course for the jealous love that she gave to her son, who threw it in her face.

Her son, no son of hers, she'd rather see him dead.

And so betrayed.

(*Traitor traitor*
We all hate her...)

The first betrayal: because I'd rather see him dead, than let her have him. So allowed police to enter the house where she thought he was, and indeed where he was though no one else knew he was there, allowed police with guns

183

in their hands, suspecting violence, even death, to be done, hoping death for her son, allowed them in there through her balcony, through her back room and over the scullery roofs because she hoped for her son's death.

The second betrayal: because he left her, her nice fugitive. And so she swore upon the Bible that she'd act as go-between, between him and his girl, finding it easy to swear on something she didn't believe in. For why should she act as go-between when he didn't have the common decency to stay for ever and be her treasure? When his girl came, she'd say she'd received no letters.

And so, when the first letter had come, on Tuesday 23 June, she'd put it in the piano stool, unopened.

When the second letter came, on Thursday, she'd repeated her action. Though relenting slightly towards the boy. Some ancient sentimental place inside the despot had warmed, and it had come to her that perhaps she might help the two. Until the night of that day's tomorrow came...

The third betrayal: this third time, she was sane again, or more sane anyway. At least not dizzy with hunger any more, and the beating torment of the children's footsteps was less loud within her head. Until the knocking that Friday night upon her door, which she opened: to find Elizabeth Cruise.

'I've come to ask,' Lizzie said, 'about Nobby. I thought perhaps you might send him a letter for me. Or that perhaps he might've written to me here.'

'Scratch out her eyes!' Job squawked.

'No,' the despot said, only then coming to her full senses and realizing who her nice fugitive had been, 'he hasn't written. But come into my parlour,' said the spider to the fly.

It was that night that the despot wrote to Nobby, making that night the first act in the treachery that went on and on through the years of five decades.

2

Traitor traitor
We all hate her
Put her in a pot
With choko and pertater
Boil her up with onion
Till she cries
Then get Pa's knife
And cut out her eyes.

Traitor traitor
We all hate her
Put her in a pot
With choko and pertater
Boil her up with pepper
Till she's nearly dead
Then chop her into pieces
And give the dogs her head.

Traitor traitor
We all hate her
Put her in a pot
With choko and pertater

When the dogs are done
Then ring the bell
Then put her down the dunny
And she'll go to hell.

3

Through the years of five decades, a boy was wandering on the track. Treading his boots in a rough circle through the back-blocks of New South Wales: Wilcannia up to Tibooburra across to Brewarrina, down the Barwon to the Darling there at Bourke, then follow the vein down through Louth and Tilpa to Wilcannia, and start the circle again. He walked on the red soil and on the black soil, through the mallee, through the scrub, along the river, increasing his swag from one blanket to three blankets and a tarp, replacing a blanket every so often when one gave out, bumming a fresh pair of boots at a station now and then, but otherwise making little change. He wouldn't carry a gun.

'You're mad you know,' men often said. With a gun he could've shot things: tucker.

He preferred to pull yellowbellies from the Darling, black bream sometimes too, in decreasing numbers though as the decades passed and the European carp ate the native fish. He preferred to set snares for possums, baiting them with a line of flour up a tree. He preferred to sneak up behind a porkypine or a goanna and knock him on the head, or run full-pelt in the early decades when he was younger and grab a squealing pig from under a burr bush.

186

He could come at a knife, for it was after all a matter of survival, and he could creep into a mob of someone's sheep and grab a lamb and slit his throat and carry him off like the cove in *Waltzing Matilda*.

Like the cove in *Waltzing Matilda* too he lived always with a nagging dread of the troopers, one two three.

'You're mad you bastard,' other men said, for with a gun he could've eaten emu and kangaroo.

They were right, he was mad.

Wandering for miles and decades, living first under false names, then no name.

In the first decade, no one noticed much, for there were thousands like him on the track: men who began as boys then grew into men as they followed a myth of work from town to town, from station to station, humping a swag of blankets and a sugar-bag of tucker, adapting in this way or that to mallee or soil or river or scrub but still in their minds tied to George Street or Martin Place and walking on a Saturday night arm in arm with their girls down a city street of shops and light, and then just a short tram-ride home.

In the second decade, though, men went to war. Overseas in uniforms they ran, to hold guns and shoot them. He thought about it, but only for a second or two one day in '41 or so, lying in his swag next to a straggly goyamutta tree; but because of holding guns and shooting them, he discarded the thought quick smart.

'You're mad you mad bastard,' said men. 'It's clothes and tucker and a job.'

By the third decade they were back from war, living in the city most of them, with lights and Saturday nights and perhaps wives, but the wives were not the girls they'd left in '31, for those were already married to other blokes. His was, he knew.

For every five years or so he'd amble into Wilcannia post office and find a letter waiting for him under the false name they'd agreed upon, and he'd learn news.

> Dear Son,
>
> I never know if you Receive my Letters, for you never Reply, but I continue to write as it is my Loving Duty.
>
> Life is the same here, very quiet, but would be Happier if you Returned. There is nothing to fear, all that is 'Long Forgotten' and the Police have other worries.
>
> I should add that your Friend Elizabeth has 'Long Forgotten' you too. I of course have not seen her for Many Years for, as I told you before, she left Home shortly after you left and she ran away to New Zealand with a man whom she married by Special Licence. I however sometimes hear News of her 'On the Grapevine' and learn she now has a number of children and is very Happy. Her Husband has done very Well for himself in Business and also served as a Lieutenant and was Decorated on the Field for Bravery, so you see 'All's Well that Ends Well.'
>
> My Wish is that you Return as it is your Duty as a Son and would give Happiness to
>
> Your Loving Mother

There was once a reference to her own new Husband, and to his Death in the War, but the letters were otherwise the same: only changing as the number of Lizzie's Children grew or the Success of her Husband increased, way off there overseas.

At night-time, most nights, questions would bite like mosquitoes. 'If we'd 've tried it, if we'd 've had a chance, would we 've made a go of it?' Questions circling around like the buzzing of a mozzy that you try to ward off before it lands. He'd light some dung to make a smoke to make the mozzies go away. He'd make up answers, lying there, *'We were always chalk and cheese. She'd 've never loved me anyway. I'm happiest alone.'* Making a smoke of answers curl around his swag so the questions might stop biting in.

They never did, but some time in the third decade at least the letters stopped. For his mother had accepted that his not writing meant his death, and had ceased to write herself.

In the fourth decade and the fifth decade he'd still front up to stations like a bagman of the thirties, ask to chop a bit of wood or do a bit of weeding in exchange for tea and tobacco and flour to last him till the next place. By the fourth decade and the fifth decade there were few of his kind left. And so he achieved notoriety of a kind in the backblocks of New South Wales, that tall skinny whitefeller who walked alone with a swag, living off bush tucker like a blackfeller, the weak cove who wouldn't touch a gun.

When darkness came he lay and thought of time. Counting off the nights since *that* night, that dawn, counting as the nights became years, then decades, then miles, then dawn, but dawn simply treading on to more nights. One night, early on, lying in the first decade in his swag beside the Darling, a fire smoking near him to ward off the night, there'd been no one there beside him, and then someone, a young *thinagulla* from a band of wandering men. He was scarred, and smelled of emu, and they exchanged some things. This one gave a tobacco tin with bullets in it; the other gave some clouds up in the sky. They were about the same age.

'Them ones, there,' said the young *thinagulla*, taking the other's hand and pointing it up at a little puff at an angle to a bigger one, 'I call them ones the mechanical clouds.' Showing the other how to tell the time at night by the circle of the little one round the big feller.

After that he'd lie there at night and watch the circle that circled like his tread upon the track. Wishing to high heaven that his arms were longer so he could reach them into high heaven and stop the circle, or move it backwards, as if it was just the clock upon his mother's kitchen wall...

And so the decades passed, and stations changed hands; and by the end of the fifth decade there was no one around who could even remember the false name he'd used at first. When people questioned him, he'd smile, then slide through the web of their curiosity as easily as his thin body slipping through the hidey-hole, many years before.

At the beginning of the sixth decade, in March 1981, he collapsed one midday in the heat on the fine hot red soil of the common at North Bourke, collapsed on the track that leads past the Bourke rifle range and down to the North Bourke pub and shop, and he was found there by an Aboriginal girl who then ran full-pelt to the phone at the shop.

An ambulance came, and then the air ambulance flew him to Sydney, all without his knowledge. He came to his senses weeks later in a white bed in Royal Prince Alfred Hospital with a tag on his arm saying: Nobby Weston.

4

On the Wednesday after the Friday when she'd first gone to see Nobby's mother, Lizzie went to Long Bay gaol to talk to her brother Mick.

'Hello.'

'G'day.'

You feel false, talking through gaol bars. Even to your own brother. Even to your only brother, Mick.

My brother, Mick. So strong, so big, so much bigger than Nobby and me. It was real good, moving in to Liberty Street, having Nobby's weight to hurl in with me in a fight against Mick. Any fight against Mick. Mick has green eyes and wild hair like mine. The identical mirror to me except he's always been a boy, and bigger and older. Pa always let him do things that he wouldn't let me do, and Ma is always telling me to plait my hair, do something with it girl, while Mick runs around with his shirt out round his bum and Ma just makes cups of tea for him and puts iodine on his cuts.

But Mick: he'd lie in wait for us up there where Crockford Lane runs into Mercy Street. Hide high up with Johnnie and Cec Kennet on top of Kennets' chook-shed, pelting poppleberries as we ran past. Nobby and I dared him down one day and took him on, and he gave Nobby a black eye. Any time, though, anyone else picked a scrap with me and Nobby, Mick would lay in fast to back us up.

'Skinny Lizzie,' they'd say about me.

'Weakie Weston,' they'd say about Nobby. 'Sobby Nobby, mummy's boy.'

'Hey that's my sister!' Mick would say.

'That's my brother!' Mick would back Nobby up.

Anyone who spoke a word against Nobby or me, Mick would get them.

Mick has green eyes like mine and I stare into them and see myself there. It's scary, recognizing yourself in someone else's eyes. He's me, except he's game and I'm not.

I look at Mick through the grill of the gaol bars. I feel real shy, and proud of him because he's in gaol, and angry because it's not me there, and I wish I was Alexandra Kollontai.

'Hello, Mick,' I say. 'How is it? Do you need anything?' There's nothing I can give.

But Mick's just happy to see me.

I look at Mick through the gaol bars. That night in the cupboard, too scared hearing the crashing to step out and look, when it came to the barricades I was not Alexandra Kollontai, I stopped in there standing up on the copper wishing for help, till Nobby found me.

I tell Mick I was scared that night.

'That makes two of us.'

He whispers now, 'What do you know about the gun?'

'Nothing.'

'What do you know about Nobby?'

'Nothing.'

Nobby. Nothing. I know the loneliness now without you.

Mick's face is my face, we stare like mirrors through iron bars with police listening and watching and there's no way we can tell lies to each other.

'If you should happen to run into him, like,' Mick says (real careful, there's warders around), 'tell him hooray from me.'

'I was a coward,' Lizzie says, her mind on something else. 'Mick, I love him,' Lizzie says. She's tight, her white hands gripping the bars towards Mick's hands as she spurts out something that is very embarrassing.

'Yeah, well tell him, Sis,' says Mick, embarrassed.

'It's too late,' says Lizzie.

5

It was the gun dream he was dreaming. Collapsing after five decades in the sun of the track, the red sand beneath his eyes like powdered blood, not far away there were suddenly bullet-bangs, and he was scared and seventeen.

Distant voices then too outside the criss-cross shadow of a bunda-bush, gun bangs, the scream of a girl, her shoes flashing past, then more legs, legs in white walking around him saying words he couldn't make out, and still the bangs that he couldn't know were simply the Bourke rifle club having its monthly target day, and then it was dark for weeks and he was seventeen. Caught inside a frozen block of movement till he came to in late

April and read his name upon his arm.

Years of fear made him jump then, expect the troopers at his bedside, one two three. He never gave his name to no one, but there was only the nice nurse.

'Feeling better, Mr Weston?'

'How'd you get my name, girl?' asked the pale thin man with sunspots on his cheeks.

'You kept saying it in your sleep.'

No troopers came, and the nurse said he was in Sydney, in Prince Alfred no less, a hop and a jump from his old stamping ground.

There were a couple of days then, and talks with the social worker, who arranged for him new shoes and a pension, for he said he was going home.

One day then in late April he walked out in the clothes and hat they'd found him in, but in new social-worker shoes, for they'd taken his boots away; a coathanger-thin man who caught a bus down King Street, got out at Newtown Bridge, stared at Uncle George's souvlaki stall, then walked slowly like a sick man or a man in a documentary, looking at the sights as he automatically followed the back route to Liberty Street.

There he made his camp.

Seeing as he came into the street a house with a Room To Let sign with a distant view of 201, he went to the door and rented the room and then began to spend his days deciding.

Deciding what, he wasn't sure.

Sitting in the winter sun on the gas-meter box watching Noel come and go, observing Evie, letting the days walk past as he'd walked past the years, walking backwards now through time till he felt the pain of seventeen.

One day, when Noel was out, this man saw the despot step onto the balcony and look down into the street. He felt sympathy.

Mother Mother, Lizzie Girl, don't snap me like a dried-out stick.

To hasten the past, he purchased a parrot. Gave it lettuce and taught it the rhymes of decades ago while he made up his mind.

To what, he didn't know.

In the daytime, watching the boy that could be him running down the street in his old black coat, with the winter air making bright warm spots on his pale cheeks, watching Evie, he planned to go away.

In the night-time, dreaming nightmares, he'd wake a coward, but his gut full of hate.

It was easier, out there on red soil, to ward off the question of Lizzie, a happy housewife with someone else as her husband.

6

That Sunday night, Evie did something strange. She stole the silver serviette ring. After it went flying off her thumb and rolling across the lino she politely picked it up, and thought she put it on the table, but when shortly afterwards she went home to her room and got undressed to go to bed, she found she'd put it in her cardigan pocket.

N...She traced the engraving with her fingernail, the flamboyant arching scroll.

Spin the ring and start again.

N

I love 4 ever, Noel Noel.

But that was wrong.

'It's Noel. Your boyfriend. Remember?'

'Lover Boy.'

The quick eyes of Ted. The smart voice of Roseanne. Evie shuddered.

Then through the quiet of a Sunday night the feeling told her again. I love for ever Nobby Weston.

Evie opened the cupboard then and had a good look at what she hadn't been able to look at since the dawn of the gun. Since that dawn, there'd been no scrabbling. Since that dawn, the girl had gone. Not far, but just not here, her wild fear no longer running through the blood of Evie, though there was worse now, now she was gone.

Evie opened the cupboard that was empty now, she'd cleaned out all the junk, and Evie studied the heart. They were old, the scratches of the heart, aged by air into the paint. But the eight in the *1981* didn't quite match. The right-hand bumps of the eight were old, but the left-hand ones were new. Evie looked, and worked it out. That was how you'd draw an eight if you'd done a three first, and wanted to change it.

Through the quiet of a Sunday night, Evie sat quiet, spinning the ring.

Through the quiet of a Sunday night Sammy screamed. A wail of terror, like police through the night.

Evie ran into the house and up and turned the light on. 'I'll stay with her,' she whispered as Mum poked her head in, sleepy-eyed. Then Evie held Sammy, held tight to the sobbing body that bucked inside her arms as the sobs wouldn't stop. Evie felt the tears plopping down onto her arms, wiped the tears from Sammy's face, but more came fast as rain.

'What's up, baby-girl? Did you have a nightmare?'

Sammy shook her head from side to side, and the tears came more.

'Are you frightened of something?'

Sammy nodded. Hiccoughed, and the sobbing dropped a bit. 'Where do you go to,' Sammy sobbed, 'when you die?'

Evie didn't know. It had never occurred to her. She held the four-year-old body in her arms and looked out the window and thought: I wonder if I wondered about that when I was four. There was darkness out there, no moon, no stars; shadow swallowed the roofs and deepened down into darker blackness.

'I don't know,' Evie said. 'What makes you think of that all of a sudden?'

But Sammy just bucked against her breast, the fearful sobbing jerking out. 'Where will I go to,' Sammy sobbed, 'when I'm a dead lady?'

So Evie told her something, not believing her own words, but just to give Sammy something to stop this. A blue place, a huge blue and white place like the sea, Evie described, where dead people fly free, like silver flames in the wind.

'Is that where she went to,' Sammy asked, 'the lady?'

'What lady?'

'The one you were telling me about.'

In the end the tears ended and Sammy slept. Evie lay there under Sammy's quilt, feeling the need for Sammy's warmth to stop her aloneness.

Through the quiet of a Monday dawn Evie heard the bell next door: ring ring. The ring-hand summoning her. Evie woke.

TELL

Evie remembered. But the despot's writing never told her what to tell.

In the darkness, she pulled out the serviette ring.

N

N for Noel.

N for no one.

N for Nobby.

The bell rang again. The ring-hand, Evie remembered. The weight of those six rings upon the finger, but six rings, not three, and two of them were gold. *'The despot's a widow, tell me something I don't know.'* I'll tell you something, Noel. Something so obvious you've always missed it. The despot was married twice. And Nobby was the son of the first time. Your mother, the daughter of the second. Evie didn't know how she knew, but she did. She knew another thing though: that she wouldn't tell Noel. Why tell him that the gunman was his uncle, when the whole thing already made him sick?

TELL, said the despot. But tell whom, tell what?

Tell Nobby, Lizzie told Evie, I love 4 ever.

BOOK FIVE
Confusion

I went to the door
And I asked for some bread,
But the lady said, 'Bum Bum—
The baker is dead.'
Hallelujah I'm a bum.
Hallelujah bum again.
Hallelujah give us a handout
To revive us again.

ANON,
TRADITIONAL SONG, EARLY 1900S.

1

Karl Marx says that history repeats itself: occurring the first time as tragedy, the second as farce. As a general theory, it's probably wrong, but as far as the Liberty Street battle went, it would've seemed right, to an outside observer. For what happened in the CYSS centre's re-enactment of that battle seemed like full-blown farce, except to a few, who sunk back into the tragedy of the first time. It was Evie, or maybe fate, who'd appointed when it would happen.

On Tuesday night, sitting at tea, Evie's mum had said: 'It's the 26th this Friday, darl. Your birthday. Why don't we go up the club at Campbelltown and make a night of it, see all our old friends, have a real celebration for once. God knows, it's been long enough.'

'You know I'm trying to save money,' Ted said, looking gloomily at a glass of lemon cordial.

'But it's my shout,' said Evie's mum.

'I'll look after the kids,' Evie offered fast, seeing the opportunity. She was serving up the steak and kidney pie and cut Ted the middle bit, with the pastry rose, and scooped him out his mashed potato and pumpkin with the icecream scoop, to make it look nice.

'I'd still rather we saved the money,' Ted said.

'But I *want* to shout you, darl.' Evie's mum touched his hand and she smiled at him.

'It's not fair,' said Maria. 'Why can't we come?'

'Yeah, let's just take the girls out for a barbecue on Saturday instead,' said Ted.

'Yeah!'

'No!' said Evie. 'It's your night, Ted.' She looked hard at Maria and bumped Jodie as she handed them their dinners. 'I'll take the girls somewhere on Saturday, to make up.'

Maria gave her a weird look. Sniffing a secret. But knew enough to shut up.

'Where?' Jodie demanded. 'Can we have pizzas?'

'Will there be swings?' Sammy said.

'There'll be everything,' said Evie.

'See, darl?' Mum said. 'It's all settled.' She looked really young and happy, Evie thought, when she smiled like that. Ted still looked as if he didn't want to go, but he made himself smile back at Mum, and then Evie's mum looked even happier.

Over the washing up, Mum thanked Evie for being so thoughtful to Ted, and Evie felt a rat inside, Might as well go the whole way, though.

'Mum,' Evie said, 'why don't you take Noel's poor little mum next door with you? She's real nice, Noel's mum, and she never gets to go out, she's probably never been to a club in her life, and Noel and I can fix tea for Noel's grandmother.'

'I thought you didn't like her, love.'

'Noel's mum? She's really nice,' said Evie, deliberately misunderstanding.

'No, I meant the old lady, love.'

'Oh? I guess you get used to her.' That was one way of putting it.

Evie's mum looked pleased. 'You're growing up at last, love,' she observed.

Evie felt dreadful. Mum was so nice, she never suspected anything, so it made you feel bad to cheat her.

But it was settled. Ted seemed to think it was a good idea to ask Mrs Cavendish – 'Might as well shout her too,' he said. 'I don't 'spect she'll drink much, and who knows, seeing as how it's m' birthday I might win the cost of the night back on the pokies' – and Noel's mum was hard pushed by Noel till she finally agreed.

'Yes, Mum. No, Mum. Of course Evie and I can fix nanna. You should go, Mum. Nanna's used to Evie. She *likes* Evie. No, don't ask Nanna, don't even tell her, just go. Of course I know the doctor's number.'

So at half-past six on the Friday night Evie and Noel waved the three of them into the Kingswood, Ted in his suit still worried because of the money, Evie's mum looking great with a henna rinse in her hair, and Noel's mum in grey silk, as excited as a child off to its first party. At the last minute, Ted turned to Evie. 'Thanks, Evie,' he said, a bit awkward.

'No, you sit in the front,' Evie's mum told Noel's mum, and at last they drove off, Ted hooting the horn and grinning and the two mums waving like mad.

'*Now* tell us,' Maria demanded. Something secret was happening. She could smell it.

'Nothing,' Evie said, feeling bad about Ted. 'Noel and I are just having some friends around, that's all, and I don't want you lot in the way.'

'Oh, let them,' Noel said. He felt jittery. I must've caught it from old Mum.

'Yeah, okay.' (How could you stop them, anyway?) 'But just don't go blabbing off to Ted and Mum, okay? You either, Little Miss.' She grabbed Sammy up and hugged her.

'What makes you think we'll be around anyway; Smartey-pants?' Ree said.

Will there be swings?' Sammy asked Evie.

A feeling of dread suddenly hit Evie. 'I told you, there'll be everything.'

2

Evie wasn't far wrong.

At half-past six, Newtown CYSS was fuller than it had ever been, for the word had got around that Roger was making a video. So now there were fifty cops dressed in blue jeans and blue jumpers, and eighteen pickets dressed in long white underpants or old trousers, and a hundred or more others dressed in raggedy gear, to be the crowd. There were two video portapaks loaded with fresh batteries, and there were two buses borrowed from other CYSS places ready to take everyone to Liberty Street.

The plan was: Roger and Di and Sharnda would go with the equipment and the pickets in the Newtown CYSS truck and set everything up, and after a while the 'police bus' would roar up and the cops would jump out and it would start. A couple of minutes later, the second bus would let the rest out at the Liberty Street corner, and they'd all run up and start booing and cheering and acting like an unruly mob.

At six-thirty, then, everyone was organized. Or as organized as an unruly mob will ever be. Roger and Di hadn't got there yet, they were due any minute.

The phone rang.

'This is Noel.'

'Hi, this is Sharnda.'

'I know.'

His voice sounded a bit odd. Distant and high and wavery. 'Is something wrong?' Sharnda asked.

'No...'

'What's up, then?'

'Nothing...'

'Then why are you ringing?'

'Oh, just to say, it's all okay.'

'We'll be over in ten minutes,' Sharnda said, but Noel had already clicked off. There was something odd in his voice, as if he was miles away.

3

In a room down Liberty Street a man who was miles away sat gazing down at his shoes. They looked strange, he thought; like someone else's feet were stuck to the ends of his legs. For years there'd been boots down there, boots to tread the miles in, boots that were always old to start with for they'd be given to him in exchange for a bit of weeding, a couple of days fencing, boots that had been someone else's until the someone else had no use for them, and gave them to that chap without a name. These black shoes, though, were new. Came from the social-worker girl, up the hospital, shiny black city shoes with cardboard soles. They looked more like they belonged to someone else than all those boots over the years that really had been someone else's.

In a room in Liberty Street the man stared down at them. Sitting inside four walls like his mate there in his cage. This was the first time he'd had the shoes on since the day he left hospital. Since the day he'd left the hospital, he hadn't left his camp.

'I've been a bit crook,' he'd said to Mrs Maria, when he arrived.

'Crook?' She mouthed the strange word on her Greek tongue.

'Sick,' said the man. 'Real no good.'

'Ah,' she'd said and crossed herself, then smiled. 'Is no good to be no good, eh?' They both grinned at her joke. After which, she'd done his shopping for him, buying him the sausages and spuds and eggs that he cooked up neat like a bushman in the cooking corner of his room.

So since that day he hadn't been out. Except (he remembered now) for that day early on when he'd brought his mate here in his cage.

'Scab, scab,' his mate said now.

'Not *me*, mate,' said the man.

'Traitor, traitor,' his mate accused him now.

'Not *me*, mate,' said the man.

'Though maybe you're right, at that,' the man said at last.

Staring down at the floor at night, a man who was stuck in the past.

4

Staring out at the ceiling at night, the despot lay in her room. With the blind half up, the blackness hit her, so she tried to pull the blind down but, like that first night, yanked too hard, and it flew right up to the top.

'*Noh!*' she called.

But no one came.

So she reached over to her magic pad and started to write to no one.

Writing her interminable letters to no one, no one could read them, so as soon as they were written, she made them disappear.

In her own room, Evie was nervous. She wished she'd never said Yes, she wished she'd never met Sharnda. Why did I have to go big-noting myself and say everyone could come round here? They'd make a real mess, turn the house upside-down, and even if she and Noel managed to get it all cleaned up before Ted and Mum got home, Sammy or Jodie would go and tell them. You could trust Ree to keep her mouth shut, Ree liked secrets for their own sake, but Sammy and Jodie couldn't help themselves, they were like the dobber's encyclopedia.

It wasn't that, though.

It wasn't really the fear of Ted that made her nervous. Ted can say what he likes. I hate him anyway. Though these last few days, since Tuesday, he'd been being nice to her.

Evie's hand felt its way to her pocket and found the serviette ring. It had been a comfort to her, this week. Something to hold to, a smooth bright silver shape to hold to in the dark. She'd been meaning to give it back every time she saw Noel, but had always forgotten, somehow. Her finger traced the scroll of the *N*.

In her room, Evie sat shivering. She'd just put on another jumper, but she still felt cold. It wasn't Ted, and Mum, and the mess that she feared, but some greater mess, she didn't know, she had a feeling. There are some things you shouldn't play with.

That feeling all this week, of being somewhere else, alone, waking in the night with a faint smell still in her mind of crusting salt, of salty breeze, of something damp that smelled like bag or rope. One morning, just before dawn, it was the hardness of the bed that woke her, a feeling of grit on her skin. Getting up, turning the light on, she saw that all the blankets had come off, no wonder she was cold; but it was more than that, for all over the bottom sheet was a fine layer of sand, not clean sand but dull gritty stuff, more a fine soil than sand. Sammy must've been in the sandpit up the play centre and brought it home in her pockets, and then mucked about on Evie's bed.

Evie felt the curl of the *N*. Tell him, the feeling told her.

But how tell, whom to tell? All week, the weight of that demand had been pressing on her. But how can I tell him when I don't know where he is? He'd disappeared, the mystery gunman, that was why he was a mystery, and if the police couldn't find him, way back then when the trail was fresh, how was she to do it after fifty years? He's probably dead by now anyway, Evie told herself to avoid even starting to search for him. For searching would start by asking his mother, and even the thought of exposing herself again to the despot's hatred filled Evie with dread. All this week, it'd grown worse and worse, the feeling of the despot thinking of her. The bell that rang to summon her, that she ignored.

But tell him, the feeling told her. And so sometimes Evie did imagine the finding, and telling him, and his joy, and then...and then...

5

The phone rang. Sharnda answered. It was Di. She was at the meeting of the CYSS funding committee that was going to decide whether or not to close down the Newtown centre.

'Hi, it's me. Look, you're going to kill me, but I can't make it. The meeting's still going, looks like going on all night. No, it seems dreadful. They're set on closing us down. I've got to stay, to keep arguing our case. Yeah, good luck to you too.'

6

Lying under the bed, Noel had the gun. They'd be here soon. Playing games. There were some things you shouldn't play with.

209

He thought of ringing Sharnda again, really saying this time that it was off. Tossed the thought around, and dropped it. He couldn't, they'd think him weak.

Yesterday he'd gone round there, to CYSS with Evie, and met some of them. Sharnda was okay, and a girl called Di, but Roger was a werewolf. This warm voice, like a werewolf, that made Evie go quiet and listen. There were blokes in the kitchen, eating spinach pie; Noel knew some of them.

'Well look who it isn't,' laughed Matt Dunkley. He was bigger than ever these days; played C grade for Newtown; was reckoned to be real good with girls.

'Hey, Sookabubba!' Tasso yelled, just as he used to when Noel was a kid and the despot sent him to Tasso's father's deli. 'Have some spinach pie. Make you big and strong, like Mister Popeye!' He laughed, as if that was funny.

'Help you see the girls in the dark,' leered Billy Greenhouse, Matt's other off-sider.

'That's no use to Noel,' Matt said heavily. Then he put on a high voice. 'Is it, Noley-Poley?'

Bang. I could shoot them.

'I dunno,' said Billy. 'He came in with a girl.'

'What's she like?'

'Not bad. Pretty good. She'd do me.'

'Probly his auntie.' Matt laughed, and bits of wafery pastry flew out of his wide open mouth. 'Little poof.'

'Little worm,' said Tasso.

'You better watch yourselves. One day the worm'll turn.'

What an idle threat. Noel walked out.

'You can be one of the eighteen pickets, Noel,' Sharnda offered.

'No thanks,' said Noel. Evie was off in a corner, with Roger. She was going to hold the sound-thing for him.

'I thought you'd want to,' said Sharnda. 'Well, what are you going to be?'

'Something,' Noel said. 'Nothing.' Then the words blurted out of their own accord. 'The Mystery Gunman.'

'But he wasn't there,' Sharnda objected.

'Well then, I won't *be* there, will I?'

Evie looked up sharply from the camera. 'Don't be stupid, Noel.' Noel's just trying to get attention, she thought. Of course he'll be there, he's got to be. The thought of doing it without Noel made her feel desperate somehow.

'*Me* stupid!' Noel said, looking at Roger, his stupid suntan.

Then Noel left, left Evie to it.

No Mystery Gunman. They'll see.

Lying under the bed, the Mystery Gunman had the gun now. He'd grown fond of it this last week. At first, it'd made him sick, reminding him of those green eyes gazing desperate into his as *quick*, he ran. With time, though, it'd grown a comfort. He'd lie there, thinking of the safety catch, imagining pulling it back, pulling the trigger, a bullet whistling out, knowing this all for make-believe, for it wouldn't be loaded, but still all the same never doing it. Sometimes even truly putting the barrel against his head, lining up, A to B, against his head. People think I'm a creep. If I did this, they'd believe me. Playing games, knowing himself as

211

gutless (freezing that night when I had the opportunity) he still got a comfort from the warm feel of brown wood, the long barrel of cold silver. It was something real, to ward off the night.

Not ward off this night, though, for nothing could do that. Except something simple like a phone call, that he couldn't do. Evie would think him weak.

7

Maria liked secrets for their own sake. Was preparing one now, with Jodie.

'We'll do it tonight,' she whispered.

'What?' Sammy demanded.

'It's a secret.'

Morning secrets and afternoon secrets and dark night secrets.

Maria knew that anything you did was vastly improved by being a secret. On dark nights sometimes she'd creep down to the kitchen and drink a glass of milk by moonlight. It made the milk taste better. One night when she'd done that – it was the night Roseanne had come around, only it was later, hours after Roseanne had gone home – Maria had seen a burglar. She'd been standing there in the half-darkness. The only light was that thrown by the open fridge door, for there was no moon that night, and she'd seen the burglar half-running, half-crawling down the stairs – really fast, but quiet as a bicycle. Then he wasn't there. Maria hadn't been scared, for how could you be scared of someone who looked so scared? And how could

212

you be scared of someone who looked like a sort of young-faced Mr Man?

Mr Man was part of the afternoon secret. Sammy called him that, the old man who lived at Mrs Maria's and sometimes sang songs from the olden days while Mrs Maria fed them cake. When Maria had asked him his name, he'd just smiled at her.

'Ask no questions and you'll be told no lies.'

But Maria had found his pension card and knew his real name. She wrote it on the fridge when he disappeared.

Tonight's secret, though, wasn't part of that secret. It was a witch secret. Ever since Mrs Maria had turned out to be nice, Maria had been looking for a witch to replace her.

'I'll tell on you,' said Sammy.

'Who'll you tell? Mum's not here.'

'I'll tell Mr Man. And Noel. And Evie.'

'We'd better let her come,' Jodie said.

Maria saw her point.

'What're we gonna do, but, when we get there?' Jodie whispered.

'You'll see.' Ree was mysterious. Secretly, she hadn't the faintest idea. But she'd think of something.

8

In her room, the despot was hungry. Hadn't eaten breakfast this morning, she never seemed to feel like eating in the mornings these days, but had looked forward to her lunch, which never came. Noel had asked Evie to get it, he wanted to go up the music shop, and Evie had said yes, though she hadn't done despot-duty since the dawn of the gun. Evie had said yes, and then the thought of that rotten face, she couldn't face it, so had left a note on Noel's door which the wind had blown away.

The despot was hungry, waiting for her supper that never came because Noel had quite forgotten. I must tell my son, she thought, calling; '*Noh!*'

But Noel lay elsewhere, hearing nothing but the memory of Matt's laughter. It'd been going on for years, for years too long.

9

The phone rang. Sharnda answered. It was Roger. Time was flying fast. All around was the fidgetiness of a crowd. Matt and Tasso and Billy and a couple of their mates were drinking beer. They were dressed in blue, policemen; in their belts, old cowboy guns from their childhood; in their words, old bullying cries from their childhood.

'We'll get Noel, eh Matt, Matt?' Tasso urged. 'Knock him down, like we used to.' He was excited, the beer going to his head.

'*You* can,' Matt said. 'I might get that girl of his. Knock *her* down.' They all laughed with him.

'Who is he, this Noel?' asked a bloke who was new to the gang. 'What's wrong with him?'

'He's just mad,' Matt explained.

Sharnda, overhearing, was jolted into a vague memory of some experiment she'd read about when she'd done Psychology. They'd got ordinary people, these Psych experimenters, and told some of them they were prisoners, and told some that they were gaolers, and within a short time the gaolers were bashing the prisoners, and the prisoners obeying.

What have I started? Sharnda worried.

10

Bang, thought Noel.

Bang, Evie hammered.

Out on the trampoline Maria and Jodie and Sammy chanted and jumped, killing time till Evie and Noel's friends came and they could go and do their secret.

> *Over the rope*
> *And under again*
> *She lives in that house*
> *And she gives me a pain...*

In her room the despot heard them. Cruel it was then.

Bang, Evie hammered. A sign up over the door. There was anger in her, though not for Ted this time, not even for the despot really, perhaps for herself. This feeling that she'd had something, and let it go, only herself to blame. She wondered where Noel was. He couldn't really have meant it, that he wouldn't come. Evie wished she could leave all this, run off through the lanes with Noel to the peace of the secret landscape. Evie slammed nails in, unused to a hammer. Ted always did any hammering around the place, one thing you could say for Ted was that he was good about fixing things. Of course, he should be, he worked for a builder. Evie slammed nails in: if this night had to happen, they might as well try to make it look proper.

> *Traitor, traitor, we all hate her,*
> *Put her in a pot with choko and pertater...*

Evie found herself chanting the words of some stupid song that Maria had come home with recently.

In his room down the street the man surveyed his feet. Had no idea why he'd gone and put his shoes on tonight, the first time in a couple of months, slippers had done him till now. It was hardly as if he was going somewhere: where was there for him to go?

Stuck inside four walls like his mate there. Thinking of that, pity took him and he pulled back the curtains, opened his window, opened the cage, and let his mate out free into winter night.

11

It was on.

The Newtown CYSS truck came, Sharnda driving, and the pickets jumped out with lights on stands and two rolls of barbed wire and lots of bags stuffed with paper to look like sandbags, and lumps of coolite hacked into the size of bricks and rocks.

'The Eureka Stockade,' Sharnda read Evie's sign. She'd forgotten that. 'Good one, Evie.'

Evie suddenly remembered that old man down the street that first morning. 'The house that was Eureka,' she murmured.

A couple of pickets started unrolling the barbed wire all over the front fence and yard. The rest raced inside and piled sandbags up at the doors and windows. The bags looked funny, in mum's loungeroom, with the white-tiled coffee table that Ted had made, with the modern vinyl armchairs. Evie had moved the vases and things, but on the mantelpiece still were the wedding photo of Mum and Ted, the baby photos of the girls, and the family photo they'd had taken last Christmas.

'*They* shouldn't be there.' Evie went to move them.

'Leave it. We'll have the light out, just set up one of these lights down here, no one will see them.'

'But it wasn't *us* that was the tenants.' But Evie left them.

'Um, Evie…' Deep down Sharnda was nervous herself. 'Here, we've got two portapaks, but you'll have to do inside the house, and I'll do outside, get Noel or someone to hold the mike for you. Roger can't get here, his wife's suddenly been taken to hospital, the baby's coming two weeks early.'

'Wife?' said Evie 'Baby?'

Sharnda looked at Evie. I'd forgotten she's in love with him. Oh well, better she knows. 'Didn't you know?'

Evie said nothing. Evie felt nothing. She paused, and examined her feelings, but no, there was no pain, at least no new pain, no pain beyond the loneliness that had been growing all this week. That thin white face, the feeling made her feel. That face certainly wasn't Roger's.

'I can't,' Evie said. Roger had shown her, sure, and she'd used the camera a few times, but she was positive she'd get all the buttons wrong. 'I'll mess it all up.'

'You'll be right.'

Round about them ran people dressed in old black and brown trousers, in long white underpants, up and down the stairs, sticks in their hands. Evie looked for Noel to get him to hold the sound-thing but couldn't find him. He might be in next door, she thought, but it was too late to go and see, you couldn't get out the front without dislodging the pile of bags. She watched Sharnda race out the back door with the other camera to get to the street via the lane, heard the pickets upstairs in Mum's room, and ran up to join them. They were laughing and arguing as a couple of guys tied onto the balcony rail a sheet with huge painted words saying:

UNEMPLOYED – UNITE AND FIGHT

Evie wished Noel was here. She'd grown used to him. Evie decided not to bother with the mike-thing, to just pick up the sound on the camera mike. She slung the portapak onto her shoulder (God it's heavy) and clicked the camera on, just as everything started.

12

Evie and most of the pickets were in the front upstairs room when someone yelled: 'Here they are.' They ran out and saw a bus roar up and then the street was full of police firing up at them.

Under the bed, Noel froze, hearing the bangs outside that sounded like real bullets here, not firecrackers.

In her room, the despot stopped writing. *No, it couldn't*

be, not again, that was last week, that was years ago. Not again, please, pray. Pray to no one.

Her hand flew fast across the page again, writing madly to erase the years, to change history. No. If I write it differently, it happened differently. '*Noh!*'

In a room down the street, drawn to the window by the bangs, the man saw the mob come running yelling, some with banners and placards, into Liberty Street. Down the other end of the street, at 203, there were shapes picked out by streetlights, blue shapes that made loud bangs. The man ran out too to join the mob.

Mrs Maria caught his coat-sleeve at the door. '*Ti einai?* What is it?' Fright in her eyes.

'God knows!' (*History repeating itself!?*)

'Where you go?'

'Home.'

And off down the street ran the man to join his past.

Up the stairs crept the girls. Giggling, nudging each other, hanging onto each other in the dark.

It couldn't be. But there they were. The cream of the Irish bog standing in her room as bold as you like. Giggling behind hands across their mouths, stepping into *my* territory, they get bolder by the year. Once upon a time, in the old days, at least they'd keep themselves to the street. The sounds they made to mock her.

Up to the window the parrot screeched, frightened by freedom, hurling his green body against this invisible thing that stopped him entering four walls and light.

'Scab, scab!' screeched the old man's mate, scratching at the glass with his beak.

219

'*Noh!*' screamed the despot. '*NOH!*'

Down the stairs terrified ran Jodie and Ree. Out the front door to the street and the noise, where kids dressed in blue were pushing back lots of other kids, and that girl who'd come to see Evie had a big camera.

'One two three four,' chanted the mob, using the chants they used at demos down the CES.

'*One two three four*
The unemployed will wait no more…'

'Pigs, pigs,' yelled the shapes in raggedy clothes at the shapes in blue clothes, laughing, jeering at their mates.

'Scum!' yelled the blue ones back. 'Dolebludgers!' Making police faces with their faces for the benefit of Sharnda's whirring camera.

Up on the balcony of Evie's house, pickets yelled down, hurling lumps of coolite. Up at them flew the bungers.

A group of blue split off into the lane to get in the back way.

'*Five six seven eight*,' chanted the crowd,
'*Get on the streets and demonstrate!*'

'Hang on!' Sharnda tried to organize things. It was getting out of hand. There must be five or six hundred here now, they must've come from other CYSS schemes. She knew Roger had passed the word on, but she hadn't expected any to come. Sharnda saw Jodie run past bawling and reached out to get her, but Jodie was swallowed into the crowd.

Filming down from the balcony, Evie saw too. *Sammy!* she thought. *Where's Sammy?* Evie ran then, down the stairs, dumped the camera in the diningroom – let it film what it likes. Went to run out the front door but that way

220

was blocked. So she ran to the back door to get to the street via the lane.

Up at the window next door, the parrot hurled its greenness at the pane.

'Scratch her eyes!'

'Persecutor!' screamed the despot, yelling a real word as she opened the window to...she didn't know what, maybe strangle, perhaps just push it away. In it flew.

13

At Newtown police station calls started to jam the switchboard.

'...some sort of wild party...'

'...a kind of demo, with banners and chanting...'

'...something to do with unemployment...'

'...a thousand kids on the rampage...'

The station sergeant put out a call to all local cars and paddy wagons; then, just to be on the safe side, made a call to central headquarters.

'We'll check it out and let you know,' he concluded.

But Mrs Maria dialled 000, terrified for the safety of her lodger out on the street. Her voice rose, hysterical, 'Boom-boom,' she screamed, 'Liberty Street, guns, bang, big fighting,' she screamed, her English deserting her as the noise in the street reminded her of the war.

As the call from central headquarters to all available patrols came through the police band of their radios, the Channel 2 Mobile News Unit was just leaving a crash at Redfern, the Channel 7 helicopter was on its way to a fire at Ashfield, the Channel 10 Newscruiser was cruising along Parramatta Road, and down at the *Herald* and *Australian* buildings journalists were just coming back from their tea-breaks.

'Sounds like a repeat of those kids who rioted at Broad-meadows!'

And cop waggons and helicopter and cameras and journalists converged upon Liberty Street.

Afterwards, Sharnda reckoned that of all of her bungling of that night, the worst bungle was not to have warned all the locals about the film. ('Though considering the outcome,' she grinned, 'it was worth it.')

14

Up in her room the despot struggled with her persecutor. Hauling her heavy body from her bed, she swiped at the green tormenting shape, ducked as its screams circled her, then swiping and ducking she finally raised the power to chase it to the stair-landing; but though darkness at last engulfed it, a screaming carried on. She felt a small softness lap against her legs then disappear, like the memory of a child, and she called then for her son, for her grandson, 'Noel!' but they were gone outside her power.

Quite outside her call, in a circle of the past, Noel was still beneath the bed. Feeling as though hours had gone, but knowing from his watch that it was barely five minutes since it began.

Since it began, though, I have been here, inside the gun dream, that's been inside my life since it began.

222

Crouching in darkness, underneath a bed. Looking up, he saw the criss-cross of the bed-wire. Not far away there were bullet-bangs. Out that way. This time, he knew where that way was. Like a magnet to a pin, the sounds drew him. He lifted up the counterpane, and peered out.

There were legs outside the bed, running back and forth. And outside too there were yelling sounds, louder than bullets.

'Here! Pass me some more!'

'Bullseye!'

'I just got Billy!'

'Pigs!'

The pickets were right into it now, hurling down their ammunition, ducking as the bungers flew, their yelling floating over the bangs. But it wasn't them that Noel heard.

Outside the bed there were yelling sounds, close and loud, the voices of a dozen men, it was them that he heard.

'They're trying to kill us!'

'It's flaming war!'

'My arm!' screamed Mick. 'They've bloody got me in the arm!' His voice pitched high with the pain, his words whistling higher than the bullets as he ran past the bed.

'Get into the back room!'

'*Help!*' screamed the voice of Mick Cruise, now downstairs.

(*Mick*, Noel thought.)

(*Mick*, thought the man in the street. Hearing the same words Noel heard, frozen inside a surge of movement, he felt his blood as something thin, not a man anyway, a boy of seventeen.)

Under the bed Noel had a gun, and this time it was real, but Noel wasn't. He was a dream.

Out in the street was a boy of seventeen hiding inside a mighty roar of voices like a tiny crab inside a conch shell. Then over the shell flew a shape screaming words, green words, etched itself like a splash of acid against a streetlight then flapped down, a beak against his ear. 'Traitor!' screeched the feathers, alighting green upon his shoulder. 'You're right, there,' said the boy, knowing the eyes of Mick he'd deserted.

All around Noel was real life but for Noel this night the thin membrane between real life and some other world had disappeared. So out he climbed, me here, balcony there, A to B, the shortest distance between two points. Walking like a part in a dream Noel climbed back through the years, out from the bed, out through the shapes that were running back and forth till I'm here.

Here.

I've been here before, Noel knew. The first time I saw this movie it was as if I'd done it all before, in real life.

Going out to go out the back way, Evie propped. Feet coming into the yard, down the side passage. Evie ran into the scullery, her private sanctuary. Sammy, Evie remembered, and then forgot. In here Evie's Lizzie, Lizzie Cruise.

15

Walking down Liberty Street that Friday night, Lizzie was scared. It was nine days ago they left, and since they left, life had been La Perouse and loneliness.

Lying at night in her blankets on the sandy soil that smelled faintly of sea, faintly of damp; listening to the sleeping of Maudie and Fee huddled up close around her; listening too to the pounding of the Pacific over there across the sand; lying there, reliving that night.

Nobby, she thought.

I'm scared, she remembered.

Pa, Mick, Nobby, Nobby, come and get me, I'm stuck here, I'm scared. Not a wild flame, climbing the barricades, but a girl in a cupboard, Nobby I'm scared.

Walking down Liberty Street on Friday a week later, the street brought it back to her, the guns and crashing and fear.

Going past 203, an empty place that would in fact stand empty for over a year, for the inner suburbs of Sydney were full of houses that no one could afford to rent.

Going past 203, she saw the rubble still in the yard, she saw her sign swinging down, she hitched her skirt up and pulled her coat straight and made an attempt at tidying her hair, then stopped, too scared to go up and knock.

16

Noel was scared. Shadows around him running, but he was alone. Out on the balcony here, looking down, it all goes whirley.

'Ya,' yelled the blue shape of Fat Tasso. 'Noley-Poley!' Hurling up at him a bunger.

'Yer little worm!' yelled the open mouth of Matt Dunkley (pushing me into the gutter, knocking me down, him and Tasso, Billy too, time and again when Nanna would send me to the shop and they'd be there, Matt's gang, knock me flying.)

'Where's your girlfriend?' yelled Billy Greenhouse.

Laughing, pushing me too far, this has been going on for years, going too far.

'Tell her I'll see her later tonight!' That was Matt.

Anger then seized Noel, wild anger; frozen, he struggled, freed himself from this ice that stopped him moving, and he was crouched, pointing the gun down into the street.

A simple act.

A to B.

The shortest distance between two points.

Noel is crouched down and aims.

Out of his dream now, back in real life, Noel sees fear upon the face of Matt Dunkley as Matt recognizes this for what it is, a real gun.

Noel laughs, the flame of his laughter gripping now, playing games, playing *games*, *who's* a coward? The joke's on them. Noel surges with free delight. Fancy them thinking this is loaded. Noel laughs in his game.

Acting/act, he remembered. Sometimes it means doing, and sometimes pretending.

17

Evie's room was no sanctuary, for Evie was Lizzie, standing in darkness, walking down Liberty Street alone.

Walking down Liberty Street feeling like a stranger, like a tourist from out of town. It was only nine days but it seemed longer than the ten years she'd lived here. Nine days since Nobby disappeared; she had to find out, had to know. So was forcing Lizzie to go now and see his mother, though she didn't want ever again to see that cruel rotten face. She felt it like a knife cutting her sometimes, Nobby's mother's hatred. What've I ever done to her. Feared her like the crashing out there like the darkness like the night. Walking down Liberty Street it was only a few yards from 203 to 201 but she felt stuck, felt she couldn't, too scared to go and knock.

In the house next door the despot ducked through the years, swiping at their green tormenting shapes. Here, along the darkness, in the corridor, down the stairs. In the background all the time was a scream like a child, like terror or police through the night.

Through the sirens in the night the boy heard the scream screaming *Help* that dragged his ear from the roar of the sea inside the shell. *Mick*, he remembered, but it came instead from the wide open mouth of a lad dressed in blue there before him.

Remembering '*the worm'll turn*' the thought rushed through Matt's brain: He's mad enough to do it. Seeing death so near him then, Matt saw the years ahead filled not with playing for Newtown, being a mate with his mates, winning with women, but with a black void like screaming in his throat.

Caught by the scream, the boy in the shell followed the gaze of Matt's eyes and saw himself upon the balcony, the thin white face, the dark believer's look, and the gun that had waited fifty years for him to come. Feeling himself

227

up there, fingering the safety catch, he saw in Noel's eyes the fervent look of make-believe, his laugh as he played games.

Playing games, playing nothing! Some things are too real to play with.

Nobby felt his blood running thin in his veins, felt the time frozen round him that he was powerless to break, but had to, this time, had to act, couldn't cockroach-scuttle off, for the sake of them both, for this blue boy here with the stupid frightened look and that boy up there that was him.

Nobby ran then, pushing through the shapes that screamed around beneath the siren wail, in through the barbed wire like a soldier at Gallipoli, shoving open the door against the pile of the bags, using every bit of strength, he was in now, through the loungeroom, through blue shapes and picket shapes that wrestled and shoved in a mine of a battle for the benefit of a whirring camera that Evie had discarded, a camera that caught a fleeting glimpse of Nobby's shape as he hurtled up the stairs, through the front room, to the balcony.

'No!' yelled Nobby, grasping the gun-barrel, wrenching it upwards, making it aim into air, into no one, as Noel playing his game had just slipped back the safety catch and now pressed the trigger of the gun that had in it still the bullet Nobby had loaded into it fifty years ago in real battle.

18

A gun went off. That was real. *Sammy*, Evie remembered, Sammy whose scream she could hear inside next door.

Breaking back from the past through the skin into real life Evie now was simply Evie, who'd had for years the reflex action of running and grabbing when her sisters screamed. So hauled open the cupboard, through the hole, the quickest way.

In the dark next door the despot moved, searching for the background shape that screamed like a memory. 'Here, boy, come here.'

But not a boy but a girl, smaller too than she'd expected, her fingers at last found the screaming fugitive that drowned the sirens.

'It's just a dream,' the despot soothed her. 'Silly men with their silly guns,' comforting the soft thing she held that let its scream drop now and let the sound come in of the knocking on the kitchen door.

No, the despot thought, knowing this to be the Friday night when Lizzie would come. 'I can't face her.' Seeking comfort in the feel of the child.

A gun went off. That was real, Noel gasped as the sirens closed in, as the real cops arrived, as a helicopter puttered in sky close by, as the news vans were down there with cameras and lights, as the yells became real as the real cops pushed as the kids shoved back and Nobby grabbed the gun and grabbed Noel too.

'Quick, boy!'

Down the stairs they ran fast in real life pushing through the shadows, Noel and Nobby, as if they were just one body or perhaps a perfectly matched pair in a three-legged race, as they raced into the scullery, hid the gun back in its place, and then *one two through*, and joined up with Evie at the door.

The door was over there. A wooden door, painted green many years back and weathered now, a door with a handle, and a bolt, there was nothing so really alarming about it. Except the way it thumped at her, wanting to come in, accusing with its handle-eye, scaring her into the corner, coming for vengeance. Ah Lizzie, Lizzie. I've been wanting you to come so I could tell you, but now you're here I'm too scared to say it. Not a witch upon a roof flying defiant as I once was, but cowering here like a fugitive, fleeing from a door.

A door's wild thumping. No, that's a heart.

Then Sammy cried. 'I'm scared,' she cried.

'There's nothing to be scared of. It's just a silly old door.'

Taking Sammy by the hand then, she took her there to show her. Pulled back the bolt, made her fingers give a twist to the handle-eye, flung open its weathered green-ness.

'I knew it would be you.' She spoke to Evie, not to Evie, spoke to Lizzie alone, her mind not taking in the others. 'I owe you an apology.' The words were hard to say, but now were said.

BOOK SIX
Interim

If I had the wings of a turtledove,
Far over the plains I would fly
I'd fly to the arms of my one true love
And there I would lay down and die.

ANON, 'THE DYING STOCKMAN',
TRADITIONAL SONG, 1890S

1

Dear Girl, I'm on the road. I'm writing to you, but don't
know if I'm game enough to send this. Sitting under a
tree like the bloke in *Waltzing Matilda* only I don't know
if it's a koolibar or what. It's funny here after Newtown.
I haven't got far, only near Lithgow, walking all the way
nearly, with a couple of lifts. I see rabbits sometimes and
run to catch them, and I think of your ma and how she'd
cook them, and I want a stew. But it seems as I don't
run fast enough. If you was here we could both run, two
ways, and corner 'em. We'd beat 'em and eat 'em! Or if
Mick was here, we'd be sure.

Say hooray to Mick for me, if he'll accept a hooray
from me (and that's if you'll even read this far to know).
He's probably told you how I let him down. I let you all
down I know which is why I run, more why I run than
being scared about the gun and the cops searching for
me, though you probably don't believe that. You probably
just think, Nobby Weston, his blood made of piano-piss,
the son of a scab. Like my mother, you must think me.

233

Though she was funny, the old mother, the last day I saw her. All love and hide me, my dear boy. I told her I'd write to you care of her, and she swore on the Bible she'd give you my letters and tell you how to get in touch with me, and not tell the police.

An ant's just stung me on the bum. It's a big'un, green, with a big green head, and I can feel a lump swelling up. I'd rather sit outside at Liberty Street where you can be sure you see trouble coming.

Well Girl, I'm on my way. Where to, I don't know. I'll go West I think. I've met a couple of blokes who reckon there might be railway work at Wilcannia. I don't know where that is, but I'm going. I won't say how I feel because you think that's soft. I just wish (if you've read this far) that Mick and your pa might not think too bad of me, and you too but you always thought bad of me anyway lately. I couldn't fight that morning, I froze, and seeing Mick there being beat I didn't help him, I run between the legs to the cupboard where you were. Of course I didn't know you'd be there and seeing you there you could've knocked me over with a feather. You seeing me scared, so I run.

A bloke's just turned up here, says he's got money for a stamp and will post this in Lithgow. I've just remembered you hate me calling you Girl but there's no time to change this. I'll write again because I'm hoping you'll read this. I love you sorry love Nobby.

Dear Girl, I've got an address now to tell you, so will tell you that. If you write care of Wilcannia Post Office N.S.W. I'll get your letter. My mother will tell you the false name to write to. I want to hear from you and know if you got my last letter though you probably didn't if the bloke didn't post it in Lithgow. I had real luck! Just after I wrote to you I was sitting there and a bloke on a truck went by going to Wilcannia so he brought me to here and here I am! Here isn't very good to be, I must say, because there's no railway work and we sit under trees near the post office, they're called pepper trees, they're green with pink berries but you can't eat the berries. I've only been here since last night and I'm sick to death of it already. It's different from Newtown where there aren't any trees, there's trees here, but I don't see the point if you can't eat them. It's not real luck to be here.

You probably think I'm a coward and don't want to talk to me, I know you must. And Mick and the other men I ran through that day, and what did you do with the you-know-what when I gave it to you? They have the papers in the town hall here and I read how they're searching but truly Girl it's you I run from more than the larruppers, you and your pa and Mick, I can't face you all.

My mother will give you this and I know you must hate her. Where are you living? Please write and tell me you got this.

Love, Nobby.

(I know I called you Girl again, but you running

and skipping, it's how I think of you. There's a river here called the Darling and its name makes me think of you and be sad.)

Dear Nobby,

I came and visited your mother tonight to see if she knows how to get in touch with you. She says it's a secret, but she'll send on a letter. It was funny to come into her house but she let me feed Job and she's being quite nice.

How are you, Nobby? We are living now in the unemployed camp at La Perouse. So if you write, write care of there. Pa has made a good camp with one tent for the four big girls and the littlies and I have got a little hut made with bags and tins. I can't write much Nobby (you know why!) and also because I'm sitting here in your mother's parlour, and about the thing you gave me, you know why. The police have been asking me over and over if I saw anything. And Pa and Mick and Ma have been asking me too, but with all of them I keep my trap shut, don't worry. The police Inspector keeps thumping his desk with a ruler like he wishes it was me he was hitting, and my bloody bronchitis has come back bad, so he thumps and I cough, you'd laugh if you saw him, going all red in the face and talking about the mystery.

Ma is in hospital, she lost the baby after the battle and it was a boy, so we're all sad. Mick is out of hospital and Pa was only in there for a day. Mick went straight to

236

gaol but the UWM got enough money to bail Pa out so he could move us into La Perouse, but then Pa was put back into gaol when they all came up in Court again on Tuesday.

This is a stupid letter. There's so much to tell you and I can't talk to you like this sitting down at a desk that squeaks in your mother's parlour. I wish we were sitting together out in Liberty Street, Nobby.

Love, Lizzie.

P.S. Ma says to give you her love and say she would have called the baby Noel after you if it had lived because you were always a second son to her, but that wasn't to be. Love again, Lizzie

Tuesday, 30 June 1931

Dear Lizzie, I'm calling you Lizzie in case it's me calling you Girl that is making you sour on me, and stopping you from writing. My mother wrote to me on Friday night and said she'd just seen you in the street and given you my two letters and you ran off reading them and laughing, like you were laughing at me. She says that after the battle you and Ma and the girls all moved back into 203 and she's letting you stop there and not pay anything for a couple of weeks till you move to another place that she got a clergyman to find for you. See, Girl? I told you she'd come round in the end, the old roof-dodger. (Though of course there's no forgiving what she's done.)

Life is dreadful here and I don't dare to come back

to Sydney, but if you just gave me one word to make me come back I would, and damn the larruppers. If you don't write, I'll take it that's the end and I won't torment you with no more letters. Please say hooray to Mick and Pa and the other men if you go out to visit them. Say I couldn't shoot, I couldn't do anything, I know you think me weak.

Regards, Nobby Weston

Tuesday, 30 June 1931

Dear Nobby,

I came to see your mother again today and she says you wrote to her to tell me you want to cut off all contacts with your earlier life so that is fine.

We are fine too at La Perouse and the girls are good. The weather isn't. It's been raining flat out since last Friday. Your mother says she will send this on to you.

Best wishes,

yours in the struggle,
Elizabeth Cruise

2

It made her lonely, Nobby did, remembering his face, that made her lonely. Sitting here, huddled up, arms clutched around my bent-up knees, making myself into the smallest possible ball to keep warm, my feet are ice, the coughing starts. Like someone jumping up and up inside me, the coughing starts and goes forever, each cough making the next one happen, like when you're skipping and your feet won't stop.

Just above me, rain on the roof, the roof just here above my head. People reckon it's soothing, the sound of rain on a tin roof, but not when the roof's so close and full of holes.

Lizzie Cruise
Of La Perouse

Skipping words started coming into Lizzie's head in time with the coughs. *Cruise, shoes, choose, lose,* rhyme words pounding to the skips inside her but the rhythm too painful to turn into a song.

Lizzie moved a few of the tins under the leaks, checked that no water seemed to be falling on the little ones, thought of the run to the tent, steeled herself, pulled a bag around her shoulders, then a bit of tarp, and out into the night.

She could hear the water in the open stormwater channel, pelting along fast, a few yards over there in the dark. A lot of the time, the other campers said, it was nearly dry: just a wide ditch in the sandy soil, bringing the stormwater down from under the road, back near the golf links, and continuing down to take any overflow to the sea. Usually it wasn't much, just a gurgle like a creek, but it'd been raining hard for five days now, raining hard since Friday night, and now she could hear the water raging down.

Pa probably should've built the camp further away, but it was getting so crowded out here that you were hard put to find a good camp site.

Lizzie ran through the helter-skelter rain, picking her way between trees in the dark, tripping, her foot caught on a tree-root. I'll be glad when Ma's back out of hospital. The girls were good, but it was a lot, being in charge of all the cooking and feeding and washing, especially since the rain, these last few days. (Especially since the loneliness these last days.) One thing, but, you could say for La Perouse, at least you didn't have to mop it.

Lizzie pushed into the big girls' tent. Three bodies curled up beneath their blankets, Maire sitting up, shivering, looking at Lizzie with green Cruise eyes.

'I'm scared,' said Maire.

'There's nothing to be scared of.' Lizzie made her voice strong.

Lizzie Cruise
Of La Perouse

The coughs started skipping fast inside her.

'What're you scared of?' Lizzie checked along the tent seams for drips, gently shoving Kathleen away from the door.

'What if the water rises?' said Maire. 'What if we drown?'

'What! In a stormwater channel?' Lizzie laughed. A real laugh, but she let it come out louder, to make Maire feel better.

'What if there's a tidal wave?' Bridget's voice was muffled, beneath the blankets. 'You can hear the sea.'

Over there, through the darkness, over the sand, you could hear the steady roar of the Pacific as it pounded on the coast. You could smell it too, a crusty salty smell, smell it as a dirty smell in the sand beneath your blanket. Though these last few days, the main smell was of wet: wet hessian, damp blankets, soggy tarp, dripping hair.

'How about you go to sleep?'

'But I'm scared.'

'Don't be a baby.' But she said it gently.

(I'm scared, Pa, Ma, Mick, Nobby, Nobby I'm scared. Not here, not scared of the wet, but there with the boots, time crashing around. There inside the cupboard, the closed air inside it, the sight of the door as I scratch on it from inside.)

Here, though, there's nothing to fear, nothing left in the world to fear, Lizzie thought, for every possible dreadful thing that could ever happen in the world had already happened.

Pa in gaol, Mick too, ma in hospital, Nobby gone.

Lizzie Cruise
Of La Perouse
Jumps the wet
In holey shoes

Walking back, too wet to make it worthwhile running, lonely night, Nobby gone, Lizzie hurdles a puddle, only to land in another one.

Lizzie Cruise
Lizzie Cruise
We're all fine
At La Perouse

241

The words of the letter she wrote last night beating like rain in her head in her brain.

It was funny, how you could have something, and throw it away, and only know you'd had it when you hadn't got it.

Like how you never knew you had a leg, until you broke it.

Like that day, years ago, when she and Nobby played Mick's trick back on him, standing up on the roof of Kennet's chookhouse, pelting chokoes down as Mick and Cec Kennet belted around the corner in their billy-cart, standing there, when suddenly the world went whirly, fear cold, a hurry and slowness, as her shoes upon the tin slipped and suddenly Nobby's face, thin and white and scared, as he grabbed her then but couldn't stop it. Only eight feet or so it was, but the depth of that distance dragged them down so fast. Two bodies, clasping stick arms, till the pavement hit, and I felt my leg.

It was funny, how you never knew you had a heart, until you broke it.

Lizzie Cruise
Of La Perouse

(Choose, lose, Nobby, lose.)

Lizzie was back in the humpy now, pushing wet straggles of hair out of her eyes, pushing words out of her brain. '*Life is fine at La Perouse*,' she reminded herself. Fine, fine, but it wasn't fine, only rain, rain, all the time, since she came back last Friday night, from the first time she'd gone to see Ma Weston.

Knocking on the door, so scared.

And saw her again last night, and today she saw Mick, and now tonight the rain.

Rain rain
Pelts again
Rushing down
The stormwater drain...

Then Lizzie ran. Hearing the great boom in the distance as the stormwater pipe split up that way inside the darkness, releasing the great pounding thrust of water, Lizzie grabbed the waking shape of Maudie and hauled her from the humpy, up here, to higher ground, pushed her screaming into the blackness, and ran back to get Fee.

Fee, Fee, here with me, but she wasn't here, the humpy was empty, there wasn't a humpy, only flat pieces of tin and hessian on the ground as the wind tore their camp to shreds.

Lizzie ran towards the stormwater channel, seeing the round shape of Fee lit up by a lightning flash as it plunged in panic running at random towards the danger.

In the danger, Lizzie didn't think of danger, wasn't brave because the thing was happening so fast there wasn't time to imagine consequences.

And so, like something fast in a dream, she grabbed Fee and slung her back to Colleen who was there now, Lizzie sliding though as she did it, her feet refusing to hold on the sandy soil that, as she slipped there, caved in beneath and betrayed her.

3

After the battle was over, they sat in the kitchen of Noel's place: Noel and Evie, Nobby and his mother. Evie made a pot of tea, pouring into cups without saucers, pouring the milk from the bottle, not bothering about the despot's fanciness and fiddle and likes.

'Thank you,' said the despot, humble, her eyes on Nobby as he read the letters for…it must be the third time. 'It's nice and strong.'

Facts blurring for the despot sometimes still, most of the time Evie was Evie, but at odd seconds time would move again and here in my kitchen she'd be Lizzie, Lizzie Cruise. Pouring tea…at least she makes a decent cup of tea, that's one thing you can say for her, I must tell her mother.

'Mother,' Nobby said, the word clumsy in his mouth, like when Mrs Maria tried to say words on an unaccustomed tongue.

Then Nobby said nothing, his hands awkward as he rolled a smoke, feeling strange, illegal somehow, smoking in his mother's kitchen. He'd just been a boy when he'd left.

Left, not left, he's back, my son, the despot thought, my lovely fugitive. 'Noel,' she said, speaking to Nobby, but her eyes on the face of Noel here, he's more the right age.

Most of the time, the despot knew and understood, but sometimes was puzzled: why are there two of them? For years nothing, neither son nor lovely fugitive, but suddenly this night, in my kitchen, there are two. I must tell my son I'm hungry, the despot thought.

Anticipating Evie, who'd just gone next door to check

on the girls in bed and came back now with sausages and eggs and bacon and tomatoes and onions. Nobby took them from her and cooked. Neat and fast in his movements like a bush cook, he mixed up flour and water and made johnny cakes while he fried the rest, and Noel and Evie began to read.

'Uncle Nobby...' Noel said (almost whispered), Noel now tasting a strange word on his tongue. All the time, when I was a kid, how I wished I had an uncle. Someone to go backstop for me.

'Don't read at the table, son. Blow me dead, the standards have been dropping around here since I've been gone.' Nobby's words came out rough, but all he wanted was to stop them from reading and upsetting themselves before they'd eaten. 'Eat, you two.' He dished up the helpings, four big shares, and plenty more still left in the frying pan. 'Here, this way.' Showed them how to slice a pocket in a johnny cake, to sit the butter in.

Evie ate. This wasn't how she'd envisaged it, the meeting, if ever it happened; but still, for the moment it was good – it was amazing – the first taste of johnny cake.

'Of course, they're no good like this,' Nobby apologized. 'You've got to cook 'em on the ashes. Not right on the ashes of course, but above 'em, on a bit a chicken wire or that, and not, like, dead ashes, you fan the coals up with your hat...' Saying words to ease his uneasiness, saying words to test the use of them, for years he hadn't used them much, for decades.

'Will you show me?' Noel was eager. 'Will you take me out one day and show me?'

245

'Sure, son.' Nobby grinned. Maybe he'd get the hang of this having a family.

Evie was quiet. Now her eating was nearly done, she was feeling again. Feeling an itch to read the letters, feeling the need to tell Nobby the message, feeling left out suddenly from these two male people who sat grinning at each other like twins.

The despot felt it too. Here they were, back at last, and any minute would run off and play their games. She coughed, to assert her power, and he looked quick, her lovely son. Looked quick, too quick, she couldn't meet his eyes, remembering what she'd done. 'I wrote,' she said, looking down, 'many times, to say I'm sorry, but when I rang, no one answered.'

'You're all right. Don't think about it.' Feelings made him awkward. He took her arm and led her up to bed.

While he was gone, Noel and Evie read. Hatred flared inside them, for along with the letters was a press clipping about the drowning. Not from one of the big papers, just on a scrappy little sheet called the *Newtown Fighter*.

How can my uncle? Noel thought. How can Nobby? Evie thought.

When he came back down, Evie had to say it: How could he forgive her?

'She's said she's sorry,' Nobby said.

'It's not enough!' Imagining herself spinning down the black water like the ring across the lino, it was Nobby now who betrayed.

Nobby reached again for his tobacco, rolled a smoke. His hands neat, thin, not wasting movement. 'Save your spit.'

246

Evie was shocked. This wasn't how he should behave. Sometimes, this last week, she'd imagined searching and finding Nobby, and she'd planned how he would be and act. Someone old, but fine, like an English actor on TV, with white skin and a wintry smile, in an elegant grey suit. She'd introduce herself, and tell him Lizzie's message, and he would smile, his eyes light up, he'd clasp her hands in his fine white hands and be speechless with gratitude. After she'd gone, he might quietly weep for joy and then...and then...but the thens didn't occur to her.

But now Lizzie was dead, and *save your spit*.

'You kids,' Nobby started again, 'at your age, you think you've all the answers. Think you've got a monopoly on morality. Well, you're wrong.'

Noel looked at him. I didn't go to all this trouble to get an uncle, just so he could lecture me. I reckon I was better off before. Nobby saw, and knew the look. Like how I used to feel, when old Paddy would talk at me.

'I'm not knocking you. I was the same.' The words stopped. You get so used to no one to talk to, your voice gets so, you forget how to use it. Nobby tried to put a gentleness into his words, but how could these two come to him for answers when all the pat answers he'd taught himself for years were suddenly questions biting him again? *If we'd 've tried it, if we'd had a chance, would we have made a go of it?*

'Lizzie...' Evie said.

'Ah, Lizzie...' As if the thought of her had only just occurred to him.

Evie hurled it at him then. All the pressure of these

247

weeks had been building up and up and now it burst. All the undirected anger focusing on Nobby now, Nobby who seemed to be the cause of all these weeks.

'Don't you care that she's dead?'

Nobby laughed, a whistling sound coming through as his lips pulled back and his teeth locked fast to keep the scream in. Then his teeth split open and the sound filled the kitchen, the loud violent laugh of Noel that twisted out of him. 'I'd rather see her dead than let him have her!'

'Him, who?' Noel said.

'Her husband there in New Zealand.'

'But she doesn't have a husband.'

'That's the point, son.' And the laugh burst now, the first good laugh for fifty years, and Nobby looked and laughed at their faces. 'Pardon me, son. Pardon me, girl.' And thumped the table in his joy.

This? But she's dead, Evie thought, then she thought:... and then...and then...

She'd never planned those thens. Had never planned how Lizzie would be, what Lizzie would do, for she was me. In all the thinking through that week, in all the avoiding of the thinking, she hadn't planned Lizzie as a real live person, as she'd planned Nobby; but nor had it occurred to her that she was dead. Evie remembered: '*Where will I go to, when I'm a dead lady?*' Somehow, Sammy had known.

Evie cried then.

Noel felt apart, for he wasn't feeling it. He'd only ever dreamed Nobby, never Lizzie. He wanted to reach out, feel like Evie, but he couldn't.

'Don't start, girl, or you'll set me going too.' Nobby,

awkward, then tried to mend it all with a joke: 'And then we'll have to mop it, there'll be such a flood.'

It wasn't a very appropriate thing to say. Black water swirled around Evie and Nobby.

'So how can you accept her saying sorry?'

Nobby looked at her: accept? After fifty years on the track alone, you learn to accept it when no fish comes jumping up to be your dinner, learn to talk to your blanket who's your only friend in the winter, learn to treat the shade as a piece of surprise. But how to teach this girl acceptance in time to stop her tears? So Nobby took the other tack. 'Haven't you ever done anything, felt anything, you're not real proud of?'

(Mick's eyes, Noel thought.)

(The years of fighting against Ted. It was me started it.)

(Mick's eyes, Nobby thought, as I run out on him.)

'Holy hell!' The words flew out of Nobby now, flying out to stop him remembering his own thoughts. 'What else could the woman do but say she's sorry? For someone like her, that's hard enough. It's not as if,' he added, his voice hard now, 'it's not as if it's a bloody fairy tale, where you can change the ending.' It's not as if you can reach up and change the mechanical clouds.

'So all's well that ends well,' Evie said, her voice adult, ironic, testing him with words Mum sometimes said.

Baiting me with my mother's words. The questions bite, now's not the time. At least the girl's not flaming crying. 'It ended fifty years ago,' Nobby said. It's just begun.

Evie looked at him, grasping still at understanding, but starting to get there. But there was the message still to

249

say. 'She wrote in my cupboard, to tell you she loves you for ever.'

Nobby nodded. 'Thanks, girl.'

'Tell me about her,' Noel said. He felt excluded.

Nobby reached in his pocket for his handkerchief and silently wiped off Evie's tears. 'Ah, Lizzie...' he said, letting his mind start, 'Well, one thing you have to admit about Lizzie, she was a proudly lousy mopper...'

BOOK SEVEN
Acts

Bury me with fists clenched
And eyes open wide.
For in storm and struggle I lived,
And in struggle and storm I died.

ANON, *THE TOCSIN*, 1930S

1

They were still yarning at half-past one when Ted and Mum and Noel's mum came in. Ted's tie was undone and he had a carton under his arm and a grin from ear to ear. Mum and Noel's mum were looking a bit anxious, but when they saw Noel and Evie they perked up.

'You're all right, then!' Evie's mum exclaimed. 'And the girls?'

'Fast asleep.'

'How's Nanna?' Mrs Cavendish said quickly.

'Fine.' Noel felt guilty about the whole thing, the strain could've been enough to give her another stroke; but it hadn't, and indeed had seemed to bring her out of the last one. She was talking. Don't tell Mum that yet. 'Better than she's been for years,' Noel added. 'And this is Nobby! He's my uncle. There's so much to tell you!'

Nobby was quiet, looking at his half-sister, wondering how she'd take to the sudden irruption of a brother.

'We saw yous on TV,' Ted said. 'Oh, not yous two, but that Sharn-what's-it girl and the rest of your Dolebludger Club.' But said it laughing, and helped himself to a chair

253

and plunked the carton on the table. 'Want a beer, mate,' he said, handing one to Nobby, pulling back the ring-pull on his own. 'We've a spot of news ourselves. Have you got any glasses there, Rita?'

'Thanks, mate,' Nobby said.

Mrs Cavendish seemed in a daze. She put four ordinary glasses on the table, went to take two back, and said, 'Oh, dear, I should really get wine glasses for the wine.'

'Not to worry, Rita.' Ted opened a bottle of Summer Wine, then poured a glass for Noel's mum, then for Mum, then for Noel and Evie.

'Ah...I don't think...' Mrs Cavendish had meant the other two glasses to be for Ted and Nobby, but they were drinking from the can.

'Once in a while,' Ted said. 'They're not kids any more, y'know. An' after all, it's not every night a bloke wins two jackpots.'

'*What?*' This on top of everything else. Evie's voice pitched up high, and she burst out laughing.

'Call me a liar if y' like, but at ten o'clock see – I was a bit ahead already – but anyway, ten o'clock comes, an I've been on the same machine all night, so I think I'll just have a go at the next one, no one's been playing it, so I put m' twenty cents in, and bugger me if she isn't a jackpot. Five hundred dollars! That puts a shine on things, I think. 'Cause to tell you the truth, well, I'll tell you later. Anyway, it's 'cause it's m' birthday, I reckon. So anyway, I stop a while, then just before midnight, I think to m'self, I'll just have another go for m' birthday, so back I go to the first machine an I put m' money in an there she blows again.

Six pineapples. Five hundred dollars. Six pineapples. Talk about knock me over. Talk about something coming when it's needed. It's 'cause it's m' birthday, I reckon.' He passed Nobby another can.

'Happy birthday, mate.'

'Thanks, mate. Best birthday I've had in years. 'Cause to tell you the truth...' He turned to Evie again, then went a bit awkward.

'Because to tell you the truth, love, which even *I* didn't know,' Evie's mum said, 'because he didn't tell me till he got the money, well, Bankcard's been going Ted because he already owed them a thousand he'd been paying the rent with, before I bought you your trampoline, so anyhow he couldn't pay them, he couldn't before, because he's out of a job, which even *I* didn't know...'

'Since when?' Evie couldn't believe it.

'Ah, since about the week after we moved here. Y'know I come down here cause the boss reckons he's got a big contract in the city, an' when we move here he lays me off.'

Evie was quiet, because you should be serious to show sympathy, it was like hearing of a death or something, but Mum was smiling, and Ted was grinning, and Noel's mum and Nobby were heating up the fry-up, and Noel was pouring wine into the two mums' glasses, and then into Evie's and his, and then Ted burst out laughing, and so did Evie.

'You secret dolebludger!' Evie said, trying to make her voice pretend to be someone on talk-back radio, but it just wouldn't, she was laughing so much.

'I *reckon*, pal,' Ted said. 'Will you give me an in, down the club?'

'Talking of which,' Evie's mum said, looking more like a mum and worried again now, 'As Ted said, we saw it all on TV.'

(Not quite all, thought Noel, thought Nobby, thinking of the gun.)

'The twelve-thirty news,' Noel's mum said, 'And they said it'd been on the ten o'clock too. Were you here with them?' she asked Nobby, feeling quite strange, there were lots of things to talk about, but she thought it best to let Ted and his family get their talking done first. Noel had said this man was family, and she presumed he must be, no one, lord knows, would come waltzing in wanting to be part of this family unless they were, it was hardly the kind of thing you'd be an imposter to. But if he was family, there'd be years and years for him to explain, and besides, Noel's mum wasn't the sort to really question things.

'Here?' Nobby said, 'That's for sure.' He glanced over at Noel and Evie who were looking a bit green around the gills, remembering suddenly the dreadful mess in at 203.

'Ah, Mum...' Evie started.

'Long as the girls are all right...'

'And Nanna...'

'God, long as you're all here okay, what's a bit of mess?' Ted stretched happily. 'You spend half your time cleaning up after the girls, reckon you're entitled to make some of your own once every blue moon.' (Everything's so much easier now I've my troubles off my chest. And Evie suddenly doesn't seem to buck against me any more.)

'We'll start on it now,' Noel said quickly.

'It's not going to run away. Your uncle here and I'll give yous a hand with it in the morning. After all, as it's Saturday it's not as if I've got to pretend to get to work, or anything.' Ted laughed.

2

The next morning, they'd just started when Sharnda and Roger and Di rolled up in the truck.

'Hey, we won!'

'Won what?'

'Whadda you think!'

Sharnda had a big bundle of the morning papers that she handed around in a rush.

UNEMPLOYED IN BATTLE FOR RIGHTS
UNRULY MOB AT NEWTOWN
WILD SCENES

Sydney police were taken by surprise last night when a thousand young unemployed workers went on a rampage in a Newtown street in protest against the threatened closure of the Newtown CYSS (Community Youth Support Scheme) Centre.

Under a banner declaring Unemployed Unite & Fight the thousand youths from Newtown CYSS yelled slogans and threats and jostled against police, who only managed to quell the disturbance with difficulty.

A spokesman for Newtown CYSS, Alexandra Byrne (32), stated during a television interview at the height of the battle that if the government were to carry out its threat to close down the Newtown and other centres, protest of this kind could be expected state-wide.

'CYSS centres don't offer much,' she stated, 'but cutting them out is yet another blatant attack on the facilities offered to the unemployed, and the unemployed are going to start attacking back.'

In recent weeks, Newtown

CYSS officers were informed that the centre would probably be closed due to a rationalization of government welfare funding.

Dr Byrne, who has a PhD in the history of unemployed organizations in the 1930s and is a Project Officer at Newtown CYSS claims however that the move to close down the Newtown Centre is political and a response to the fact that Newtown CYSS staff and unemployed have been active in organizing rallies against the alleged inadequacy of the dole. The reason for holding the demonstration at that time was that the main funding committee that controls CYSS was meeting last night to decide the future of the Newtown centre.

CENTRE GAINS REPRIEVE

The Chairman of last night's Committee when contacted late last night at his home stated that after much deliberation the Newtown Centre had been allocated funds to continue its activities subject to review after 12 months, but asserted that this decision was taken independently of any pressure exerted by the Newtown youths.

However Miss Diana Vassey (24) the representative of Newtown CYSS at the committee meeting, stated 'We were losing hands down till we went out for the supper break and they saw the news on TV, and then when they came back in they voted the funds.' When asked the reason for the change she said: 'They seemed scared.'

One puzzling aspect of the demonstration is that it was held in Liberty Street Newtown, an ordinary residential street with no connection with the CYSS committee's meeting place. When asked why it was not held at the CYSS headquarters and the press informed before the rally in the usual way, Miss Byrne replied that the unemployed would fight where they liked, and that 'the press had all come anyway'.

Nobby reading it could hardly stop laughing. 'Good work, girl.' He shook Sharnda's hand.

'But it wasn't a *real* demo,' Noel objected.

'Don't be a pedant, Noel,' Sharnda said. 'If they believe it, then it was. Besides, when the cops got here it was real enough. I've got bruises all over. Where the hell were you two?'

'Um,' Evie said, suddenly remembering the film too and how she'd just dumped the camera.

But any immediate inquiry was stopped by a man who rode up on a bicycle. He was big, not tall like Nobby but built solid as a tank, and despite the June nip in the air was wearing an old blue work singlet and work shorts and thongs. His chest hair was curly and grey, sticking out above his singlet, and the hair on his head was wild and thick. You couldn't help noticing his green eyes.

'G'day,' he said, nodding to Nobby as if he'd seen him only yesterday. 'Had a feeling you might be here. When I seen it on the box last night I think to m'self, couldn't just be a what-summy, coincidence. So I decide to ride over. Have to keep m' weight down,' he explained the bike, 'ever since I retired.'

Nobby searched around for what to say. Noel too, recognizing. Evie knew: those eyes like mirrors of Lizzie's.

Ted shifted a bit, uncomfortable. They were all being a bit backward about coming forward. 'Ted's the name, mate.' He stuck his hand out.

'Mick Cruise.'

'*The* Mick Cruise!' Sharnda said. It was as if a ghost had walked out of history.

Mick's hand went the rounds.

'It's been pesterin' me for years, y'know,' Mick said to Nobby, 'where the dickens you ever got to.'

Afterwards, after the cleaning up and then the barbecue that Ted slapped on for his birthday, they all sat in the backyard on the trampoline.

'Strewth it's funny,' Mick's eyes were roving over the yard, 'being back in the old place.'

'You're not kidding.' Nobby still felt a bit uneasy with him.

Evie suddenly remembered. There were things she wanted to ask.

'But for all that effort it failed, but,' she said. 'You didn't stop the eviction.'

'Struggle never fails,' Mick said. 'It's always better than nothing.'

Better to be alive and flying, Evie remembered, than so given-up you're dead.

'Besides,' Sharnda added, 'a week after Newtown, the government was so worried by the publicity, it changed the laws. Made it harder for the landlords to evict people.'

'Really? Unreal!' Noel had another sausage. Victory made him hungry.

There was something else to ask that didn't matter, but just to be polite. 'What was the baby?' Evie said to Roger.

'False alarm. Come back in two weeks, they reckon.'

'Tell us when it's born,' Evie said, a bit patronizing, 'and we'll all bring flowers and stuff.' Imagine being so old you were nearly a father.

Then Evie asked something she really did want to ask. But it was Sharnda she asked this time. Not quite sure how to phrase what she meant, she said, 'What did you mean, that first day, when you said something about Newtown being left out of history because it's dangerous?'

'Dangerous? Oh yeah!' Sharnda laughed. 'Not to us. To the other side. You've just seen the proof of it. If the unemployed of now know that others fought before, it makes it easier to resist.'

'Like, history on your side?' Noel said.

'Something like that. Shit.' Sharnda spilled tomato sauce down her front.

Mick passed Nobby a beer. 'Here's lookin' at you, Sunshine.'

'Here's lookin' at *you*, mate,' Nobby agreed.

3

It was a blue day, a bright Newtown winter Wednesday, when they made the final act. Evie, Nobby, Noel. Walking, the three of them, slowly, with Nobby in the centre, a tall thin man in a coat and pants that didn't quite match, a shirt without a tie, in his unaccustomed city shoes, but in his stained felt hat. Walking slow, not because of age, not because of sickness now, but walking slow in that rolling, steady mooch of the man on the track who has no need to hurry for destination is not his aim: there is no aim, but to fulfil the endless destiny of the track.

Walking slowly, then, even though this day there was a point in Sydney's geography they aimed for, walking like tourists with all the time in the world; Evie, being used to Sammy, slowing her pace to Nobby's tread, Noel on the other side bounding forward, pulling himself back, swinging the duffle-bag from his shoulder.

Nobby suddenly touched his hand out to a fence. 'This was the Kennet place.' A done-up terrace now, with drifts of maidenhair in hanging baskets, with gums and wattles growing at the front, and clinging native creepers. Nobby glanced as they passed along the lane, but the chook-shed had given way to an aluminium garage hidden behind a screen of more gums.

'Do the trees make you homesick for the bush?' Evie said.

'What d'you think, girl?' Then Nobby smiled to ease the shock of his voice.

Homesick for the rotten scrub? Give me Newtown concrete any day, and if you must have some greenery, stick some privet in a pot! I'm home.

'I'm sorry,' Evie said, getting his meaning wrong. 'You've made me really want to go out there too, one day,' added Evie, Evie who just a couple of months ago had had absolutely no ambitions.

'Is that right, girl?' Nobby said, thinking: Evie. This girl who barely came to his shoulder, a real nice girl with quick darting eyes, a girl who'd have something alive and strong in her for ever more as a result of being mixed up in Lizzie.

'It's this way.' Noel darted left.

'Teaching your uncle to suck eggs!' But Nobby stopped now, stepping back out of step to cross over to a corner shop. He'd run out of tobacco.

Noel stayed put. This bad place of the past. But Matt and Tasso ambled out anyway and saw him on the corner here, standing here with Evie.

'Hey look...' Tasso started to cross over but Matt tossed his head to show that he was to stay on this side.

'G'day,' Matt muttered across at Noel, averting his eyes and hurrying on away. There was something about the shape of something in that bag that reminded him of something he didn't like to think about.

'Okay, son?' Nobby was back, his eyes on the fast-moving figure that he recognized from that night.

'Why wouldn't I be?' Noel laughed, so happy all of a sudden, not quite knowing why Matt and others like him weren't going to get him down in future, but just knowing that they weren't. It's funny, all those years of wishing for an uncle or someone to go backstop for me, and now I get one, for some reason I can suddenly backstop myself.

'You'll start sprouting any day,' Nobby said, as if irrelevantly. 'You've got the same build as me. Year I was sixteen-seventeen, I remember, I went up five inches in that year. God, the hell of that, being a beanstalk!' Nobby promised himself that, if he could, he'd try to protect this boy; then shrugged. What the heck. You can only grow by growing.

Noel looked at Nobby's tallness, only half-assured. 'You stayed skinny, but.'

'That's much better than having a beer gut,' Evie said warmly, and Noel felt good, as if she somehow saw him already as he'd be in the future.

And so they walked on, the three, and caught a bus into town and then another to La Perouse, where on this Wednesday that was the fiftieth anniversary of Lizzie dying they stood in sunshine on a high rock and hurled the gun, and then the letters, and the terror of the past, into the bright blue pounding of the Pacific.

EPILOGUE

The days after that Wednesday settled down into ordinary days. The past was still there, but no longer pressed itself relentlessly through the calendar. A stranger to the story could come into the street and observe a flow of unremarkable activity lapping in and out of the two houses.

First there'd be Ted, at half-past five, setting off to the building workers' day-hire pick-up in Enmore Road. Sometimes he'd get a start, sometimes he wouldn't; the days when he didn't, he'd be back again and out with the ladder, working on the years of neglect that had crept over the despot's two houses, for the despot had made a deal that Ted could work for the rent.

Round about seven, Nobby would bring him a tin mug of tea, and then Evie's mum and Noel's mum would pop out the doors at eight and mag away together as they headed for the station. Noel's mum was much easier these days, had started to relax and laugh for the first time in years, for with Nobby living there she didn't have to worry about leaving the despot with Noel.

It was Jodie and Ree's turn next. Out they'd belt, yelling in their uniforms, yelling up to their dad on the ladder, and then Ree would be off, running like blazes, with Jodie's stumpy legs chasing after her.

At about nine, there'd be Evie and Sammy, and Noel too; for Nobby made Noel go to school regular these days, but that didn't mean that Noel didn't delay the getting there, slowing his pace to match Evie and Sammy as they headed down Noel's back way to the play centre.

After a bit, Evie would come back with the milk and bread and things for both houses, and then they'd have morning tea, Ted and Evie, Nobby and Nobby's mother, all crammed onto 201's front balcony, eating fried scones or brownies if Nobby made it, eating peanut-butter toast if Evie or Ted made it, eating baklava and yoghurt cake if they invited Mrs Maria up too. It took a long time sometimes, morning tea, sitting in the sun with the despot and Nobby telling yarns of Liberty Street, and Mrs Maria joining in with stories from back in Greece, and sometimes Mick would ride over and join them and talk of struggles and strikes on the wharves, and there'd be Ted with his tales of when he was an interstate truck-driver, that would sometimes link up with Nobby's tales of the track.

'One night, see, at Brewarrina…' Ted would start.

'Have you gone fishing down the Black Stump there?' Nobby would cut in.

'The Black Stump?' Ted would scratch his head. 'At Bre? Can't say I know it. Down the weir, now. Caught fish there, heaps a times…'

'Yeah, the old fisheries, mostly fished out now, no, I mean the Black Stump. A funny thing happened to me, camping there one night…'

And they'd be off then, miles away, their voices bringing to the balcony the places that Evie would get to one day, if it killed her.

Though these days, right now, it was the music shop

she had to get to by twelve o'clock to do the afternoon shift, so she'd set off, and everyone would remember the time, and Ted would race back to his tools and Nobby would belt down to peel the spuds for the despot's midday dinner and Mrs Maria would go home to clean the room of the new lodger who'd taken Nobby's place, and Mick would pedal into town to some union meeting. The despot would stay there on her cane chair in the sun, her hands in her lap lying at peace now her words had come back, now her son had come back, and there was no longer the need for the desperate writing.

Round about one o'clock she'd go in for a feed and a nap, and then it would be Nobby's time to potter about with a paintbrush, giving Ted a hand till it was half-past two and time to go and get Sammy.

She loved it, Sammy did, the new routine. Instead of Evie twice a day, taking her there, hurrying her back, there'd be Dad there now at pick-up time in the Kingswood, honking a triple honk on the horn so she'd know he was excited to see what pastings and things she'd bring home today. Or Mr Man would be there, and that was just as good, because his steps were slow like hers and they'd explore back through the lanes. Often they'd find things like a cardboard telescope or a nearly-good thong that she could take up to show Nanna. Sammy loved Nanna because she'd once found her when it was dark.

And then when Maria and Jodie got home it'd be time for afternoon tea. Out on the front porch watching Dad and Mr Man or out the back on the trampoline where they could yell up to Nanna at her window to watch them be a circus. Or they'd run down and have it with Mrs Maria for old times' sake, or sometimes even, on special rainy days, Nanna would let them have it in her front parlour with a silver teapot and a silver tray and the piano. Maria sometimes got annoyed because Nobby and Mrs Maria weren't secrets any more and she couldn't plan witch-things about the despot, but Jodie reckoned it was better because now Maria could openly earn money from everyone so she'd get her BMX bike all the faster, and then Jodie would inherit the ancient-history dinosaur.

Round about five the two mums would come back, one a bit before the other, or sometimes both together, Evie's mum with her neat case of make-up samples, Noel's mum maybe carrying a parcel of fish from the fish shop near the station because Nobby loved fish.

'Knock-off time, mate,' Nobby would yell up the ladder, and he and Ted would sit out on the step and have a beer and admire what a difference their work had made today, while Nobby would gut and scale the fish.

Then it'd be Evie and Noel, back from the music shop. Noel still went there after school to hang around and Evie liked him being there. It seemed okay to be seen with a guy who was still at school, because now she had a job (even if it was only part-time and eighty bucks a week). She could feel as if things she did were *her* choices, not something foisted on her. She could even move out if she wanted to, because Sharnda had offered her a room at her place for twenty bucks, but now that she could, she didn't want to. Ted had built her shelves and lined her room, and the girls didn't come in any more because they had Nobby and the despot to visit.

Besides, there was Noel next door, and something about Noel really grew on you. Evie couldn't imagine how she'd put up with life at Campbelltown, with Roseanne's silly giggle instead of Noel's wild laugh. When things got one of them down, the other one would sense it, and they'd find themselves meeting in the lane and heading for the secret landscape. They'd go there other times too, just when they happened to be around the station; as they happened to be for example on Christmas Eve that year.

On Christmas Eve that year, Noel and Nobby had just bought all their presents in the last-minute late-night Coles rush and were back at the fish shop near the station buying three kilos of prawns as their present for Ted and Evie's mum, when they spotted Evie laden down with bags from Centrepoint coming out from the station.

Noel and Nobby looked at Evie's bags, and it was obvious she'd thought up better presents than they had, but it was too late now.

'Let's go down the landscape,' Evie said to Noel without thinking.

Noel didn't say anything. His uncle was there, and he didn't feel like sharing it, even with Nobby.

Evie knew, and went quiet herself, wishing she hadn't said anything, remembering that other time when she'd sort of betrayed it to Roseanne.

So they stood there, the three of them, in the bit of waste land in between Uncle George's and the station, and Nobby was quiet too, remembering back to that other late-night-shopping night when he'd stood here, in this very spot, listening to the voice of Jack Sylvester and watching Lizzie over there on the other side of the crowd. Lizzie tense as a cat, keeping an eye out down Australia Street to the cop shop, spoiling for a fight. And then that row she'd had with him. The first row they'd ever had. That night, that had been the beginning. The beginning of the end, you might as well say. It didn't do to dwell on it, but maybe just this once.

Nobby moved past the souvlaki stall and down through the waste land, swinging the plastic bag of prawns to remind himself that he was here, in this time, not following the fierce clatter of Lizzie there before, but here and now, with Noel and Evie close behind. 'D'you know this place?' Noel said as Nobby headed up the steps.

'Do I know the back of me hand?'

Up then, on the stage, dangling their legs down over the criss-cross lights of the suburbs, they could hear the intermittent roar of the trains cutting over the sound of the Christmas carols floating down from the railway pub.

Oh Come All Ye Faithful...

Evie started to hum along without realizing, thinking of Lizzie.

Noel shifted, embarrassed somehow, the Bethlehem side of Christmas not fitting in with his opinions.

As if he could read both their thoughts, Nobby said: 'There's nothing wrong with faithfulness, son.' Thinking of Lizzie. I love forever. 'You just have to pick the right thing to believe in.'

'Yeah but...'

'It's a bloody damn sight better song than that answer-in-the-wind stuff *you* play. Answers in the wind! As if any old answer 'll do. You don't get answers from the wind, son. This is what you get from wind.' And Nobby farted. He liked to shock them sometimes. Liked to pull himself down to earth too, when these two made the old questions start biting him.

'So there *is* an answer?' Noel desperately wanted one.

'Don't you know it, son?' Letting off a laugh through his teeth. Feeling good suddenly, joy.

Looking down on the criss-cross of the lights of the workers' suburbs, Botany, Redfern, the backside of Newtown, Alexandria, the houses down there with people living and working and fighting and us up here too, swinging our legs. Us all in a circle that no one can reach to stop, like the mechanical clouds up there that the *thinagulla* taught me that night beside the river.

Nobby searched up, but there was too much smog, you couldn't see them here; they were still there, but.

What he could see, what even the city couldn't blur, was the blaze of the Southern Cross, belting its bright Eureka sign like an ad across the sky, as if up there too people were living and fighting.

'*Live and work, work and fight, live and love life...*' Nobby chanted softly.

'What's that?' Evie said.

'Something that a woman called Alexandra Kollontai once wrote.'

Evie reached in her bag to feel the silver serviette ring she always carried. She'd never told Noel or Nobby that she had it. The words fitted how she felt but couldn't say. 'But why'd she write it, what for?'

'Ah…well…to end off a story she was writing.'

Noel considered. Up here on the stage. 'It's a good ending.'

Evie considered. It was just how she felt. 'It's a better beginning.'

Nobby swung his legs still with these silly damn social-worker shoes and said, 'D'you reckon your mum and Ted would mind if we made a start on these prawns?'

HISTORICAL NOTE

Although this is a novel, the history in this book is real.

In the late 1920s Australia, like most western countries, entered a period of severe economic depression. By 1931 at least a third of the country's workers had been given the sack—not because of their own inadequacies, but because of the failure of the system.

Unemployment relief was provided by the state governments, and both Labor and conservative parties kept it at a bare subsistence level. In those days, moreover, the dole was not given in cash. At first the unemployed had to line up with a sugar bag at the relief depot, where they would be given the actual goods: meat, bread, tea, sugar, soap etc. By 1931, a system of coupons had been introduced. Unemployed workers would go once a week to their local 'dole dump', where they would be given coupons for meat, groceries, and bread. They would trade these with a designated butcher, grocer and baker.

Obviously, with no cash, there was no money for fares, shoes, clothes, doctors' bills, medicines and other essentials—let alone for a luxury such as a bottle of beer or a bar of chocolate or a bag of oranges. While this made the physical side of life very tough, it also increased the humiliation of unemployment.

Yet the most disastrous aspect of the 1930s relief system was its effect on the housing of the unemployed.

With no cash, paying the rent was a weekly nightmare for the jobless. In those days, most working-class Australians rented their homes, so thousands of unemployed workers lived under the threat that they could be evicted for failing to pay their rent. In working-class suburbs it was common to see bailiffs forcing a family onto the street, together with their bits and pieces of furniture and clothing. After being evicted, some families were able to squash in with relatives, who were usually already living in overcrowded houses. Others were forced to shift to the shanty towns of bag and tin humpies that sprawled on unwanted land along the coast. Sometimes the young adult members of the family took to the track, and spent the years of the Depression moving between the country towns where they collected their weekly rations.

The sense of injustice aroused by evictions was increased because most of the rental property in working-class suburbs belonged to wealthy landlords and investment companies who owned housing on a vast scale. Many people wondered why poor families should be thrown onto the streets, when the rich lived an unchanged lifestyle in their mansions in the affluent suburbs. While the housing crisis highlighted the cruelty of capitalism, it also dramatised the stupidity of the system: in the inner suburbs of the capital cities, there were strings of terrace houses that had been boarded up because no one could afford to rent them. The real-estate companies usually preferred to have their houses untenanted to allowing the unemployed to receive a free roof over their heads.

Given the extent of the economic crisis and the

inequities of the relief system, it is not surprising that all over Australia a proportion of unemployed workers formed organisations to protest against their economic and social plight, and to demand improvements in their conditions. While some of these protest groups were confined to a single area or a single demand, in 1931 there was a nationwide body called the Unemployed Workers' Movement (UWM), which was made up of hundreds of suburban and country groups. By mid-1931 there were about seventy UWM branches in Sydney alone, with perhaps two hundred members in each branch. Although this was a fraternal organisation of the Communist Party of Australia, in any branch there would only be a handful of Communist members. The platform of the UWM included demands for a 100 per cent increase in the value of the dole, a rent, fare and clothing allowance in cash and the end to evictions.

Over the first six months of 1931, Sydney branches of the UWM mounted a strong campaign against evictions. In a number of cases throughout the metropolitan area, the organisation used petitions, deputations and street pickets to pressure landlords and real-estate agents to allow defaulting tenants to remain in their accommodation until they were able to find work. This campaign was so successful the large landowners worried that the idea of free accommodation would catch on. At first they attempted to pressure the Lang Labor government to send in the police to enforce evictions. Though the ALP saw the radical UWM as a threat, the Lang government did not want to upset its working-class electorate by directing the police to do this unpopular job. The large real-estate companies turned next to the magistrates, whose task it was to make out the eviction orders. They were quick to oblige. Given heightened class tension, the rich feared a backlash if the legal system sent in the full force of the law in defence of large property owners. And so small landlords—and in particular landladies—became pawns in the game, as the first test cases were enacted.

On 30 May 1931, in the inner-city suburb of Redfern, the UWM was taken by surprise when police, rather than bailiffs, arrived to evict a family. Moreover, the police brandished their guns and used their batons against the tenants' UWM supporters. This was the first fight that the UWM lost. Over the next couple of weeks, the campaign rapidly escalated as both the unemployed militants and the police took stronger and stronger measures. The bloody climax took place in the inner-west suburb of Newtown. By this time, popular support for the anti-eviction fighters was enormous. The crowd that spontaneously gathered in the street to cheer on the 'Newtown boys' (as the anti-eviction fighters were popularly called) stretched for half a kilometre in each direction. These hundreds, if not thousands, of supporters were not Communists, but ALP voters, and even ALP members. And they were jeering at Premier Lang's police.

It is no coincidence that a couple of hours after the Newtown battle a meeting of the New South Wales Labor Council called for legislation to protect the unemployed against eviction. Although no provision for rent was made in the relief system, the legislative changes made it harder for landlords to evict people.

*

Historical fiction allows writers and readers to play with hypotheticals. It lets us measure what did happen against what might have been.

In this book, the reports of the Redfern, Leichhardt and Bankstown fights are taken from the newspapers of the time. The Newtown battle was also all too real, and I have based my account on a great deal of primary research, as well as investigation of the battle site.

However, the characters living at 201 and 203 Liberty Street and the 'mystery' of the nineteenth picket are fictional. So is the story of the gun. Although some UWM members had access to guns, the occupation of the houses was a tactic of defence rather than offence. It was also a campaign based on principles of family and community: the UWM would not have done anything that risked injuring children and neighbours in the crossfire.

In order to bring out the fact that the UWM did not use guns, I needed give them access to one. While I wanted to find out what role a gun might have played in such a situation, I could only do this through a character such as Nobby, whose youthfulness placed him outside the discipline of the organised unemployed movement. Once the gun appeared—it immediately had to hide itself again. Yet just by being there, it provoked tragedy.

For dramatic purposes, I shifted the timing of the Newtown battle to the night after the Bankstown fight. It actually occurred at noon, two days later. Though the law stated that evictions had to be carried out between 9 am and 5 pm, a house at Glebe was stormed by police before daybreak, so my change is within the bounds of possibility.

And after all, the Redfern attack happened illegally on a Saturday, and at Bankstown the police went in twenty-four hours before the warrant was due.

Despite these fictional changes, the violence done to the pickets has not been exaggerated. The account of the storming of the house is based on the statements that the eighteen pickets made to their solicitor. Newspaper photographs show police gathering up bullet shells from the street, as well as holding off the crowd with guns.

A number of the background characters are real. These include Jack Sylvester, who was National Secretary of the Unemployed Workers' Movement; Richard Eatock, an Aboriginal activist who was shot by police at Bankstown; and Alexandra Kollantai, who was an early Russian Bolshevik, feminist, and writer...

But Evie and Noel and their problems are just as real. Sometimes it is only through fiction that we can read between the lines of history.

Nadia Wheatley, 2013

ACKNOWLEDGMENTS

A number of the epigraphs in this book were originally published anonymously in a broadsheet called *The Tocsin*, which was produced and distributed by the Balmain branch of the Unemployed Workers' Movement (UWM) in the 1930s. Copies of this publication were kept by labour historian and union activist Issy Wyner, who as a teenage boy was a member of the Balmain UWM. In the 1970s, Issy encouraged me to include this material in my historical research and publications about unemployed workers in the Great Depression. The fragment of verse about the 'Bankstown and Newtown boys' was compiled from various sources. It is typical of the kind of anonymous verse that sprang up spontaneously in response to political events.

Other material used as epigraphs comes from popular songs (also anonymous) that were sung in this era.

Readers wishing to know more about the history on which this novel is based could consult my article, 'Meeting them at the door: radicalism, militancy and the Sydney anti-eviction campaign of 1931' in Jill Roe ed., *Twentieth Century Sydney*, Hale & Iremonger, Sydney, 1980.

Text Classics

Dancing on Coral
Glenda Adams
Introduced by Susan Wyndham

The Commandant
Jessica Anderson
Introduced by Carmen Callil

Homesickness
Murray Bail
Introduced by Peter Conrad

Sydney Bridge Upside Down
David Ballantyne
Introduced by Kate De Goldi

Bush Studies
Barbara Baynton
Introduced by Helen Garner

The Cardboard Crown
Martin Boyd
Introduced by Brenda Niall

A Difficult Young Man
Martin Boyd
Introduced by Sonya Hartnett

Outbreak of Love
Martin Boyd
Introduced by Chris Womersley

The Australian Ugliness
Robin Boyd
Introduced by Christos Tsiolkas

All the Green Year
Don Charlwood
Introduced by Michael McGirr

They Found a Cave
Nan Chauncy
Introduced by John Marsden

The Even More Complete
Book of Australian Verse
John Clarke

Diary of a Bad Year
J. M. Coetzee
Introduced by Peter Goldsworthy

Wake in Fright
Kenneth Cook
Introduced by Peter Temple

The Dying Trade
Peter Corris
Introduced by Charles Waterstreet

They're a Weird Mob
Nino Culotta
Introduced by Jacinta Tynan

The Songs of a Sentimental Bloke
C. J. Dennis
Introduced by Jack Thompson

Careful, He Might Hear You
Sumner Locke Elliott
Introduced by Robyn Nevin

Fairyland
Sumner Locke Elliott
Introduced by Dennis Altman

Terra Australis
Matthew Flinders
Introduced by Tim Flannery

textclassics.com.au